WITH DUST
SHALL COVER

PAUL O'NEILL

Dear Moranda,
   Whether you like it, love it, or loathe
it, I really appreciate you giving me
your time.

   May your shadow never grow less,
                              Paul O'neill

DEDICATION

For Grandad Spitfire.
For teaching me you don't have to be loud to be a powerful storyteller.

CONTENTS

INTRODUCTION

Well, here we go again, my friend. Or if this is your first time, welcome.

How can I tell you how much I love short stories? How can I express what they mean to me? How much it means that you are here on this journey?

I'm a quiet guy. I find it hard to speak. Some days it feels my brain and my mouth aren't linked up at all. In a very real way, these stories are my voice.

There are stories in here that were written in two days. Some took four years to finish. Such is the nature of short stories. Some fly out of you. Some need time to simmer.

Forgive me for coming across all vulnerable, but this collection is a personal deal. There are big parts of me in each of these stories. The messed up, creepy parts? Well, I'll leave you to decide that one.

On Dream-Wings Float started as a longing for the old conversations my brother Joe and I had when we were drifting off to sleep, talking about all the stuff we would buy if we won the lottery.

Midnight Machine stemmed from playing the guitar in music class with my buddy Martyn and a lie I told (sorry, Martyn!).

The Swirly People was a recalling of the strange fear I had of faces appearing in the ceiling if I stared too long.

Time's Shadowy Tide is about dementia (there's no worse word in the English language).

Above all else in this set of thirteen stories is fear. There's popular belief among writers that all evil must have a sympathetic bent about it. You have to understand the villain, they have to be messed up for a reason. While that rings true in most cases, I don't believe it's the case each and every time.

Sometimes you're in the wrong place at the wrong time. Sometimes there is no *why*. Pure evil exists. I've seen it. It can be beyond explanation, comprehension.

Sometimes these forces are human, sometimes alien.

So, come wander through my messed up mind.

Are we the same, you and I?

May your shadow never grow less,

Paul O'Neill
August 2022

THE SHATTER BOX

A knot of emotion almost screamed its way out of my lungs as I shifted my legs under me, my thigh muscles quivering. The hardened blood on my hands cracked in the creases of my palm as I rolled my fingers. An invisible force held us down, not allowing us to move from our spots as the ancient board game demanded we hurt someone. Four of us knelt around the coffee table as a misty darkness drew nearer with every roll of the dice, blotting out the world.

It was just us and the game.

I looked at the empty space where Craig once sat. His playing piece lay toppled over on the table. He'd ran into the darkness, screaming that he couldn't take it anymore. I could still hear the wet noise of some alien thing ripping him to pieces. In the silence that had followed, I leaned back and stuck my hand into the dark, jerking it back as a hundred moist hands swarmed over my forearm, trying to pull me in.

Diana and I had a cracker of an argument yesterday. I'd stormed out for a stroll to clear my head. I found myself in the middle of a car boot sale when the game, this *Shatter Box*, caught my eye with its glaring neon letters. I asked the old man how much it was. He threw it at me and weaselled into his car like it was the only thing he came to sell. Later, I realised I hadn't given him any money for it.

The objective of the game seemed simple enough. First one to move their piece around the snaking path and into the see-through cube that was arched on the centre wins. The board was a long rectangular box that covered most of the coffee table we huddled around. Brown felt fuzzed at its edges. When I traced my finger along it, I swore I felt it breathing, like I stroked the pelt of a slumbering bear. The squares our pieces moved along were once white but now shone with a splattered maroon that reminded me of dried blood on bathroom tiles. The path wove around the outside of the board, spiralling in on itself until it ended at the cube that sat on its centre like a gemstone.

Its old wood smell that reminded me of teak benches in church hit me as I gazed at the electric words that swam inside the cube.

Roll the dice.

"I told you not to open that box," said Diana, my wife. She sobbed, glaring over the knee-high table at me with haunted eyes. "But you had to, didn't you, Dan?"

She tucked a strand of black hair behind an ear, a gesture I'd smiled at a million times before. Her fingers touched the ruined blob of waxwork that used to be her ear. She flinched and sucked in a shaky breath, knuckling her eye and willing the pain away.

"It was supposed to be a bit of fun," I said. "Like when we used to play that Atmosphere game with those creepy videos. How was I supposed to know it'd end up like this?"

"Craig's gone. Got that? Slashed up like a damn horror flick."

"It's an alien conspiracy," whispered Pauline. She clutched her side with both hands like her innards would worm out of her. "Spaceship's sucked us up and now they're toying with us, testing us. Only explanation."

"Shut your hole, you stupid woman," said Tam to my left, thumbing the screen on his phone. "Dan's just having a laugh with us. Couldn't take the fact that the rest of us are off having kids, so you thought you'd plot a wee bit of revenge. Boil us up a bit because you're jealous." He slammed the phone on the table. "Whatever this black thing hovering about us is, it's royally messed my phone."

The game clicked. A low hum shook the chess-like pieces, a noise that set my nerves slithering around the back of my neck. I picked up the dice with its eight uneven sides, wrapping my trembling fingers around it.

"We just keep playing the game, that it?" hissed Diana. "We don't try to get help or—"

"You heard what it did to Craig," I said.

We fell into a stony silence. The only sounds were the wincing from pain and a buzz like a swarm of wasps that rose in pitch, vibrating inside my skull.

"I don't want to find out what happens when we run out of time," I said.

I shook the dice, its chipped edges scratching my palm. Its marble surface stayed cold no matter how long I held onto it. A shard of ice anchored at the base of my throat upon glimpsing the venom in Diana's perfect blue eyes. I steamed out a sour breath then sent the heavy dice clinking along the wooden board.

The green words faded from the cube as the dice spun and clattered about. We all held our breath. A crimson four landed face up. Diana, Tam, and Pauline turned to face me, mouths hanging open.

The playing pieces were intricately carved. They reminded me of knights on an ornate chess set though their faces were hidden behind scowling masks. Each had a different colour that flowered out the carved slits of its eyes and the square holes that ran along its mouth. The masks made me think of Hannibal Lecter though there was something sleek and alien about its edges.

My piece pulsed a violent red. I gripped it between my fingers. A small river of electricity shot up my forearm as I moved it around the path. The piece was wooden, but there was a crisp texture covering it that felt like dead snakeskin. Touching it froze the lining of my stomach.

My hand trembled as I settled back on the carpet, sucking in a lungful of humid, sweat-stained air. Diana glared at the middle of the board game, her face scrunched up as red letters swam in the glassy cube. A command would often appear after we finished our turn.

"What's it say?" Tam leaned over the board, a sharp laugh blasting out his rubbery mouth as he read the flowing words. "Aye, right. Just you try it, you lanky bastard. See what happens."

A slab of a meat cleaver phased to life on the table. I grabbed its warm, moist handle. I closed my eyes and leaned my forehead on my palm, the cold of the thick blade chilling my cheek. "You've seen what happens. When you put it off, it only makes the punishment worse."

"Aye." Pauline twirled her long auburn hair between her fingers. "It's alien mind control. Like when it told me to burn Diana's earlobe. I tried to hold off, but you saw what happened. It ticked down like some mad oven timer. When it buzzed, it was like the aliens just... took my hand and made me do it. I'm so sorry, Diana. I—"

"My arse," Tam exploded. "Just because you chose to burn half her ear off, doesn't mean it's aliens. All it means is you're in on whatever fuckery this is. And you're not chopping off my fucking thumbs!"

Diana glared down at her piece that glowed a sickly purple. I had tried to get to my feet, but my knees stayed glued to the carpet as Pauline stomped over to my wife, a small black lighter in her hand. A jet of fire like a flamethrower engulfed my wife's ear and most of her cheek. I could still taste the sizzled meat of her baked skin. The game paid double when you defied it.

Take his thumbs, glared at me in murderous red letters, urging me on. Its cold light shone against the wet sores that seeped up the side of my wife's face. She flicked her gaze at me, her watery eyes trembling as she fought back the tears. She gave me a slow nod.

"Look," I said, "I can chop them off, quick as you like, then we'll blast through the rest of the game. Once it's finished, we'll—"

"I'd rather keep my thumbs, thank you very much," said Tam. "I'll wait."

"You can't hold me responsible for what happens."

"If you come at me with that cleaver, I'll chop your knob off. Got me?"

Diana let out a mirthless exhalation. "Doesn't work properly anyways."

Tam whooped a great belly laugh. I stared down at the game, shame billowing through me. I opened my mouth to spit something back at her, but slammed it shut.

Our inability to produce a child had torn at each of us these last two years. We'd been trying for ages, smiling dutifully as our friends all announced their future offspring. I tried not to melt too much whenever we got the chance to hold them, but it only got harder.

We were good at blaming each other, which was why I found myself wandering into that car boot sale and bringing this hell-forsaken game back with me. Board games used to be our thing. Tonight was supposed to be about having fun and getting back to how we used to be.

Tam feigned wiping the corners of his eyes as his laughter simmered down, then scooped up the dice in a meaty fist. "Ah, that's a good one, Diana. Let's get this game done then, shall we?" The dice rolled, hitting the centre and making a hollow ding. "Hmm. Ain't ever rolled a zero before. Something weird about that. Hey, maybe the game's having a dig at your balls, Dan. Big fat zero children for you two, ha!"

I tried to relax my grip of the cleaver to let it fall, but something made me hold its handle even tighter until my knuckles popped. "You're not hel—"

Diana sprung over and yanked the cleaver out my hand. She held the blade high, then spun, her hand outstretched as she swung a backhand slash. Hot, sticky blood splattered up my cheek. Tam gargled as he clutched the gaping wound along his throat, a red river sluicing over his fingers as he tried to catch the blood. I hacked up the contents of my lunch over my knees, staring down at the frothy mixture of beer and BBQ chicken.

Tam worked his mouth, an inaudible croak escaping him before his eyes rolled in the back of his head. He slumped to the floor, a final breath relaxing out of him.

Pauline glanced at the wreck of our friend, his blood pulsing out onto the carpet. She picked up the dice, rolled it, then clinked her piece seven times along the winding path.

"Diana, what—" I said.

"M-maybe the last one standing wins, eh? Thought about that?" Diana pointed the dripping cleaver at me which fizzled out of existence. She stared at her empty hand, then sat on the floor, wiping her hand furiously on her jeans. "Or do you know more than you're letting on?"

"How many times? I don't know anything. Would you just help me out? I thought we were a team."

"We've not been a team for a long time."

"What's that supposed to mean?"

"Forget it. Hardly matters now."

Pauline stared at the cube, a silent prayer on her sallow face. After a long moment, she breathed a hefty sigh. She leaned over and handed Diana the dice. "Roll."

Diana cupped the dice in her palm, then sobbed into it. "Fuck. I killed him, Dan. I killed him."

"We play as a team from now on, alright?" I said, looking at my wife and then Pauline. Neither of them made eye contact. "Alright?"

"Maybe she's right," said Pauline. "It's like we're being tested to see who the strongest one is. We're just playthings to them."

Diana threw the dice. It rumbled across the table, coming to a stop in front of me.

"Five," I said.

Diana shook her head then picked up her piece. A low buzz emanated from somewhere inside the board, growing stronger, setting the fillings in my teeth on edge. I looked up, my balance wavering like I'd mistimed a step on a staircase. The darkness crept in closer. I was close to leaping into that blackness and into the clutches of whatever had ripped Craig to shreds.

"Oh ho," chuckled Pauline. "I guess that's not referring to Tam."

I turned to ask what she meant when Diana's steely fist cracked my nose. My head jerked back, a tang of coppery blood cascading down my throat. Diana flicked her wrist and sat down. Through stinging eyes, I saw the fading words: *Punch him.*

"Didn't waste any time there," I said, the sound rumbling through my now thick nose. A trickle of blood swam down my nostril and onto my lip. I batted it away with the back of my hand, then wiped it on the carpet. Tam's cold, open eyes glared at me. "We should move him."

"Feed him to the aliens, you mean?" said Pauline.

"You want to leave him here to rot?"

"Better than sending him into whatever's out there," said Diana.

"Aliens, man," said Pauline. "They'll eat his face."

"I know he was a bit of a prick, but still," I said. "It was Tam, you know?"

The board clicked impatiently. Liquid writing screamed the word: *Roll.*

I flung the dice, rolling a six, holding my breath. No instructions appeared.

"At least Ronnie's at home with my sweet little Jake," said Pauline as she shook the dice in a tight fist. "Little guy picked the perfect night to have the shits. Do you think the aliens will let us go free when we're done?"

"Well—" I started.

"No," said Diana. "No."

··•••·••··

We continued for an unknown time, the deep ammonia smell of urine stinging the air. The only things that changed were our position on the board and the encroaching darkness. The game hurried us along with its ear-piercing clicks and buzzes.

I leaned over the board to pick up the dice when my hand exploded with red agony. The memory of Pauline driving a silver trident through the back of my hand made acid coil up the back of my throat. I picked up the dice with my other hand. It rolled to a stop, inches from my wife, the harsh lights of the game blazing up her chin as the words formed.

Tell her.

"Tell me what?" Diana snapped her head up, blood trickling out her closed swollen eye.

"I... I..."

Pauline leaned over and slapped a hand on the table to stop from fainting. She picked up the dice, dropped it, then lifted it again. Her skin was yellow as a corpse as she broke down in her gentle way, calling her son's name over and over. She rolled a three and moved her piece along the snaking path that neared the glass dome, close to the end of the game.

"Tell me what, Dan?" Diana spat, her head lowered like a drunk.

My mind slipped like a balloon on a thin string as my wife, my beautiful wife, stared at me over the evil board game, her skin dripping with fever sweat. "I don't know wh—"

"Don't. Don't even try that. We're in this together, right? That's what you said."

"Right."

"And it'll make you tell me anyway, right?"

My jaw wobbled as I stared into the hideous words on the cube that ruled our existence. The words tumbled out. "I had an affair. A long one. Ashley at my work. Started as a bit of fun. Got heavy."

My jaw ached as I fought against the invisible fingers that pried my mouth open. "She got pregnant. She got it... taken care of. I..."

Pauline sucked in a breath and covered her mouth as new words blazed from the cube. I couldn't bring myself to read them, not after taking a knife to my marriage.

"I'm so sorry," I said. "She didn't mean anything to me, promise. I—"

"Don't give me that," said Diana, voice cold. "Least we know which one of us is to blame for us not having kids."

I looked over my shoulder and into the dark, willing myself to be anywhere but here. This was all my doing. I was responsible for the deaths of two close friends and for butchering my wife's heart.

"Dan?" said Diana.

The note of panic made me turn to face her. She stared at me as Pauline clawed at her own face, ghostly wails escaping her. Diana nodded down at the game.

Jake is dead.

"No," I said. "No, it can't... it can't possibly have—"

"How do you know?" screamed Pauline, spittle hitting my face. "My little cupcake, dead. All because of you. Next time I get a sharp blade, it's coming straight for your fucking veins. Then I'm coming for the aliens that did this." She craned her neck, roaring at the blackness. "You hear that, you sick fucks? I'm coming to slice you up for even thinking about touching a hair on my superboy's head!"

Diana picked up the dice. "Quicker we finish, quicker we can check on Jake, right?"

She flung the dice, a four, and it clanked along the board. She handed me the dice, the look in her eye telling me she'd forgotten all about my confession because her best friend needed her. It made me hate myself on a whole new plane.

I rolled a two and went around the board. "On the home-stretch now, see? Just, what, twenty more steps until we reach the end and get out of here. It..."

The fiery words in the cube prickled my skin.

Scalp the player to your left.

Pauline cried so hard into her hands that she struggled for breath, her long hair shaking over her face. Beside my leg, a drill clattered on the carpet. Only, it wasn't a drill exactly. It had a circle of serrated metal atop it.

"No..." I said as my hand moved toward the blue handle. "Roll, Pauline. Quick."

Diana looked at me. A river of pain warped her face as she saw what I reached for.

"Pauline, come on," pleaded Diana. "Jake is fine. How can the game possibly have him? How—"

"I can feel it in my bones," said Pauline. "I'll be seeing you soon, my little gingersnap."

"He's at home playing his Sega, Wii, or whatever the fuck he's always playing when I try to talk to him. We'll get out of this. You, me, and shit-cunt over there."

"And the other two? What about them, eh?"

A pulse tensed my hand, tightening my grip on the handle. The plastic creaked in my palm. "We're only a few rolls away from finishing this thing. Pauline? Pauline, look at me. You need to roll the dice."

"No," said Pauline, staring down at the floor. "I can't."

My finger twitched against the trigger. A high-pitched shrill sliced through the thick air between us. They both flinched, bodies leaning away from me, unable to get up and run.

"It's alright, Dan," said Pauline, her shoulders slumping. "Honest."

My finger tensed on the trigger, sending a deafening squeal into my brain like a dentist's drill rumbling in my gums. My hand raised itself into the air, no matter how hard I pushed it down with my other hand.

"No," I heard myself repeat over and over as I moved steadily toward Pauline.

"It's alright. It'll all be alright." Pauline lowered her head as if in prayer, presenting the crown of her head to me. Below the roar of the spinning blade, I heard her soft singing: "Kittens and lollies, and all things nice, sugar plum fairies and rolling the dice. My sweet little angel, he comes to me, he sings la and fa and diddle-dee-dee."

"Pauline," I roared, close enough to smell the coconut scent of her shampoo.

"Fight it, Dan," screamed Diana. "Don't. Don't. No!"

The high-pitched whine lowered as the blade found hair and then went into her skin, blood spraying everywhere. The drill struggled as it bit into bone, making a low grinding noise that made me gag as I desperately tried to hold my hand still.

Pauline shoved her head forward, the saw squealing and squelching as it sliced into the soft mass of her brain. A nightmarish wail escaped me as pieces of white meat blasted out of the coin-slot hole I'd made. I let go of the trigger and fell back.

I touched my mouth. Thick blood coated my bottom lip. Pauline's body slumped to the carpet, the drill sticking out the top of her head.

I kicked at the floor, attempting to scuttle back into the damp blackness.

"No!" shouted Diana. "Stay here and finish this, you bastard."

With a sob, I watched my wife pick up the dice. A scowl was etched on her face as she chucked it against the board, rolling a seven, her piece clinking around the squares, nearing the end.

· · · · · · · · · ·

"This is it." My thin voice scratched out my throat like raw fire. "Just need a two."

My wife exhaled. Her head hung so low her forehead almost touched the table. "You've said that every fucking turn, I—" She clutched her ear, sucking in a pained breath through gritted teeth. "We never get the right number. We'll keep going forwards and backwards forever. How much longer can we sit here and torture each other, Dan? My hand..." She sobbed, holding it up, her fingers bent like snapped twigs. "Won't be using that anytime soon."

"Do you have to?" My tongue touched the swelling gap where three teeth used to be. An explosion of white-hot pain roared up my jaw. I closed my eyes, riding it out. "You think I enjoyed mashing up your hand like that?"

"It's never going to end, is it?"

I could still see her in there, beautiful beneath the blood and her swollen, puss-filled eye. She would have made a great mother.

I scooped up the blood-stained dice. "I love you."

"Fuck you, you prick." She let out a keening, agonised note, spittle running down her chin. "Fuck you."

"We'll go back to how we used to be. We can have our family."

Diana winced like every breath knifed her lungs.

I closed my eyes and prayed. *Two, two, two.*

The dice skittered along the board and swirled on the spot, taking an age to settle.

"One," said Diana with an awful chuckle. "Least you're one step closer. That's progress, I suppose." She wiped her cheek with the back of her hand, leaving a trail of curdled yellow that made me think of custard.

My playing piece shone its horrid red light, buzzing the skin on my fingertips as I lifted it and placed it one space in front of the cube that sparked to life.

I wanted nothing more than to reach over and take my wife's hand as we waited on its next command.

"It'll be alright," I said.

Go back to the start.

"What?" My heart thundered. "What? No? No, it can't..."

Water stung my eyes as I stared at my wife. She looked like a deer trapped in headlights.

"That's not fair. No!" she wailed.

The table shook, vibrating through my palms like an earthquake. Our two pieces exploded with colour as they slid backward, tiny squeals like fingers on clean glass as they snaked back to the start. The three dead playing pieces came back to life, joining ours, a rainbow of sharp colour lighting up the ancient board.

My brain was on fire. I closed my eyes, a high-pitched screech reverberating around my skull.

I caught the scent of woody aftershave. Craig knelt at the table, happily taking the spot next to my wife, his jolly smile shining from under his bushy beard.

"Woah, why the long face, Dan?" said Craig "You're the one who wanted to have this game night. Let's just get pished instead."

"Nah, let's play," said Pauline, sitting up from the floor where she'd fallen, the hole that I'd drilled into her skull gone. "It'll be fun."

"Fine." Tam sighed, not taking his eyes from his phone as he sprung up next to me. "Anybody know the rules?"

"D-Dan?" whispered Diana, her eye healed but twitching like it still caused her great pain.

The darkness pulsed in around us, disintegrating our humble living room. I tried to stand, my legs held by an unseen force.

The pieces shone with a hideous light.

Diana let out a muffled sob. "I can't... No!"

The swirl of letters screamed inside the cube.

Roll.

STATION MASTER

Tall, skeletal plants hunched in each corner of the hotel lobby, licking the ceiling with their yellow leaves. They screamed in dry desperation, clawing at the air for moisture. Henry had the sudden urge to set the plants alight, to put them out of their misery. He gulped as he passed them by, his own throat itching for a drink.

A handsome lass with panicked eyes greeted him, talking deliberately as if he had a hearing problem. She fidgeted by his side when he walked down the line of strangers who congratulated him on his retirement.

He eyed the double doors that led into the main hall and the bar. He did his best to ignore the banners that screamed *Hero Station Master Retires*.

"Help me," said Henry, shaking a moist, dainty hand. "It's not too late."

"Y-You've been an inspiration, sir," said a lady with smeared, red lipstick. "We won't forget you."

"It's gone. I can't remember any of it."

She smiled demurely, bowed, and stepped back. He hadn't seen a familiar face yet.

Forty-one years. That's what he'd given Kirkness railway station. Forty-one years, and Station Master for twenty. They'd forced him into retirement, saying he was blocking the line like an old, mangled train. Retirement yawned like a cavernous tunnel with nothing on the other side.

"Suave suit," said the next in line – a man with teeth and eyes like a rodent.

Henry turned his head and almost saw the mirage of his wife. *Looking fair dapper, my goodnight sir.* His heart twisted.

"You should be here, Maggie," Henry said aloud.

"Huh?" said Ratface under a hairy, furrowed brow.

Henry felt his eyes go sad as he clasped the man's thin hand. "Let me at the bar before I kill everybody."

"Ha ha. Scotland's finest. What a legend."

The air on the other side of the double doors was as dry as a Greek island. He kept a smile on his face despite the sweat beginning to slide down his temples. At the far end of the hall, beyond the sea of people vying for his attention, rows of amber bottles glistened.

A frizzy-haired lad with scattered jerky motions placed a hand on Henry's shoulder, pointing him at another group. The mouldy reek of puke phased up from the carpet with each step. Inside his trouser pocket, he clawed at the side of his thumb with his index finger. The urge to light a cigarette roared within him. He'd quit ten years ago – wife's and doctor's orders. His lungs yearned for sweet smoke.

"Henry Campbell," said a weaselly voice.

A rotund man turned to face him, tucking his thumbs into his braces. The movement was done with the flair of a Bond villain.

"Mr. Garrity," said Henry. "Are you here to end it? Exile me to the sheds never to be seen again. Quick! Lock me in."

"Ha, funny," said Mr. Garrity with not a trace of humour.

When his boss leaned closer, Henry caught the mustard-like tang of body odour.

"Just smile and say thank you," hissed Mr. Garrity. "You're a hero in these parts. Wouldn't get away with a simple card and flowers. You seem a little edgier than usual. Not planning on dying on us tonight, are you?"

Henry eyed the bar, doing his best not to wet his lips. "That depends. You know what's funny? Forty-one years and I can hardly mind fuck all. Not a single good memory. And I used to argue about how important the almighty railway was to my Maggie. She deserved better."

He slapped his boss on the arm as he slid past. The slight blow made Mr. Garrity jerk like he'd been stabbed.

"Some shindig this is for an old geezer like you, H."

Henry turned, a smirk tugging the corner of his cracked lips. Dahlia, the crone who ran the WHSmiths attached to the station leered at him beneath eyebrows like white caterpillars.

"Kill me," said Henry. "Kill me now, ha ha."

"Surprised Mr. Garrity's smell didn't do that for you."

"Being serious."

"Aye, right. You go get yourself a drink before you erupt, you handsome—"

"Ladies and gents," said Mr. Garrity, leaning onto a lectern on a small stage. "Old engines and new."

This drew titters from the crowd. Henry shook his head.

"Everybody please take your seats," Mr. Garrity continued. "We'll get our Henry up on stage after we've filled our bellies. Please ensure you keep all luggage and belongings with you."

The crowd spurted cheesy, overthrown laughter. Dahlia rolled her eyes and slunk off like she wasn't planning on coming back. The ashen perfume of cigarette rolled over his face as he watched her go.

"Take me with you," he said. "Please?"

"Mr. Campbell," said a bothered young man who seemed an iota of stress away from a stroke. "Your table is front and centre. Table one, if you please. Make your way to your seat. Please. Table one."

"Jesus, how much does Fife rail make? If we took all that money we'd make one hell of a bonfire, eh? Watch that baby burn all night."

He ordered a double whiskey, no ice, and was still waiting on it by the time the mains were done. The bar had shut up shop while the dinner was served. Shards of the driest chicken were stuck in his teeth as the seven strangers at his table peppered him with questions. He continued to give the servers the eye, but none saw him.

"Describe your hardest day at work," demanded a man across the table who sat like a card shark.

"Hardest day?"

Henry studied the mottled scars on the back of his hand. It still sang of the searing pain from the day he'd hauled passengers from a burning carriage. An echo of the heat stung his eyes.

"You wouldn't know a hard day if it sniffed your arse and bit your knob," said Henry. The man's jaw hung open like Henry had just socked him one. He sighed and gave them what they wanted. "No such thing as a hard day at work if you're prepared."

"A-any advice?" shook a reedy boy not long out his teens.

"Find your soul and hold on to that bastard. I lost mine when I took up Station Master."

The guests stared at each other, then giggled. Some looked as if they held off the urge to clap.

Two thuds pounded from speakers at each corner of the stage.

"This thing on?" Mr. Garrity said, almost splitting Henry's ears open. "Woah, guess I don't have to be that close, huh? Look at you all. Packed tighter than a Virgin train in here."

The crowd guffawed and slapped their knees. Henry eyed a waiter, holding up a pretend drink and pointing at it.

"Station Master is a serious duty," Mr. Garrity continued, "and Mr. Campbell has been the utmost example of the values we represent. Though many of you have never met him, you have all heard the heroic tale of the great rescue of '98, when he pulled burning victims from a fire that engulfed an entire carriage, saving women, children and many others."

A round of applause catapulted Henry's senses. His face went red as he flexed his burnt hand, almost able to taste the cloying smoke from that day. He had never needed a drink more in his life.

Mr. Garrity droned on. Service this. Commitment that. What a load of prattle, especially coming from the bloke who signed off on the budget cuts that had turned the railway into a shadow of its former self.

"You deaf, Henry?" boomed Mr. Garrity. "Come on up here, you goof."

His spine cricked three times as he rose to his feet. The crowd slapped their eager mitts like seals. He imagined the way Maggie's eyes would've crinkled with joy had she still been alive to see this.

When he got to the stage, Mr. Garrity slapped him on the back with a hot, meaty hand. The stench of cigar and body odour roiled off him as he leaned close, whispering in Henry's ear. "Show them what Station Master meant to you."

Another round of applause circled the room as Mr. Garrity stepped to the side of the stage, leaving Henry in the limelight.

He leaned on the lectern. The spice of a freshly lit cigarette caught his nostrils. He breathed deeply of the phantom smell.

"I haven't prepared anything," said Henry, "and thanks to this fucker's speech, we're running late. And you know how I like to keep time."

The crowd exploded with raucous laughter. Some pointed at Mr. Garrity who nodded politely, although Henry saw the big man wring his hands behind his back.

"Well, this is it, I guess. Since I'm drier than a train to Aberdeen, I'll see you at the bar."

He walked to the side of the stage. The crowd stared up at him with vacant, confused eyes. A few clapped slow and unsure.

Mr. Garrity ambled over and grabbed his wrist. "Where you going? Stay right there, you old baboon. Embarrass me in front of the workforce. Can't believe you. After everything."

Mr. Garrity let go and walked to the lectern, a jolly smile back on his doughy features. "This man, eh? Always brief. Always so... humble. Do you think we'd leave you without sending you off properly? Now, on behalf of the railway service of our glorious Fife, I present to you—"

Mr. Garrity whipped out a small silver thing and placed it in Henry's hand. It slumbered coldly in his palm. The intricate engraving on the metal made him squint his eyes. For a second, it looked like a picture of him hauling kids from a smoky carriage. It morphed into the image of the Flying Scotsman rolling through the countryside.

Henry held it up to his face. The crowd stood, slapping their hands together.

"A lighter?" said Henry, closing his fist around the gift. "I haven't smoked in—"

"Least you could do is say thank you," Mr. Garrity hissed in his ear. He jabbed a dirty finger at the lectern.

The ground seemed to tremble up Henry's calves like a train rumbled beneath him. His tongue almost stuck to the roof of his mouth as he stared beyond the crowd at the joyless plants that clawed the walls in each corner of the room. Sweat gleamed on the guests' foreheads as they leaned on pale tablecloths, ready to bark out dry laughter.

The lighter grew hot in his grip.

"You know something?" he said into the mic. "I never liked trains. Hated the bastarding things."

The glittering eyes of the crowd darted about nervously before a ripple of giggles flowed through them. The sound picked up speed, turning into a collective belly laugh.

"I mean it," he continued. "Worst thing I ever did."

"You're roasting us right good," cackled a bespectacled young man near the front.

"Should never have become Station Master. Hated every arse-kissing moment of it. Cost me everything."

"Stop, stop," wheezed an elderly lady from the back. "You're killing us."

The crowd boiled over in hysterics. The noise made something pulse deep within Henry's brain.

He opened his hand. Two lines of dents showed red on his palm where he'd pressed into the metal.

Forever a part of us the lighter said in scrawled writing.

He flicked the lighter. A wholesome flame sparked to life. Warmth prickled up the scarred skin on the back of his hand.

"You find that funny?" said Henry. "Laugh yourselves dead, then. I want those years back. I want my Maggie. I want the bairns we should've had."

With his free hand, he rolled up a sheet of paper from the lectern, holding it over the still flame.

"I hate you all."

The crowd continued to roar.

MIDNIGHT MACHINE

Sydney tapped the strings on her guitar, wishing something true would pour out of her. No matter how frustrated she got, only a swarm of knock-off Megadeth riffs spidered out her fingertips. She longed to be a musician, a heavy metal goddess, but grey sludge clogged her brain when she tried to create something of her own.

Midnight had come and gone by the time she placed her beloved Gibson Explorer with its lustful cherry finish in its stand. The skin on her fingers thrummed with the silver strife of runs and solos. At school, they called her Sydney Shredder – a name that drew a smile each time she heard it.

She leaned back in her seat, holding her hands in front of her, spreading her thin, calloused fingers. Now she'd stopped playing, the January cold seeped its way into her.

"Just a bunch of copycats, you lot," she said to her fingers. "Never make it out of here unless we pen some hellish tunes that'll break necks."

She swiveled her small office chair towards her desk and opened her laptop. Its glare lanced her eyes as it loaded up. Battle of the Bands was two days away, and she promised Martin she would smash him in the ears with a new song that would win the competition – the first stop on their way out of this Scottish dump before taking on the world.

Her forehead burned. The sound of harsh scratching filled the small, dark room as she clawed at it, her nails digging through skin and into slippery blood.

"Damn it, Syd," she said, wiping her fingers on her jeans.

She clawed her brown hair from the right side of her face, sticking it behind an ear stuffed with piercings. The crescent-shaped scar had hung above her right eye since she was six. It drew stares, but she'd never told how her real dad tried to carve 666 into her skin, the voices telling him she was a 'devil child.' He'd stopped halfway through the first digit when her mum burst through the door. That was the last time she'd seen him.

Down in the nether-regions of the internet, she looked for inspiration. She imagined what her stuffy stepdad would say at her browsing photos of murder victims like she flicked through a catalogue.

The screen glitched, flashed, then died.

She blinked away the purple outline of the dead girl that had been on screen. Nothing happened when she tapped keys, no matter how hard she pressed. The burning smell of spent battery smoked up to her.

A symbol glowed in the centre of the screen. The letters *MM* appeared like a werewolf had clawed them there.

"What the…"

Down-tuned guitars thundered from the laptop's tinny speakers. The heavy, churning noise vibrated the hairs on her arms. A moan of ecstasy escaped from her pursed lips.

A grainy photo pixelated on the screen. Of the four leather-clad men, only one looked at the ancient camera that must've snapped the picture. The man's eyes held nothing but shiny malice. A scar split a river down the side of his face, carving into his beard.

"The singer," she said.

Words scrawled across the bottom of the photo:

The Midnight Machine calls you,
It kills inside let it drive you,
The Midnight Machine needs you,
Get inside let it take you,
The Midnight Machine.

"The Midnight Machine." Sydney cupped her hand over her mouth. She breathed in the scent of metallic guitar string. Cold scurried at her windpipe.

The singer's smile widened, showing moistened, pointed teeth.

The movement made her stand, tipping over her chair. A disbelieving laugh whooshed out of her.

"What's happening to me?" she said, leaning on the desk, feeling like her hands were floating a million miles away.

The photo disintegrated.

An electric buzz filled the room. A red light caught her eye. Her amp had switched itself on. She sat on her bed, nestling the

Explorer on her lap, and plugged in its cable. The amp crackled as the connection was made.

She didn't think, letting her fingers march up and down the different notes. Delicious pain seethed in her as she bit her tongue and closed her eyes. It was as if her heart was connected to her fingertips. She bled music. Something flowed through her, used her.

"The Midnight Machine calls you," she mumbled.

The amp spewed out the sweet mana of heavy metal. Dense, thrashy, break-neck stuff. She resisted the urge to lean her head back and howl as the power grew unfathomable inside her.

Footsteps snatched her from of the lightning storm in her head. John, her stepdad, stood with his arms folded, tapping his foot like an angry headmistress. She continued to pick strings until John reached over and flicked the amp's switch. A final note choked off into nothingness.

"Bit early for all this racket, isn't it darling?" said John. "You know your mother gets the head monsters if she doesn't get her nine hours."

"Fuck Mum."

"Well, I tried, but she told me no in a most unpleasing fashion."

"John! Not what I meant—" Sydney shook off the image and leaned over, switching the amp back on. "Wanna hear something? Don't worry, I've turned it down."

A ball of energy seemed to grow from her chest, glowing down her arms. It smacked into her fingers, and they danced along string. The aching noise that blasted from the amp was like nothing she'd ever heard.

"Well," said John, tapping his chin as the notes died away, "that was... crunchy."

"Crunchy? I can dig that."

"It's no Elton John, but there was something about it. Something, I don't know, frightening. Was that the aim? Feels like a nut-job just rattled me in the face and ran away. Enough of the show and tell. Back to sleep, pet. School tomorrow."

"Sleep? I gotta get this stuff down before it's gone. John? John? Your nose. Is that—"

"Huh," said John, running the back of a dainty finger under his nose. The finger came away glistening. Blood streamed down the digit, falling to the carpet. "Oh, dear, would you look at that."

"You alright?" Sydney set the guitar on the bed like it was a newborn babe.

"I-I think I'm gonna go—" A single line of blood zig-zagged down his smooth cheek. He wiped it and stared at it for a long time.

"John? You still with us?"

He shook his head, snapping out of his trance. "I'm, ehm, just gonna pop my boots on and head out for a wee stroll, I think."

"You what? It's the back of two in the morning. Only jake-balls and alkies out at this—"

"Nice night to clear my head." Blood dribbled from the corner of his eye and down his chin joining the stream made by his nose. "You stay here and sing your heart out."

· · · · ·●·●· · · ·

The next day, a wet dog smell wafted around Sydney as she sat opposite Martin, both plucking their guitars. They always spent their breaks locked away in the music annex with its thin walls. Outside, lunchtime mania had struck the kids of Kirkness High School. The remnants of a groaning chord thrummed in the air.

"Woah, Shreds. That's hella gnarly," said Martin. "Where'd you come up with that? Sounds so… evil."

"It's not evil! I'm not—" Sydney covered her mouth, inhaling the sweet sting of metal on her fingertips. It calmed the anger that had burst from her. "Figured it was time I showed you how awesome we can be. Ready for some more?"

It was like a river bursting a dam. It gushed out of her soul, onto the guitar in slides and hammer-ons.

"Easy, Shreds," said Martin. "Cut your fingers open doing that."

"Can't stop. Needs out. Needs—"

The plastic chair creaked as he leaned over and laid his fingers against the strings, muting the sound. This close, she could smell the stench of rotten apples coming from him. It made her crinkle her nose.

"Out with it," said Martin.

"What?"

"Something's itching at you, man. Looks like you've sunk forty Red Bulls. Eyes all popping and wild like."

Sydney took the guitar from her lap and placed its bottom on the floor, wrapping her arms around the neck.

Instead of following her stepdad as he sauntered out into early winter in nothing but his t-shirt and shorts, she'd turned back to her laptop and searched *Midnight Machine*, trawling obscure forums.

They'd been the heaviest of heavy metal bands judging by the comments. None of their music was on YouTube or Spotify or anywhere. Deep in the coves of her search, she found an interview with a wide-eyed, bespectacled producer.

"Shame what happened to those lads," the man said, his trembling hands making it impossible for him to light a cigarette. "They were well into rites, and seances, and all that bollocks. Found in that van with all that blood… They were gonna be the next big thing, I tell you. Music was killer." The guy lifted his specs and clawed at the corner of his eye. Sydney zoomed in on the finger. It was red. "I haven't been able to get their songs out my head."

Something thudded the window, shaking her out of her thoughts. A glob of yellow-green mucus snailed its way down the glass. Hooting boys shouted that she and Martin were goat-shaggers then ran into the crowd.

"My stepdad didn't come home last night," she said.

"I've hardly seen that old fud leave the house. Where'd he go?"

"I've no idea. I…"

Martin looked at her from under his mop of hair. She noticed his gaze flick up to her forehead. He flinched and looked down at his Fender, grinding out a low, stilted rhythm. The scar taunted her, begging to be itched. She ground her teeth as he played his plodding notes.

"Read somewhere that Kirkness has the highest levels of dads leaving their families in all of Scotland," he said, tongue sticking out his oily mouth.

"Shocker."

"Think he's done a bunk?"

Sydney picked her guitar up and nestled it back on her lap where it belonged. It made her feel whole again. "He wouldn't do that."

She twisted the volume knob and punched out a grinding, desperate riff. Rows of eyes gathered at the windows as the power exploded out of her. She churned out riff after riff in a blur of fingers. When she hit the start of a solo, the muscles in her left hand ached, refusing to keep up with the need inside.

She stood and kicked the amp over, letting the guitar hit the floor. Feedback squealed.

"The what machine?" said Martin, gawping up at her.

"What?"

"Mumbled it when you blissed out there. Is that who we are? Is that our band name?"

A crowd of eyes shone through the window. For the first time in her life, she felt as if anything was possible. She could ride any stage with these tunes that bled out of her. The metal world would raise their horns. A green feeling circled her bowels.

"Aye," said Sydney, gulping. "That's our name. Midnight Machine."

"You're onto something here, Shreds. We'll win Battle of the Bands for sure if we can—"

"Your nose."

Martin knuckled his upper lip. Blood trickled down his wrist. "Woah, did you do that with your guitar?"

A gleaming, maddened smile rose up his face before he toppled from his chair.

·········

Cold shocked through the soles of Sydney's socked feet as she walked through the park late that night. Rain made small, sludgy craters in the grass that squelched under her.

"What the hell you doing out here, Syd?" she said, hugging herself.

A hulking figure lumbered a few paces ahead, his long hair dripping in the rain that bellowed off the ground. She followed, John's voice in her head telling her to watch out for glass, used needles, and condoms.

"John," she whispered, a trickle of tepid rainwater sliding over her lower lip.

Her fluffy pyjama bottoms and Metallica t-shirt were sodden, clinging to her like a second skin.

She shook the fog of sleep away as she studied the man ahead of her. This park where children played had been witness to vile rapes and murders, yet she didn't feel the urge to bolt. She followed him further into a dark corner.

The man stopped before a looming oak tree. He stared up at the leaves and spread his arms wide in supplication.

"H-Hello?" she called.

An angry song had dreamed its way through her fingers since she'd gotten home from school the night before. She'd let it rip, ignoring the questions her mother spat at her about John, why didn't she care, how she could be so cold, so evil. Her skin seemed to turn in on itself when she thought about what could've happened to him, yet she'd kept on hammering away at her strings.

The man turned. Black tar curdled down his chin as he moved his lips. The drumming rain swallowed his words.

"What? Can't hear you," she said, moving closer.

He pointed a crooked finger at her. "You took the name. Finish it."

A putrid smell of churned worms made her gag as she looked into his dead eyes. "What does it all mean?"

"The Midnight Machine calls you."

"No, I can't—"

Ashen blood glooped down the back of her throat. The man burst into a cloud of a thousand black flies. She covered her face as the swarm cycloned around her before taking to the sky. The rain continued to needle her shoulders.

"You can't be real," she said, her hands trembling through her hair. "Get a hold of yourself."

"Get away," a panicked voice wailed. "What did I ever do to you? Please. No!"

Sydney marched under the dome of leaves. A figure writhed at the base of the tree, clutching his side, face screwed up in agony.

"John! What happened?"

John's eyes grew wide as he shuffled away from her, holding up a bloody palm. "Why Syd? I did everything for you."

"What?"

"A-Always knew there was something in you. That song. That was the real you." He turned and coughed a line of spit into the dirt. "You go rot in hell."

She crouched, leaning closer. "What's happening? What are you talking abo—"

The weight of the knife in her hand stopped her cold. Warm blood trailed from the wooden handle, over her hand.

"We got on swell. What did I do wrong?" said John, each word an effort.

"No, no. It wasn't me," cried Sydney.

Her knees protested as she fell beside him, setting a hand on his quivering shoulder. He flinched like she'd stabbed him again.

"I gave you everything," he wheezed through ragged breaths. "Evil…"

"I'll get you an ambulance." She patted her pockets. Her phone wasn't there. "Shit. John?"

A long, sighing breath escaped him. His whole body seemed to deflate with it. Two dead eyes pleaded up at her.

A voice boomed from above. She felt its bass in her belly. "The Midnight Machine feeds."

Sydney leapt to her feet. Blood pounded in her ears. Four figures hunched over John's dead body. They held hands, forming a semi-circle.

"Get away from him," said Sydney.

She darted her hand forward, but the knife phased through one of the ghostly figures.

The four men bowed their heads. Strands of long, black hair covered their faces as they chanted something that made Sydney's skin crackle.

The ground rumbled up her calves. Earth churned around her stepdad, drawing him down. The stench of mud and lank rain circled her as she watched the chocolaty ground swallow him.

"No!" she sobbed into her hands.

The band turned their lurid attention on her. They all pointed with dirty, gnarled fingers.

"Let it drive you," they said in grating unison.

She ran.

·······

The next morning, Martin twitched at the end of the gravelly driveway like a junky waiting on a fix. Sydney's guitar case had never felt heavier as she walked to meet him, white breath wisping out her mouth. The cold bit into knuckles that she'd scrubbed until the skin broke, unable to rid herself of the stench of blood and rain.

Martin grabbed her by the shoulders. "Where'd you hear that name, Shreds?"

"Get off, you wee prick." She shrugged him off and marched to the end of their shady street.

"Midnight Machine? They existed before. Think I gave my laptop herpes, but I managed to find out about them. There was so much buzz about their shows, but I can't find any of their songs. You know they sacrificed a goat on stage? A goat! How metal is that?"

Her shoulder trembled with the dead weight of the guitar. The piney scent of evergreen trees from a nearby garden stung her nostrils when she took in a long breath.

Martin droned a song under his breath. "The girl wears 666. Thrusts a knife quick, quick, qui—"

Sydney dropped the case and grabbed a fistful of his polo shirt. "What did you say?"

"Calm it, Shreds. Jesus."

She leaned in close, unable to keep a trembling snarl from worming across her lips. "Where?"

"They came to me. Sounds mental, I know, but—" he blinked then stared into her eyes. "They came to you, too, didn't they? That's how all this started."

She let go. "Who?"

"Who? Who do you think? Santa? Midnight Machine. Next thing I know, I'm thrashing this mental song out of me like someone just jacked me into a plug socket, you know? Still feel it now."

She hacked at her burning scar with a ragged thumbnail, chasing away a vision of the singer and the malice in his eyes. The back of her thumb came away with blood. "We need to stop this."

"Stop it? Shreds, we just getting started. We're so gonna win Battle of the Bands. Let's get Dana and Donnie and practise later. Put on a screamer of a show tomorrow."

"It's all wrong. It's the reason that Jo—"

"Wrong? How can anything that feels that good be wrong? Don't ruin this, Sydney. We can ride this all the way to rock

Valhalla. How many years have we resorted to playing shitty covers? This is our chance."

She stared down at the stickers plastered all over her worn guitar case – the bands who'd carved a name for themselves against all odds. She clenched and unclenched her aching hands.

"Truth time," said Martin. "You played for him, didn't you? Your stepdad."

"Aye."

"He bled, didn't he?" Martin clapped his hands together, laughing up at the still sky. "Ha! Perfect. Think about it, Shreds. Ultimate PR right there – the band that rocks so hard you bleed. Your stepdad and my granny all bled out their ears or whatever. We'll be famous in no time."

"You played it for your gran?"

"Och, don't give me that. She's alright. Just sleeping it off."

"We have to stop this. What's gonna happen when we play in front of everyone? I can't."

"But it's everything you ever wanted. You've always dreamt about having command over a festival crowd, making them smash each other senseless in a circle pit. How's this any different?"

"How's it the same?" she yelled. "Mosh pits are just for funsies, you fucking moron. This is evil. Don't you feel it? The energy makes me sick."

"Makes you wanna lift that guitar and rock out though, right?"

"I…"

He was right. A large part of her wanted nothing more than to be on stage and have the crowd roaring her name. She longed to unleash the songs that whispered inside.

"I've told the committee what our band's name is," said Martin. "Midnight Machine is ready to take over. Too late to back out now."

·· • • • • • • ··

Dana clutched his bass, weeping blood and Donnie's nose dripped red on his snare drum when they practised. They'd skipped class to spend most of the next day practising in the frigid annex. She'd have spent that night at Martin's house rehearsing had it not been for the police crawling all over her home. John's disappearance had officially become suspicious. The way the detective had raised his bushy eyebrows at her heavy metal posters told her she'd be top of their list if she didn't act like a good wee lamb.

After school the next day, Battle of the Bands begun.

Sydney stood in a dust-laden backstage area, listening to a girl shriek a Britney Spears song about hitting it one more time to painful wolf whistles. Next to her, Dana thumped his drumsticks against his thigh, his thick lips moving to a count in his head, while his twin Donnie thumbed at his bass guitar. Both had painted double Ms over their bare chests. The paint was red.

"Ready to go, Shreds?" said Martin, peering from behind a side-curtain at the crowd. "They're gonna go bat shit when they hear us after this shite. Shreds?"

Last night, she'd dreamt they thundered their song, reveling in the crowd's calls for more. An eye-shaped rent had appeared at the back of the hall. The four members of the ghostly band stood around the portal, summoning a red-eyed beast. The creature had massive horns and a glowing symbol on its elongated nose.

"Syd?" said Martin. "Don't wang out on me now. We're so close."

Her knuckles went white as she squeezed her beloved guitar's neck. "Call it off. We can run through some Metallica tunes. Give them what the want, and—"

"No."

"We don't know what forces we're dealing with."

He turned, spittle hitting her face. "When are you gonna see it, eh? This is who you are, Shreds. Be the person you're meant to be. Who I need you to be."

On stage, the whorelet did one last twirl, pencil skirt whipping above her pimpled arse. The crowd clapped dutifully as she clambered off the stage.

They started pumping their fists, a chant building and building. "Midnight Machine. Midnight Machine. Midnight Machine."

"How?" said Sydney.

"That's for you, Shreds. Everyone's been going nuts after hearing us jam these last few days. Breathe it in." He punched himself on the jaw. "Oh, baby. Feel that ride. It's now, Syd. We're onto something here. And you're the star."

"I'm the star," she looked behind her at the twins and their wicked grins. "It's in all of us now."

The crowd erupted as she stepped onto the stage, the surge of energy adding a bounce to her step. Chairs squealed as the crowd leapt out their seats and shoved themselves at the stage. The thick, scarlet curtains had been drawn, pitching the hall into darkness. She plugged her guitar lead into an amp and stood by the mic. The silver taste of it was on her lips as she closed her eyes.

"This one's called—" her fingers hovered over the strings.

The crowd pressed towards her, all wide-eyed and waiting. The dead whites of John's eyes echoed in her mind. What was she doing playing around with a power like this?

"This one doesn't have a name yet," said Sydney.

She turned to her bandmates and pointed at herself – a sign to say they should back her improv if they could. She ignored the WTF riding Martin's face.

The musty scent of hall dust clung to her nostrils as she ignored the whispers and looks of confusion. The energy of the Midnight Machine begged to be set free. It itched at her, irritating her fingers.

Always knew there was something in you. That's what John had said right before he perished at her hand. No. It wasn't her. This wasn't her.

She'd show them something else.

Her fingers slid along the fretboard. A churning, raucous riff pounded out the speakers. Dana started smacking the drums behind her.

The crowd surged, raising their horns up, nodding their heads.

This wasn't the Midnight Machine playing. This was her. The noise came from her soul. She rode the feeling, leaning back, letting the ecstasy pour forth. It was a drug.

She darted her fingers up the fretboard in a spiraling crescendo before picking at the start of a solo that pulsed within her spine.

She thrashed it all out, baring her soul to the world.

Then it was over.

Her forehead was slick with sweat as the final note rung out over the awed crowd.

The ghostly singer stood in the dark corner of the hall, smiling its lecherous smile.

"No," whispered Sydney.

The crowd stared up at her, a thousand gleaming stars in the darkness. She turned to Martin. His jaw hung loose. His eyes stared into oblivion. Blood trickled from his ears.

"Midnight Machine," hummed the crowd in unison. "Midnight Machine."

"No," said Syd, covering her mouth.

She watched a large boy elbow a frail girl in the nose. A teacher fell to the floor, clawing at her long braids. A girl reached into her pocket and flicked open a penknife, slicing the blade along her own cheek. Fights and malice erupted everywhere. All while the four members of the dead band smiled from shadowy corners.

"What have I done? Stop it!"

Sydney was lifted into the air. Her bandmates carried her to the edge of the stage as carnage broke out below.

They didn't throw her. Instead, they marched off the stage, falling onto the crowd.

The back of her head cracked off the wooden floor.

Rows of blood-soaked faces stared down at her with glee.

THE SWIRLY PEOPLE

Cuthbert Watson wasn't sick. He was the only one in his house who could say such a thing. His dad's racking cough barrelled down the hall as Cuthbert lay on his pillow, arguing with himself about phoning an ambulance. As long as he could hear his mum and dad spluttering the night away, they should be fine, he hoped. It was when silence fell that worms seemed to wriggle under his skin.

He clutched the top of his covers, an electric buzz swarming inside his skull. The sound built as he clenched his eyes shut.

"Go away." He punched himself in the head as he spoke. "Go away. Go away."

The noise melted away, and the pressure in his temples faded. Sounds of distant coughing and spluttering returned.

Since they locked their home off, shutting out the outside world, Cuthbert tortured himself, imagining they'd cough their souls right out of their bodies as he dialled for an ambulance, watching them perish one by one. In his mind, the ambulance always arrived too late. Then, he'd be the man of the house – a mantle he did not want.

Duncan, his older brother, slept on the bunk below him. Cuthbert leaned over the side of the bed, hanging upside-down, blood pressing in his temples. Dunc's sweaty face glowed in the streetlight that spilled in through the drafty window.

Cuthbert focused on Dunc's chest, unable to detect any movement. He narrowed his eyes, ignoring his pulsing, protesting brain. He'd never seen his brother look so pale, so weak. Dunc snorted, and Cuthbert almost fell off the bunk.

A giggle escaped him as he sat back up in his own bed, the edges of his vision pulsing in the aftershock of his fright. He tasted the salty stench of sweat and dirty tissues as his breath returned to normal.

Rest was what his family needed. Since the bug descended on the house four days before, he'd barely slept two hours at a time, bursting awake at every cough or wheeze.

His brother continued to haul in wet breaths as Cuthbert gazed up at the white ceiling. His eyes went wide as he stared and stared, not blinking, wishing with all his bones that his family would wake the next day feeling spritely, ready to leave the house and take in the Scottish springtime air. He longed for a kick about with his dad. He'd even settle for a bruising from Dunc, as long as they were outside.

The white landscape above shifted and swirled as his eyes went dry. Cascading dots of light fell down like rain. A wave of dizziness crashed into him, eyes screaming for moisture.

He ignored the pain, continuing to stare. From that spot on the top bunk, he could almost touch the ceiling. It was one smooth lick of white paint, but when his eyes gazed into it, it changed. Swirls and grooves transformed, shifting around like thousands of fingerprints twisting, pushing down on the ceiling, reaching for him.

He hauled his race car duvet over his head. In his mind, he could hear the moist rubbing together of those shapes like maggots squirming over each other.

"Pull yourself together, you idiot. They don't exist," said Cuthbert, sour breath steaming in the darkness under his covers. "You're not a kid anymore. They don't exist."

The Swirly People. That's what he'd named them when he was a wee boy. They'd always been there, their faces swirling and dancing above him. His mum wrote it off as some weird version of an imaginary friend.

"Go play with your Swirly People, sweetie," she'd say whenever she wanted rid of him.

They were a trick of the mind, a childish fancy. On New Year's Day, he'd resolved to rid himself of them, to finally grow up. Since that day, the Swirly People came every night, screaming their mute agony down at him.

He pulled the covers down below his eyes, something inside still curious as to what the creatures were. If he squinted the right way, he could see into their pulsing, static universe.

A face burst down at him. The contours of the ceiling ran over its toothless gums as if someone held a plastic bag over its head, suffocating it.

He hauled the covers over his head. The contents of his stomach were ready to catapult out of his mouth if he made the slightest movement. Under the thick cover, he realised he couldn't hear Dunc or the rest of his family.

He cursed the stupid illness that held his family in its grip. As soon as Dunc had taken to sleepwalking in his feverish state, Cuthbert swapped bunks with him, assuring him he was fine to sleep up top after refusing for so many years.

Oh, the Swirly People? They don't exist anymore. They never did. Just a fragment of his imagination is all they were.

He whipped the covers off, keeping his eyes closed, listening intently, relief flooding him when he heard his brother's pig-like snoring. He slowly opened one eye.

A hand pressed down from the ceiling as if the roof was white cellophane. It shook with effort as it reached, its long fingers splayed like it would burst through and grab him, crushing his skull into dust.

He leapt from the bed. A little *oomph* of pain jangled up his spine as he landed on the balls of his feet. He glanced at his sleeping brother, checked he still breathed, then tiptoed out of the room to check on his parents.

·· • • •· • • •··

Cuthbert glared at the ceiling in his parent's bedroom. It'd been years since he spent any proper time in there. Running the length of the ceiling was a minuscule crack. As he concentrated on it, the familiar wriggling patterns emerged, shadows dancing around like shapes behind static snow.

The Swirly People phased into life, pointing and screaming down at his father. He'd never seen them outside his own room before.

Cuthbert held his breath. The muggy air of the hot spring day mingled with the harsh scent of cigarettes. Broken shapes slithered about on the ceiling. Handprints pushed down. The ceiling bowed under the pressure as if it were melting toffee. Pointed edges like alien fingers almost pierced their way through it, ripping into the real world.

"Spider up there, dude?" said his dad, struggling to sit up on his elbows, a dazed light in his normally bright eyes.

Cuthbert shook his head. The falling shapes vanished. He turned his attention to his bare-chested father, at his stubble of a beard that grew in rough patches like sickened clumps of grass.

"No," said Cuthbert. "Just… Never mind."

"Huh. Minds me how you used to be terrified of—" A gargling cough erupted from his dad, his face turning beetroot red. He whacked at his thin chest and lay back on the bed, catching his breath. "You were just a couple of months old the first time. Screamed so loud I was running before I realised I was even awake. You just… gazed at the roof, all dreamy eyed, you know? Like you hadn't just screamed your lungs out. Had to shake you out of it. Never quite knew what you saw up there. Took you a while, but I'm glad you're over all that."

Molten pain built in Cuthbert's temples. He slammed his eyes closed. A murmuring, shifting noise built inside his head. They weren't real; they couldn't be real. Just a leftover from his childhood imagination, that's all. He was over all that now.

"You need anything from the kitchen?" said Cuthbert.

"No, I'm—" Another cough exploded from his dad. "No."

Cuthbert walked out the room, pausing in the doorway. "Dad? You'll shout on me if you feel any worse, right?"

He waited. The tension in his shoulders felt like two boulders hunched beneath his skin. He focused on the puddle of sweat that shone in the centre of his dad's chest as his lungs sucked in air like they'd forgotten how it was done.

He strode through to the living room where his mum slept fitfully on the couch, the alkaline odour of snotters and saliva lining the air. He didn't like that his parents slept in separate rooms. They'd decided not to "share each other's germs" so they didn't keep each other sick.

"What?" his mum croaked, sitting up, chucking her covers off. "Tell me it's not got you, too? My strong boy."

Cuthbert stared down at the discarded tissues dotting the carpet like sick snowballs. He wanted nothing more than to fold himself in the crook of his mother's arm and have her hum gentle melodies in his ear.

"I'm fine, Mum," said Cuthbert. "It's—"

She sighed. The act of keeping her eyes open looked a monumental effort. "Your father said you were the weakling. Sure proved us wrong, eh? You've been a superstar. Doing a fine job of being the man of the house."

Cuthbert cleared his throat, puffing out his chest. "As soon as you're all fit and ready, we'll take a nice long walk. As a family. That's my orders."

"That's my boy."

She closed her eyes and collapsed back onto the couch. Cuthbert hauled the covers over her, tucking her in. Her skin was hot enough to alarm the empty pit of his stomach.

He did his best not to look up, but soon his neck hurt as he glared at the moving ceiling. He could almost taste their dead earth smell as they raved above.

He marched into the kitchen. A wooden seat creaked under him as he stared out the window. He longed to run outside, the fresh air swirling around his bare neck, the green pine scent of the forest enveloping him as he entered the cool shade of the trees.

In the forest, he'd be free of the constant weight pressing down on his shoulders. Were the Swirly People there to take his family away? Was it a punishment for attempting to banish them from his life?

"You're making it up, Cuthbert," he said to himself. "No such thing, young man. You're letting your imagination run away with itself. That thing always had legs. Just another few days and we'll all be out of here. Just a few days, that's it. Don't lose it. They're relying on you. Step up, man."

He dug his nails into the palms of his hands, white crescents staring back up at him. "They don't exist, silly bones."

From down the hall, a nightmare whimper came. From his dad or Dunc, he couldn't tell. He stood, hovered for a second, then sat back down.

"There you go again, you big bairn. No need to jump at every wee sound. They're fine. Everything will be fine." He tugged at his nest of hair, a sharp pain burning his scalp. "Get your act together."

It was his job to make sure death didn't claim any of his family. He was on watch, the "man of the house" as his mum had said.

White pain lit the centre of his forehead. He closed his eyes, rubbed his temples, wishing away the flood of heat that built up inside his skull. The scent of oil and iron was strong on the air.

Again, the nightmare groan came to him from the hall like a ghostly breeze.

"Dunc?"

He ran, shoving the bedroom door open. Dunc stood, swaying beside the bunk beds, his neck craned up at the ceiling. The strong, pungent sting of pee tweaked at Cuthbert's nostrils. A dark stain appeared over his brother's crotch, a growing oval spreading down one leg.

A sack of taut, translucent skin dropped from the ceiling. Swirling masses of agonised faces pressed against its rubbery surface. Their shrieks punctured his brain. The sack dropped inch by slow inch like melting rubber, as if some alien creature was about to give birth.

"Dunc?"

Cuthbert stepped forward. Shivers jolted up his arm as he held Dunc's wrist, his slow, weak pulse on his fingertips. He blinked away a heavy, dizzy spell.

Dunc's arm tensed. His entire body vibrated like he'd stuck a finger in a plug-socket. His eyes rolled in the back of his head, and he toppled back. Cuthbert held him upright, tightening his grip.

"You can't have him!" Cuthbert roared at the ceiling.

"What's that?" mumbled Dunc. "I won, didn't I? Now, I get my prize."

"Did you talk to them?"

"I don't wanna be here no more, all mushy inside. Take me."

"Take you where, Dunc?"

Dunc pointed up, his head lolling like it was too heavy for his shoulders. "Up there in the forever place."

The drooping mass had vanished. The ceiling was a smooth desert of shifting white sand. Hands slapped the other side of the ceiling, a sound like an army on the march.

"Snap out of it!" said Cuthbert, shaking Dunc.

Dunc convulsed, a shudder running all through him as he jolted awake. He glared at Cuthbert, a nasty bite in his eyes. "What is it, you wee pillock?"

"The Swirly People, they—" Cuthbert looked up, his mouth hanging open as his words fizzled out.

Nothing.

"They were right there, I swear."

Dunc tugged at his oily hair, then drummed his fingers against his wet trouser leg, his eyes going wide. He darted under his covers. He'd smelled like an unwashed sock soaked in piss.

"Dunc, I'm sorry. I can't just let them take you."

"I'm sick of your crap about those damned people. Know how childish you sound? Wake me again, you prick, and I'll knock your teeth out the back of your head, got me?"

Cuthbert glared up at the unending white of the ceiling, clenching and unclenching his fists. He felt his eyes go together.

If he focused hard enough, he could see what was *beyond* the ceiling.

Shifting faces appeared, flying around like ghosts yelling in the night, mouths hung open in endless screams. A buzz like white noise filled his skull. One face peered down at him, the swirling mass of it drawing closer, its flame-like tail of a body trailing off like glistening waves.

"Numb skull. Get to bed," whispered Dunc.

Cuthbert let go a breath he didn't realise he was holding onto. His family needed him. Needed him to grow out of that nonsense.

He stepped to a chest of drawers, took out a pair of Dunc's pyjama bottoms, and lay them on his pillow. Cold from the metal steps buzzed through his soles as he climbed into bed.

He closed his eyes tight, promising he wouldn't open them until morning.

"You never existed," said Cuthbert. "Now, go away."

· · • • • • ♦ • • · ·

In Cuthbert's dream, he ran through a white world of shifting quicksand, the blank sky making his stomach twist and turn. The ground enveloped him as he waded through the mushy surface. The harder he tried, the harder it pulled him down. Soon, it covered his neck. No Swirly People gazed upon him with their screaming, desperate faces.

He gasped in a final breath, sinking. He hammered against the hard bottom of the world, slapping his palm against it. With all his might, he shoved down. The ground turned to goo under his touch. He was almost able to touch his own sleeping face.

"Dunc…" he whispered, his mouth full of bitty, tasteless sand.

Four Swirly People huddled around Dunc's bed in the real world below him, touching his sweaty face with their blank, white fingers.

They snapped their attention up at him, pointing.

He fell through the ceiling, springing awake in bed, sending his covers cascading down to the floor. He leaned over the side of the bunk bed, blood rushing to his head as he hung, staring at his brother.

Dunc's covers moved with each irregular intake and release of breath, a nasty click sounding in his wide-open mouth.

Cuthbert grasped his hair with both hands, hauling at it until his follicles screamed fire at him. Tears sprung to his eyes as he slowly glanced up, his neck muscles protesting. Empty eye sockets pressed against the white, warping the ceiling. The faces bumped against each other, fighting to push through.

He climbed out of bed and set a hand on his brother's quaking covers. He picked up a tissue and wiped the thick mucus that clung to his brother's chin.

"I can't be the man of the house anymore," said Cuthbert. "I need you to wake up strong and look after everyone, alright?"

The faces continued to shove their slow way through the ceiling. A noise like a pelting thunderstorm echoed inside Cuthbert's skull. His mind skittered, the image of those empty faces reminding him of playing whack-a-mole at the arcade. A giggle escaped him as his sanity threatened to float away like a black balloon.

Cuthbert bolted down the hall, almost able to taste the VapoRub scent on the air.

"Dad?" He pushed his parent's door.

His dad lay on his back, eyes open, his skin a mothball shade of yellow, the scratchy fuzz of his beard growing on a jaw that hung open wider than Cuthbert thought possible. His father's chest didn't move.

Cuthbert stood by the bed, his hand covering his mouth. He held his breath, praying at his dad's chest, his feet stuck to the ground as if encased in concrete.

"D-Dad?" said Cuthbert. "No."

His dad's hands shot up. He gulped in a huge, gasping breath as if breaking out of water into fresh air. Pain crawled up Cuthbert's arm as his dad grabbed his wrist, drawing him close.

"Can't," said his dad, eyes still fixed on the ceiling. "Can't..."

"I'll get an ambulance. Sit up. Breathe, alright? There you go. Breathe. Dad? Look at me. Breathe. I-I'll be right back."

He wrangled his way free of his father's clinging grip. He gazed up at the ceiling, fearing what he might see, helpless to look away. Eight points jagged the surface, pushing down, almost ripping the shiny material of the thin veil that held the Swirly People in their own world.

The creature's mandibles and eight bulbous eyes shoved down in the middle of the ceiling. He fled to the living room, seeking his mum's phone to call an ambulance.

"Mum? Where's—"

He could almost feel the two halves of his brain being yanked apart. He stood, staring down at his unconscious mother on the floor, her legs cocked at an unnatural angle like she'd slipped off the couch, the fall not enough to wake her from her slumber.

Her phone lay on the floor like a black pebble. He picked it up and dialled 999.

"H–Hello?" said Cuthbert.

The voice hazed through the phone as if the woman spoke through a marshmallow. "999, what's your emergency? Hello?"

"Yes, hello? I need an ambulance. They've come…"

"What? You're breaking up, kid. Say again?"

He nearly said Swirly People were there. That'd be a fine way to deny an ambulance when his dad lay choking on his own breath, and his mum lay unmoving.

"Ambulance. My dad. He's choking, can't get a breath. 27 Kirk View. Mum's hurt, too. Hurry."

"Kid? You still there? Kid? If you're there, press a button for me, will you?"

Cuthbert's forehead creased as a spike of squealing feedback sputtered out the phone.

"H–Hello?" he said, clenching his teeth as he put the phone back against his ear.

Fetid breath steamed out of the phone. The velvety voices made a shock of squirming electricity jolt down his neck.

"What did we ever do to hurt you, Cuthbert?" they said. "We'll kiss your family, one by one."

The red end–call button warped as he pressed it. He launched the phone across the room. He backed away, and his back hit the wall. A seething giggle spewed from the phone in the room's corner.

He clamped his hands over his ears, drowning out the demented screams. Faces pressed against the living room ceiling, their cavernous mouths upturned in promising smiles.

"Go away!" he shouted.

"Oh, do shut up, Cuthbert," his mum said, head cocked round to near breaking point. "Leave us to sleep. There'll be time to be a selfish wee brat later."

He hauled his mother up on the couch, then he burst out of the living room, stumbling over his own feet, the sludgy nightmare settling over his shoulders like a cold blanket.

Dunc stared at a drooping sack that came down from their bedroom ceiling. Its swirling mass danced like ants gone crazy as it lowered itself inches from Dunc's nose.

He grabbed Dunc's arms, leading him back to his bed. Dunc mumbled something as he set him down on the protesting mattress, shoving the covers over him.

The tear-shaped thing bubbled down from the roof, almost reaching the floor. Beyond the thin membrane, faces and hands punched out, nearly bursting through. A long finger pointed at the bed.

He looked at his brother who slept on his back, his chest hitching as his lungs clawed desperately for air.

Cuthbert turned to the mass, now inches from his face. Its smell reminded him of the taste of bitter cello tape. Leaning in, he peered into its depths. A face screamed at him, almost touching his nose. His knees gave in. A small jolt of pain ran up the length of his spine when he landed on his backside.

He punched the floor and got back to his feet, glaring at the monstrous Swirly People trying to reach his world.

"Take me instead."

··· • • • • • ···

Dunc walked into his bedroom, the sour stench of sweat and other unfortunate stinks on the air. It'd been a few days since he'd snapped out of his funk. His inner oven was back to normal, no longer flipping from Antarctic freezing to hellish fire every two seconds.

The wee guy had come through. If it hadn't been for his little brother calling an ambulance when he did, their mum and dad would probably have died. It still plagued him how frantic Cuthbert had looked.

Untrustworthy, fevered memories played in Dunc's mind like a broken film. White beings had hissed at him, begging him to come up. He recalled the urge to hug his wide-eyed brother as he'd stood by the side of his bed. In his snot-addled condition, he chose not to comfort Cuthbert when he'd needed it most.

He stroked the covers on the top bunk where Cuthbert had slept, giving up his usual spot on the lower bunk despite being terrified of the ceiling. He'd given it up, all for him. It was Cuthbert's sacrifice that saved them from being overcome by their mysterious illness, keeping the family tethered together.

Dunc let out a long, shaky breath, running his hands through his recently washed hair, locking his fingers behind his neck. He felt like a new person when he'd gained his strength back. The scent of coconut shampoo smelled like heaven compared to the reek coming off him when he'd first came back to his senses.

A twitch of movement like a snake sidewinding across sand caught his eye. He blinked, not able to shake the feeling he was being watched. He peered at the ceiling, the blank canvas transforming into swirling fuzz.

A face appeared pressed down, its mouth twisting out silent screams.

"It can't..."

He stumbled into a lopsided chest of drawers. Rivers of ice shot up his legs, darting up his spine.

Dunc shoved his hands over his ears, a sound like teeth grinding together itching the centre of his brain.

"It was all real."

"What was?"

Dunc gasped, his heart flashing in alarm. "Cuthbert. Y-You scared me."

"You're being awfully strange, Duncan," said Cuthbert, tilting his head.

Dunc looked at the ceiling, hot blood throbbing in his ears.

Nothing but smooth white.

He let go a giggle as he turned his attention back to his little brother—the rock of the family.

Dunc felt shame stab him as a sickly feeling waved over him. An icy breeze trickled over the back of his neck.

He couldn't explain it, but Cuthbert had changed. Maybe he'd grown up a lot over the past few days. The way Cuthbert looked at him with vacant eyes—

"Duncan?" Cuthbert smiled. "Whatever is the matter?"

Duncan. He'd called him Duncan. He never called him that. Dunc or booger-face were firm favourites but never Duncan. His voice lacked the sizzle and pop Dunc was used to hearing. It was as if his vocal cords relaxed too much when he spoke.

"Still a little woozy from being sick, I guess," said Dunc. "Say, Cuthbert? Know how you used to go on and on about those Swirly People? W-When I was sick, I think you shouted at me to get away from them. Did… Did that really happen?"

Cuthbert's smile warped into a grimace. "No, it did not."

"I saw you in there." Dunc pointed up. "I swear it was—"

"We don't look up anymore."

"I saw you."

"You must've imagined it, Duncan."

"But I sa—"

"Don't turn into a big baby. There's nothing up there, okay!"

"Right." Dunc stared out the window at the bright day that lay ahead, the trees at the edge of Kirkness swishing back and forth like a green sea. "Mum's out of the worst of it. Says we can go out again. Let's get the fudge out of here."

"Out there? Outside?" whispered Cuthbert.

"Just to the forest for a wee walk. Fresh air. I haven't been out in so long I might get drunk on it."

Cuthbert clutched at his t-shirt, his eyes almost jumping out of their sockets. He ran one hand over his face, clawing his cheek, pulling that side of his face down. The pink part of his lower eyelid unfurled as he wrestled with himself, his eyes darting to the ceiling, then down again.

"We can't go outside," said Cuthbert. "It's too... *big* out there. You can't make me." Cuthbert dropped to the floor, clutching at his knees, dragging them close to his chest. His small body rocked back and forth, grinding his teeth like a fevered rat. "Don't make me. Don't make me."

Dunc walked over, throwing an arm around his quivering shoulders. "I'd be worm food if it wasn't for you. You saved us all."

As his brother buried his face in the gap between his knees, Dunc stared up at the ceiling. Figures rippled across the white, screams dead on their faces. They swarmed around a lone figure who flailed, batting them away.

It was Cuthbert up there. The shadow of his little brother punched a hand toward Dunc, his bony fingers digging through the latex-like substance of the ceiling, reaching.

"Cuthbert? What? I—"

The hand retracted as the other Swirly People clawed their arms around Cuthbert's neck, hauling him away, up into their own universe. The ceiling returned to its blank white nothingness.

"Whatever is the matter," said Cuthbert, standing inches from him. "Brother?"

GREEN WORLD

The summit of Ben Chonzie waited, lonesome in a hazy sky. Gina inhaled a lungful of green summer, delighting in the way the sheep scampered around the mountain. She could taste the sun-warmed water that burbled in streams nearby and the purple heather that swayed in the breeze.

"Don't have to be up my arse all the time," said Sadie, stepping to the other side of the gravelly path. "Give me some space, man."

"Sorry." Gina tried to strangle the rising smile from her lips. "It's just... I can't believe you're actually here, you know?"

She tucked her thumbs under the sweaty straps of her rucksack and waited for a witty retort, but Sadie only grunted and stared at her dusty boots as they crunched up the stony incline.

"Toni's super bummed she couldn't make it," said Gina. "Sickness crept up on her all of a sudden."

"Aye, I'm sure." Sadie scratched the side of her shaved head, looking as mad as a bulldog. "Hope she feels awful. Cop out."

"Hey, that's not very nice. Don't worry. The Trio will be back together soon."

All through high school, boys hurled a tv jingle at them. *Trio. Trio. They are lesbians, they're going to hell.* Instead of slinking away hurt, they took that name and made it their own. A puff of laughter escaped her lips as she remembered Sadie yelling back at one gang, saying that the Trio liked to eat boys, and not in the way they'd prefer.

Since Gina met Sadie and Toni, she rarely left their orbit. Then one moonstruck November night, Toni spun her round and kissed her. It'd been all she'd ever wanted. She'd been glued to Toni's side ever since, wanting to just burrow inside her pale skin and live there.

A butterfly fluttered inches from her nose, brilliant blue in the sun. She sighed from the top of her lungs. Could the day be any more perfect?

"Must've been terrible, not having anyone," said Gina. "I'd have gone off my trolley if I had to do the pandemic on my ownsome. Toni was my saint. Sadie? Sadie?"

A chill rose up her calves and the backs of her legs. She turned, holding a hand over her chest. Sunlight bounced off Sadie's pink hair.

"Don't do that to me," said Gina. Scree slid under her boots as she stepped down to where Sadie had stopped. "Thought I'd lost you."

"I'm, like, five feet behind you."

"Trio got to stick together."

"We're down to a duo if you hadn't noticed. Keep up your crap, I'll make you singular."

"Please don't ever do that."

Sadie's jaw tensed. Her dark eyes seemed to throw a bunch of swears at her. Gina felt the sting of them as Sadie turned her attention to a cluster of tall trees by the side of the path. The trees cast a dark shadow across half her face.

"Last time I trekked old Chonzie," said Sadie, "these trees weren't here. I'm sure of it."

The forest spread thick across the side of the mountain. Treetops swayed every beautiful shade of green, making a sound like waves crashing a beach. A waft of hot fumes sighed over Gina's face as if she stood beside a rumbling double decker bus. She leaned forward, peering into the cave-like entrance of the trees.

"What?" said Gina. "They just magically appeared?"

Sadie adjusted the straps on her rucksack. Her face turned full dark as she entered the forest's entrance. "Time for a wee detour."

"Don't!"

"Where's your sense of adventure?" Sadie ambled forward, swallowed by shadow. "Come on, scaredy-cat. Live a little."

"Wait up."

The air changed as she followed Sadie into the forest. Her breaths quickened like she'd shot up into a whole other altitude. She caught up to her friend who craned her neck up at the canopy of leaves that sheltered them from the sun. Gina had never seen anything so beautiful. It was like being plonked in the midst of a Tolkien tale. Each tree was an ideal, perfect version of a tree. Everything around them was tinted as if viewed through a kaleidoscope.

"It's the green world," said Gina.

"You what?" said Sadie.

Gina scrunched up her nose. "Do you smell that? Like diesel or something. It's like someone perfumed everything to cover up the stink."

"You're weird."

"That's why you love me."

Sadie marched ahead.

"What's got your rat?" she said to Sadie's back.

Total silence wrapped around her. No birds. No wind. No leaves rustling. Just her and her ragged breaths. All alone.

When you're all alone, the demons smell it. The badness comes for you, draws near, Gran Malya was so fond of saying. *Stick to my shadow always and you'll be safe, minha garotinha.* My little girl.

Gran Malya was proud of her Portuguese roots. Gina had her to thank for the whistles and comments she got when she got her legs out. She'd lived in Gran Malya's safe shadow until she passed on. She'd died without Gina getting the chance to come out to her.

The air felt like it had become thinner, less substantial. The heat was baking. A rivulet of sweat dripped down her temple.

"Sadie?"

Gina sprinted. Small, wiry branches scratched at her face. She ran straight under a tunnel of leaves, seeing nothing but green darkness in the distance in every direction.

"Watch—" said Gina.

Sadie stepped from behind a tree, gazing up in child-like wonder. Gina collided into her, bouncing off her sturdy frame, and crashed to the soft forest floor.

Sadie groaned, rolled her shoulder, then offered her hand, yanking Gina up like she was a ragdoll. "Why you tight as a banjo string all the damn time?"

The forest breathed to life again. It was like someone had pushed a button and restarted the system. Fresh air satisfied her lungs, settling her galloping heartrate.

"The green world lives," said Gina.

"Woah. Ever see a gold butterfly before?" Sadie leaned forward, squinting. "What the…"

Gina had once seen starlings perform their hypnotic sky dance. These shining, impossible critters did the same thing. They swarmed the two of them like a mob of wasps. The sound their collective wings made was like someone rifling through pages of a laminated catalogue. Gina hid her face behind her arms.

As quick as they'd appeared, they vanished.

Gina slowly lowered her arms, her heartbeat thud-thudding in her ears. "We need to get out of here."

"Out? This place is black lace."

Gina covered her mouth, stifling a gag. "Not supposed to be here."

"Relax for once in your stressed-out life." Sadie slapped her arm. "Back to nature, baby. Just what the doctor ordered. And I'm filling my prescription pad."

Sadie went ahead, ambling along a straight path. Trees curved their branches perfectly over her, making it look like she walked through a large, green pipe. When her image started being obscured by branches and leaves, Gina hurtled forward.

She caught up with Sadie and they walked in silence for a time, going deeper into the forest.

"Cooking in here. Is it just me?" Gina pinched her top, tugging at it, airing it out. "Feels like we've been walking for ages, but the sun hasn't shifted one bit." She giggled and sang. "*Trees, trees, go away, come again another day.*"

"Whatever." Sadie stepped over a log and continued on. "Stuck in the forever forest with Mrs. Weirdo. Great."

Gina's boot made a rubber thud. Pain jolted up her foot. The forest floor came to meet her. She couldn't get her hands up in time to stop her fall and scraped her chin across small twigs and moist dirt. She rolled over and looked behind her. She'd kicked a stone that jutted out of the ground like a hand. A pained whimper escaped her. The stone hand slowly lowered itself into the ground, disappearing.

A wave of sickness crawled its slow way through her stomach. It felt as if she'd gone drink for drink with Toni all night – a game she always lost. She turned and spewed, retching out green, globulous lines onto the ground. From somewhere behind her, Sadie tutted.

Gina gazed at her hands. They looked alien, like they were a million miles away. Along her forearm were four sets of red dots. Each had an angry, red iris that bulged with pus. She blinked her eyes hard, struggling to keep them open. "S-Sadie?"

"Come along, pukey-pants. Shift butt. Gina? Gina?"

The world seemed to flip and flop around her. She lay on the welcoming grass, staring up at the perfect, lolling leaves above. A faraway pain surged up her arm.

She felt the ground move as Sadie knelt beside her, holding her face in her hands.

Creeping numb spread over Gina's face as she tried to talk. She fought against the dark, but it claimed her, forcing her eyes closed.

·········

Gina spun among cold, lonesome stars. Her stomach lurched. Pressure built up in her temples. It was hard to tell if the universe spun around her or if she was the one doing the spinning.

Cold fingers seemed to grab the base of her spine.

Alone.

All alone.

The badness comes for you, draws near.

"No, Gran. It's not real." Her voice was pathetic against the great ocean of space.

The icy stars flamed green. Not Christmas wreath green, or the bright green of Quality Streets, but a promising, leering green that made her want to rip her own eyes out.

"Gina? For fuck's sake," said Sadie from somewhere far away. "Come back to me. Shit. Wake up!"

Dreaming. The stars were a dream.

"It's under the trees," Gina mumbled, eyes still closed. A line of hot drool ran down her cheek.

"Holy fuckery. Y–You're back."

The piney scent of the forest floor seeped up to her. Through the swirling leaves above, she felt the sun lay its radiance on her face. Sadie muttered under her breath then wrapped her muscled arms around her, tucking her chin against her shoulder. Gina's hand shook as she raised it to pat her panicked friend on the back.

"I was in space," said Gina. "I was in space, and I was alone. I don't like being alone."

Sadie let go but kept a hand on Gina's shoulder. "I lost you."

With effort, Gina sat forward. A burp of sick swam out her gullet, forcing her to slap a hand over her mouth. The world shimmied unsteadily about her.

"Butterflies," she said once she felt able. "Bit me. Knocked me out. Feel like I'm wasted."

"What do you mean, knocked out? You were dead as fuck."

"Dead?"

Sadie shook her head, then got to her feet, looping her rucksack around her shoulders. "You were gone. Least ten minutes. I checked your pulse. You didn't breathe. Nothing. I tried to call for help, but do you think I can get a signal in here?"

"Dead? But I wasn't... I'm not."

Sadie turned away and tugged at her lower lip. "Mind my grandad Barry? Died back when we were at school. When he decided to go, I was the one in the hospital room. Typical that he would wait for me. Well, you turned that yellow way he did. Rigid. As sure as Angelina Jolie is perfection, you were dead."

Gina gazed at her arm where the butterflies had bitten her – nothing but smooth skin. No red welts like jellied eyeballs peered at her.

"Let's get shifted, princess," said Sadie. "Get you looked over. Should never have agreed to come here after Toni backed out on me."

Gina leaned over to her pack and took out a bottle of water. Refreshing cold trickled down her gullet. The water hit the bottom of her stomach. She finished half the bottle, then stood.

"Give Toni a break," said Gina. "Probably best she didn't make it now, considering." She caught a flare of rage in Sadie's eyes. "What? What did I say now?"

"We were gonna... Never mind." Sadie started walking in the direction of the tunnel-like path cutting straight through the forest. "This place is too beautiful, if you get me. Like one of those plants that suckers you in and chomps you up. Getting that vibe."

"We should call somebody."

"Tried that."

"Try again."

"What we gonna say, eh? Hello, mountain rescue? We're stuck inside an impossible forest up the side of Ben Chonzie. Golden butterflies bit my friend. Killed her, but she's alright now, just a wee bit piqued."

"You don't have to be such a cow about everything."

"Cow? Know what? When we get out of here, I'm leaving you on the side of the mountain. Done dealing with your whiny face. Done with this whole Trio shite."

"Done? You can't be done. What about Toni?"

Gina's voice wavered as she tried to stand her ground, telling herself not to look away. A river of nerves jangled down her arms. If she had to raise them in defence, they'd be flimsy and useless.

Sadie reached into her pocket, pulled out her phone and danced her forefinger along its screen in short zigzags. "It wasn't supposed to be me doing this on my own."

"Do what on your own? Sadie?"

A dry, dusty hiss crackled from the phone. Sadie's hand jerked like it had stung her, though she held onto it. A wail whimpered out her lips. Steam rose from it as the plastic melted, covering Sadie's hand in black syrup.

Gina gagged on the sizzled meat smell. "Throw it!"

Sadie leaned back and screamed a note of agony at the trees. The sound ricocheted back at them. Gina grabbed her, held her up. The skin on Sadie's blackened hand continued to sizzle.

Gina brought out her own phone. Her heart flipped at the cutesy picture of Toni with her tongue stuck out and the sight of her bright green tongue-bar.

As she thumbed the screen to dial for help, she felt the phone's case going hot and gangly. She launched it. Where it landed, it steamed into a black puddle. A sound like children laughing came from it before it vanished into the forest floor.

"It's mocking us," said Gina. "It has eyes behind every tree. Eyes of stars, everywhere."

"Shut the fuck up and help me."

Sadie knelt on one knee. Sticks snapped beneath her as she clutched at her wrist.

The skin between Gina's shoulder blades prickled. Someone, or something stared at her. Silence fell as she looked around.

The forest waited, exalting in Sadie's whimpering, like it was breathing in her pain.

"It's still burning," said Sadie. "Holy mother of shitting fucking cuntery, it hurts."

"We need to get you out of here. Go buy you one of those robotic hands. Be the talk of Balekerin with one of those."

Sadie chuffed like a bull about to charge. Gina saw the war of words waiting to whip out of her friend's mouth and braced herself to take them on the chin. They didn't come. Sadie set her feet and stood, clutching her forearm just above the black mess of her hand. When her eyes rolled in the back of her head, Gina darted forward to catch her, but got a stiff arm in her chest for her trouble.

"Don't fucking touch me," said Sadie. "Walk."

Gina stared into the deepening green of the forest. Diamonds of neon-green opened, multiplying in pairs among the darkening trees.

"They're here..."

Sadie jerked and slapped her away.

"Stupid, stupid, bitch," yelled Sadie, clutching her hand. "Argh!"

In her panic, she'd grabbed Sadie by the injured hand. Sadie's forehead lit up with veins as she doubled over, rocking in pain – pain she'd caused.

"You stupid," Gina whispered to herself. "When will you learn? You deserve to be in the alone place." She clutched her fingers, feeling a ghostly pain beneath her fingernails, like something tried to pry the nail off. "The alone place..."

Back when she'd been super into her My Little Pony figures, she walked to her Gran's car at the Glen when a Bad Man grabbed her by the ponytails and hauled her into his rusty Ford Escort. She still dreamed of that car. How patches of brown against its once proud white had looked like maps. How it reeked of something stronger than cigarette smoke. How broken she'd looked in the window's reflection as she kicked and screamed while other parents watched, only shaking their heads. What a bad girl she must've been.

Gran Malya had saved her. Sconed the fucker with her huge bag. There was a standoff where she was sure the Bad Man would charge at her gran, but he only tutted like someone had spilled a drink over him, then leaned into the seat of his boy-racer car and zoomed away, leaving Gina tasting bits of dirt.

She was a stuttering, hitching, sobbing wreck of a girl. Gran Malya knelt on one knee, grabbed her by the chin and made her look into her stony, grey eyes.

"*Minha garotinha*," she said, "I warned you not to be alone. See what happens? The Bad Man came to get you. You invited this. I want you in my shadow at all times. If you're always with me, the badness can't get to you. Got that?"

And so she had. She'd even slept in the same room as her gran, the rhythms of her snores drawing her to sleep each night. It took her years to stop going to the bathroom with her gran in tow.

"You need to be taught a lesson," said Gran Malya years later, grabbing her by the shoulder, her thumb pressing into bone.

"What? I didn't mean to," cried eleven-year-old Gina. "Honest. W-Where are you taking me?"

Gran Malya shoved her down the hall, opening a quaint, slanted door to the cupboard beneath the stairs. "Get in."

"What? Granny, no. I only sniffed the booze, honest. I wasn't gonna drink any. Gran. No!"

Complete darkness cloaked over her as the door creaked shut. Gina punched and scratched at the door, but her gran clicked the lock.

"Bad girl," said Gran Malya, her voice on the other side of the darkness, far, far away. "Maybe some time in the alone place will make you regret being bad."

"Don't leave me alone. Don't leave me alone. I can't be alone. They'll get me. Gran? Gran!"

She could still feel the way her fingernails had bent to snapping point. She'd clawed at the wood like a rabid animal, her flight mode on full. After that, she did everything she could to make sure she stuck to Gran Malya like a shadow and never set a foot wrong. She couldn't bear another long hour in the alone place.

A sigh breathed its way over her face, bringing her back to the forest. When she looked at the trees, the green-eyed creatures were gone.

"We can't be here when the sun goes down," said Gina.

They walked back the way they'd come, the scenery crisp, green, unchanging. Gina's calves groaned after an unknown time, walking by tree after beautiful tree.

The sun's warmth radiated along the back of her neck. She turned her head up, staring at the leaves. "Surely, it's almost sunsetting time, but it's hotter than Kelly Clarkson's face in here."

Sadie walked beside her, hunched over her hand. "All I wanted was to come here, to tell you the truth. My hand... It's ruined. It's fucking ruined and you're talking about Kelly Clarkson."

"Tell me the truth? What do you mean?"

Sadie stopped, opened her mouth to speak, and closed it again. By the side of the straight path, another way opened. Branches popped as trees parted like two fancy butlers ushering them through.

"No!" said Gina.

"Where else we gonna go, eh? Maybe it's helping us."

"This forest, this place, doesn't help people. It's unnatural."

Sadie ignored her and walked into the narrow space made by the parting trees. The forest flowed around Gina, guiding her to where it wanted to go. Leaves brushed her arms as she stepped forward. Some tugged at her skin with tiny, barbed endings.

Minha garotinha...

The sound whispered along the small hairs on her neck. She looked about the trees, searching for the impossible image of her grandmother. Nothing. Her heart beat so loud she felt its thud in the bottom of her ears.

"Woah," said Sadie from somewhere ahead.

Gina sprinted and the green world opened up once more. They stood underneath a dome made by the treetops of ancient oaks. Gina craned her neck to look up at the impossible height of the trees that seemed almost fake, like they were special effects in a Hollywood blockbuster.

In the centre of this dome, white mist covered an egg-shaped stone that sat on its side. The oozing tang of battery acid crept towards her. The stench was so thick she could almost see it ripple the air.

"It's a meteor," said Sadie, moving closer to the dark stone.

"Don't go near the heart."

"Heart?" Sadie turned to her with fever-lashed eyes. "You been licking frogs back there?"

"I... I don't know why I said that."

Gina stared into the stone. It was blacker than any stone had any right to be. She wanted to run her palm over its smooth surface. Tendrils of white ghosted from it like dry ice.

"I read somewhere," said Sadie, dropping her burned hand by her side, "that the meteor that killed the dinosaurs landed where the Amazon is now. The impact created a tropical paradise. What if this is the same type of thing?"

"You mean, all this was brought from some alien world?" Visions of the cold void she'd swam through when she'd been poisoned came back to her. "We need to go. Like, now. Right now."

"Go? We tried that already, babe. Ain't no *go*, here. Only *stay* is here."

The childish cadence of Sadie's voice was something Gina had never heard before. It made the contents of her stomach swirl.

"*Stay, stay, stay*," Sadie chimed, "*ain't no windows here. No way out, don't you cry no tears.*"

"Sadie? We need to get out. Your hand."

"Your face."

"What about my face?"

"Nothing." Sadie turned to eye the black rock. Sweat glistened from her temple. "Just that I hate that fucking thing. Always with the lost-me eyes. Always me and Toni bailing you out. And now you and her, cooped up all cosy."

"You're not right in the head."

"I get it now."

"Get what?"

"You're a pup. A rescue pup. Must've been hell stuck with you all that time, with your needy, bastarding shite. No wonder she's gonna—" Sadie turned and kicked the base of a thick tree, wincing in pain. "She should be the one to do this."

"Do what?" Gina stepped closer, sensing the watching silence of the forest. "Do what, Sadie?"

Sadie walked until she stood in front of the stone. She took a sharp breath and then placed her palm on its smooth surface. An ecstatic shudder seemed to roll through her as she closed her eyes.

"You're a big girl, right?" said Sadie, eyes still closed. "Can't believe Toni crapped out on me. Plan was to tell you together."

"Tell me—" Gina spidered her fingers over her mouth. She looked away, up into the towering trees, unable to shake that prickly feeling they were being watched. "Tell me what?"

"When she snuck out for those long walks during the height of all this virus pish, who did you think she was coming to see, eh? Tried to get her off the idea of bringing you here to tell you. Her idea. Tell you in person. Keep the Trio strong and together."

Gina ran a hand through her hair and turned her back on Sadie and the stone. She fought against her jelly knees that wanted nothing more than to collapse. If she did that, she knew she'd lose it, sobbing like a little girl.

"I thought she needed space," said Gina, rolling a knot of hair between her fingers until follicles screamed at her. "It was hell. All this time. She was seeing you."

"You and your crazy drove her to it."

Hot, manic energy seemed to flow up her calves from the forest floor. An image of bouncing Sadie's thick skull against the rock thrummed within her. A giggle tripped its way out of her lips. "This was a break-up hike, that it?"

"Until Toni shat out on me, aye. Can you turn around and face me at least?"

"Why'd you have to sneak around like that? Like a couple of... a couple of whorelets."

At the sound of the last word, the charged up fury evaporated. The tension slunk from her shoulders. After Gran Malya's heart gave out two years ago, Toni and Sadie were all she had left in the whole world. Without them, she was nothing.

She talked back over her shoulder, shame flushing its way up her neck. "I'd have stepped aside, you know. Let you be happy, if that's what Toni wanted."

"I think we both knew that."

Gina turned. She could hear the scratch of skin Sadie's hand made as she moved it over the stone. She wanted to run forward and hug her old friend and tell her it would all be okay. She wanted to rush forward and squeeze that burned hand until her friend's face went purple.

"We need to get out before something serious happens," said Gina.

The forest went dark.

"Sadie? You there?"

The world returned to light. Gina blinked away the dizziness and strobing images as her brain adjusted from sudden night to sudden day.

The stone lay on its side. Sadie wasn't beside it.

"Sadie!"

Something crashed through the brush beside her. She shoved her head back, feeling her neck click. A black and white shape flapped inches from her face. A magpie glided into the high treetops.

"Och, you scared it away." Sadie appeared at her side, staring up.

"Did you see it get dark? Like the sun just blew up."

Sadie fixed her with glassy eyes. "Dark? Middle of the day, hen."

Gina gazed up at the magpie. It turned, clicked its tail-feather at them, then soared across the space onto another branch. It flew too smoothly, mechanical, like it was pulled on a zip-wire.

Every time she saw a magpie, it stirred something in her. Toni had a tattoo of a small magpie on her shoulder that she'd spent countless hours tracing with her fingertips. Her heart swelled. She gulped in a deep breath. The memory of Toni's sharp, blue eyes. The dancing Toni on drunken Fridays. Toni with the zap, the energy, the best hugs. Toni telling her she'll never have to be alone again.

The green air stung her eyes.

"Can't trust the bastards when they're alone." Sadie took in a breath and roared at the magpie. "Hey, fuck-face. Why'd you not have any pals, eh? Two for joy? Two for get us the fuck out of here, more like. Show us the way." She lowered her voice. "Magpies are from hell, you know. The devil himself. You hear me, Gina? Gina?"

Gina peered into the forest. The way into this large, dome-like space had been a tiny entranceway made by moving trees. Now, the trees had parted, the ground smoothing over like a road.

"The forest changes," she said, leaning forward, ear pointed toward the road, listening. A sound like a lawnmower revving buzzed its way to them. "Are those... headlights?"

"Don't be dumb."

The harsh roar of an engine split through the forest. In the distance, two diamonds of light grew. A car was racing its way towards them, through the impossible road in the trees. It was white.

"The Bad Man." Gina turned, tried to run for the big stone, but her legs turned soft and useless. It was him. Come back to get her. Unfinished business. "Sadie, get out his way!"

"What are you blethering about? Nothing there."

Everything slowed. She saw the way Sadie scrunched up her mouth and shook her head as she gazed into the trees. Her face lit in awful white from encroaching headlights, yet she didn't seem to notice.

"Get out of the—"

The Ford Escort hit Sadie at speed, sending her spinning through the air. Her body crunched to a landing by the big stone. Gina had to paw at the moist grass to keep herself from falling as she raced over.

A line of black blood trickled down the side of Sadie's face. Her neck was at an impossible angle. Two blank eyes stared into Gina, seeming to beg for help before life deflated from them.

"No!" screamed Gina. "No."

A car door clapped shut. Gina stumbled her way back to her feet. The Bad Man stood by his Escort with its cancerous rust.

"You're not real," she said.

"Why don't you come for a ride, eh? Got lollipops in here. All kinds of things you can suck on. Ha-ha."

The oily smile that split his face made her gag. She held a hand over her face, willing herself to run, unable to move.

"Enough talking, babes. Let's go."

"But—"

She was about to scream that she was too young when he darted forward, grabbing her by both arms. She kicked and squirmed, but he had her in a vice grip, throwing her over his shoulder. The door opened and the reek of cannabis circled her as he chucked her in.

"Just you stay there for me, honey-bunch," he said. "Stay sweet for me. Let's go to my quiet place. My alone place for a while."

"A–Alone place?"

The door slammed closed, and he sped away, leaving her in the back seat watching the trees blur by. She tried to pry the door open, knowing that if she fell out the car at this speed she'd die, but anything was better than what his eyes promised. The door stayed locked.

She eyed the road. Massive trees stood before them, looming large. "Watch out!"

She wrapped her arms around her head, bracing for the impact. The car crashed through the trees as if they were made of cardboard.

"This baby can handle anything," the man said, one hand on the wheel, one hand between his legs. "Bet you can handle anything, too. Can't wait to find out. *Minha garotinha.*"

"What did you just say?"

The man turned his head around slowly. For a split second, she thought the skin slipped, showing something grey and metallic beneath.

"You're a fake," she said. "You're not real. Get back in your box."

Her neck snapped back, hitting the headrest. They'd hit a jump. The car's engine red-lined as the contents of her stomach rose. As the car's bonnet dipped, she saw the black body of water they were headed for.

The man smiled knowingly at her. Then he melted away, his body turning into soft wax.

The car exploded into the water. Churning water gushed in, consuming everything. She sucked in a final breath, kicking and punching at the door, unable to move it. The car tipped. Above her, giant bubbles of air burst out the car, floating their way up to the shiny surface.

The rusted white coffin dragged her into the dark.

·········

Gina gasped in a long, guttural breath. The oxygen spread warmth through her chest. The grey taste of water clung to the back of her throat. It was only when she blinked, she realised how dark it was.

"I'm still in the forest," she said.

Soft, green smells pawed at her face, but she couldn't feel the air anywhere else. The rest of her was stuck inside something. Whatever it was, it held her tight. The squishy, oily sound she made when she moved her arms was like swirling a knife round a jar of goose fat.

"I died again," she said.

The imploding pain in her lungs came back to her. She'd been pulled into the deeps. Drowned. She'd drowned. It was every bit as awful as she'd imagined it could be.

Green dots flickered to life far below. Her eyes ached as the lights multiplied, turning darkness into bright, sickly light. The green dots begun shooting up the barks of the trees all around her.

She was high off the ground, inside a tree. Her face peeked out of an oval gap in its bark.

"I'm the creamy centre."

She started to laugh, but cut herself off, not liking the torn, loopy quality of the sound.

The tree she was stuck inside had a heartbeat. It thumped every three seconds, jangling her spine. Each time it beat, it cancelled her thoughts, sending her into a moment's panic.

"They landed it here on purpose," said Sadie somewhere to her right. "Playtime, babes."

"Enough of that, where are you?"

"*Look at me. I'm a tree,*" sang Sadie. "*I'm as happy as can be. With a nick-nack, paddy-wack, give Toni a bone. This old hack's a jolly gnome.*"

Gina moved her arms through the moist, warm goop. She placed her palms against the inside of the tree's bark and pushed. A sliver of the bark cracked loose like pork crackling. She punched at it, chopping her way free. The air chilled the gloopy substance caked over her arms as she hauled herself out of the cavity and onto a thick branch. The bark irritated her fingertips until she had to resist scratching the skin off them.

She pulled herself along the branch like a careful caterpillar. As she neared its end, it bowed, lowering her to the ground. She let go of it and landed on the forest floor.

"Sadie?"

Mist steamed around her boots, dancing across the bright lights. The air had a sweet, fluffy taste, like pink candy floss.

"Did you get in the car with a yucky boy?" said Sadie, somewhere close.

Gina looked around the electric forest. In the centre of an oval outlined in brilliant green, Sadie's face appeared from inside a tree like some sleeping deity. Her arms dangled loose from two holes.

"I'll pull you out," said Gina.

"It was me that died this time, wasn't it? Smacked by a boy racer in the middle of a forest." The merriment in her voice turned sour. "What did we step into?"

Gina gripped Sadie's forearms and pulled. The tree split open like a rib cage, spewing Sadie out on top of her.

"I-I died, too," said Gina, letting go, sitting up. "Drowned. Sadie?"

"Aye?"

"Your hand. It's fixed."

Sadie held the hand up. The green light made shadows crawl over her face. "Am I supposed to be happy about that?" She dropped the hand and sighed. "Sorry. I'll try to stop being such a dick. I just… I just hope…"

"It's alright, you don't have to."

Sadie took a breath and tried again. "They say death is this mythical thing, like it washes all your pain away. It wasn't like that at all. I can still feel it – the fire of that pain as I died like roadkill smacked by a truck."

Beneath Gina, something rumbled like the ghost vibrations of a distant train. "It's a machine. Keeping us alive. So it can toy with us."

"We shouldn't have snuck around behind your back. I'm so sorry. We didn't mean to—"

"Stop. We'll survive. Nothing can split the Trio up."

"Really?" Sadie sniffed. "You really mean that?"

"We stick together. No matter what."

Gina looked around for their rucksacks but couldn't find them. They walked through the dark forest, guided by the lights. As they went on, the lights behind them switched off so they were only able to see the snaking path ahead. Gina crossed her arms, trying her best to suppress shivers.

"If I die again, I'm gonna lose my—" Sadie flinched. "G-Grandad?"

Gina followed her stare. Nothing. "He's not there, Sadie. It's not real." She clamped her hand around Sadie's soft wrist. "Sadie?"

"*If you're alone in the woods today,*" sang a dusty voice, "*you better not go at night.*"

"S-Sadie?"

A prickling sensation fizzled up the arm she'd grabbed Sadie with. Loose flaps of skin hung over her knuckles. Her lungs forgot how to work, how to take in air. Gina had never been able to touch her own fingers together when she'd clutched onto Sadie in the past. Now, her thumb and forefinger touched with room to spare. She screamed inside, telling her neck muscles not to look up at the figure she held on to, but it was no use.

A crone leered down at her. Its eyes were black moons. Wet skin blubbered off its hideous nose. When it opened its mouth, dry words hissed out. "*If you're alone in the woods today, no standing on the green light.*"

"What?"

The light around them increased in intensity. It showed every line and pock mark on the witch-like face. Her song sighed out of her open jaw, bringing with it the scent of deadly, whitened mushrooms. "*For Gina Gregor and Sadie will die and die and die and die again. Today's the day, that Gina's alone foreeeever.*"

Gina's whole body trembled. Her mind teetered on the edge of some precipice. She couldn't tear her gaze away from those hungry, all-consuming eyes. She tried letting go, but her grip tensed as if an electric current passed through her.

"What do you want from us, you sicko?" she said.

The thing leaned in, slowly drawing closer and closer until she could feel its hot breath tickle her ear. Curls of mist rose from the black cloak that flapped languidly around her skeletal frame.

The crone's tongue clicked wetly. "*Minha garotinha.*"

The form stumbled forward, reached its clawed fingers out to grab her shoulders as if to stop itself from falling. Gina jerked, balling her fist, ready to crack the thing on the jaw, but it collapsed in on itself, crumbling like it was made of dirt.

She sunk to her knees beside a mound of earth. As she sobbed, the gravity of the world seemed to press down on her shoulders. The way the lights zipped around her made her feel as if she were stuck in some futuristic computer.

"Sadie?" she called. "You dumb animal. Stop leaving me."

Gina groaned, then punched her fingers into the soil. It crumbled like warm chocolate cake. Anger boiled out of her as she ripped at the ground, tearing clumps of grass and dirt.

The impact of something solid jarred her fingers. She'd struck something that felt like a glass windshield. Seeing its glint, she dug some more.

Below her, a massive piece of machinery worked, pistons pumping, sparks flying. The engine looked as big as a house. It sent vibrations tracking up her palms.

"How do I switch you off?"

The machine below picked up speed.

She peered into the trees. At the furthest point, the lights flickered out.

Gina stood. "Don't."

A noise light a door slamming closed echoed toward her. The darkness stepped closer like someone hit a switch. She turned. Darkness crept in from that direction, too.

The sound crashed again. More lights blinked off. She tugged at her hair, standing in the only remaining circle of light. It was an island floating in a starless sky. "Please."

Total darkness consumed her.

Her skin prickled with heat. She poked and clawed at her face, making sure she was still here, still alive.

When you're all alone, the demons can smell it. The badness comes for you, draws near.

"Gran?"

When you're all alone, the demons can smell it. Stick to my shadow always and you'll be safe, minha garotinha.

"It's not you. It can't be you."

Stick to my shadow always and you'll be safe, minha garotinha.

Gina sucked in a breath that tasted more like spilled diesel than forest. "Stop!"

Stick to my shadow.

She dropped to her knees. "I'm in the alone place, Gran. Save me. I... I wish I told you the truth about me and Toni. How much she makes me happy. How much I ruined that, too."

Stick to my shadow. Stick to my shadow. Stick to my shadow. Stick to—

"It's not you!" Gina slapped at her head, trying to drive the voice away. "Whatever you are, come get me. You hear? I'm not scared of you. I won't play this game."

Sobs rocked through her as she set her forehead on the warm earth. A pang of homesickness hit her so hard it felt like a physical blow. She'd kill to be able to sit on their wee couch, watching crappy telly, nuzzled into her Toni. Never again would she comment on Toni's collection of bird ornaments that covered every available surface. She'd hug her and never let go.

The green world returned. Fresh, summer air flittered about her nostrils like a dream. She gulped it in.

"Why are you so beautiful?" she said to the forest and its soft, kaleidoscopic colour.

Sadie's scream blasted through the trees. The broken note in that scream clawed at something in Gina's soul – no human should ever make such a noise.

After searching for a long time, she split open another tree, catching Sadie as she fell out the womb. The white substance on Sadie's skin smelled like roses mixed with turpentine.

"Dead again," said Sadie, leaning her head against Gina's shoulder. "All dead again. Where'd you go, drumstick?"

"Where did I go?" Gina shoved Sadie off her. "You left me there with that… thing. We stick together from now on, alright? I want you in my shadow."

"How did we get in this mess, Gina? I don't wanna die again. It's too much. Just leave me on the other side next time. You hear that, forest?" Sadie's chin wrinkled and she bent forward, sobbing from her stomach. "If I wasn't a girlfriend stealing cow, we wouldn't be here in the first place. I—"

Gina slapped her. The sound cracked around them, rebounding off the shelter of leaves above. It had been the first time she'd hit anyone. The skin on her palm ached as she watched Sadie lift a hand and rub her jaw.

"You're supposed to be the strong one, damn it," said Gina. "If we don't make it out of this hell, neither of us gets the girl. I'm not sticking around until it gets dark. I'd rather die than be alone again. We stick together, got that?"

Sadie stared down at the mossy floor, refusing to meet her gaze. "I just love her, you know? I love you, too."

The earth rumbled beneath Gina's feet. She shot her hands out, expecting the ground to open up and claim her. The trees in front of them changed. They creaked and twisted, making a sound like wrung leather and popping sinews. It morphed in front of them.

"I can't be seeing this," said Sadie, standing next to her.

Five cave-like entrances appeared before them. Each way was obscured in shadow.

"I want to die again," said Sadie, her voice hoarse. "For keeps this time. You got a knife? Stick me with it. I can see you want to."

Gina glanced at Sadie's stomach, imagining the clean blade of her pocketknife slicing through skin, its handle flowing red. The knife was in her rucksack that had been lost several deaths ago. She rubbed her moist palms on her trousers.

"W-Which way?" asked Gina.

"Does it matter? Spoiler alert – they all kill us."

Gina studied the entrances. She had the strange sensation of floating up, watching herself and Sadie pick a direction as if she played a video game set in a fantasy world.

As she walked past each entrance, the air changed. The first smelled of a desert landscape. The second was of acrid swamp. The third of lavender and—

"Toni?" said Gina, staring into the dark tunnel. "Hear me out. That's Toni's perfume smell coming from that one. I'd know it from anywhere. Hard as sin to find, and just as expensive."

"Pish."

"No, lavender, actually."

"Funny cunt. You think this forest, this 'green world' as you keep calling it zapped Toni in here?"

She gazed into the shadow of the third entrance. The purple taste of lavender wound its way around her, filling her with memories of their first picnic date where she'd been so excited she couldn't touch a single sandwich. The sun had shone so bright that day.

"You're right," said Gina. "It's messing with us. We—"

You two coming to play or what?

"T-Toni?" said Gina.

"It's her," said Sadie. "Toni, wait there. I'm coming."

"Stop." Gina stood in front of her, guarding the entrance. A spike of chill air blew against her back. "That's what it wants."

"But you heard. It's her. Let me past. She needs me. Toni?"

Gina planted her feet, pushing Sadie away as she tried to muscle through. Sadie slapped at her, landing open-palmed blows on her arms. They crashed to the floor when Gina wrapped her arms around her, taking her down.

"Let go," said Sadie.

"You've gone off the deep end. You—"

Sadie landed an elbow on Gina's chin, making her head crack back. The world fizzled back into place slowly. As she came back to herself, she saw Sadie march towards the entrance.

Gina rubbed her jaw. "We didn't want you around. We never did."

Sadie stopped, turned. "What?"

"You heard me. We never wanted you near us. Nothing but a gooseberry. Couldn't wait for you to leave."

Gina closed her eyes and waited for the blow. A calm settled upon her, cooling her from her shoulders down to her heels. She inhaled the taste of lavender. Its flowery, violet smell coiled around her tongue, her lips. It was as if she'd spent the night kissing Toni's neck, getting lost in the best way.

She opened her eyes.

Sadie wasn't there.

She wrung the collar of her t-shirt. Her breath came out in quickening gasps. Ahead of her, the chasm of the entrance waited.

"That wasn't very nice of you to say that."

"Toni?" Gina stumbled to her feet. "Toni, w-where are you?"

Toni's husky voice seemed to come from the very trees. "Especially when it wasn't true. You're not the one I wanted. You did the trick for a spell."

"You're the alien thing. Not my Toni. Why are you torturing us?"

"Because you're a tight bitch who always gets her way, and you deserve to suffer."

Toni's lilting giggle echoed around the trees. Both of Gina's hands tugged at her hair as she marched around, seeking the source of that terrible laughter.

When it spoke again, it was all soft and honeyed. "Just popping for a wee walk, snookums. Don't worry. I'll be back soonish. Need me some outside time, you know? Some alone time."

"You want to break us," said Gina. "I was already broken."

"And don't I know it."

The forest plunged into darkness. Green lights crawled over the ground. The corners of Gina's vision began to strobe. She stottered about the trees, bouncing off them. Cut into a bark was Toni's face. Her smooth, touchable skin glowed green.

"How do we get out, babe?" said Gina.

Toni's face vanished into the hollow of the tree. Another Toni appeared in the next tree, lit again in green.

"You don't," the Toni-thing said.

"There has to be a way."

As it spoke, multiple Tonis buzzed inside Gina's skull. "We have you now. This is your home. Your forever place. What's wrong, dearie? Don't you like it? Don't you like what we've made for you?"

"I can't take it anymore."

"Oh, I think you'll be surprised at how much you can take."

The green lights switched off.

"Don't leave me." Gina stumbled forward, catching her foot on a branch. She made a small, pathetic oomph as she hit the forest floor. "Toni? Sadie?" She crawled forward, tapping at the moist ground. "Anybody?"

Her breath wouldn't stay in her lungs. It panicked out of her. She felt her mind slipping into madness. The feeling took her back to being locked in the alone place.

I love you, minha garotinha, her Gran's voice echoed in her mind.

"It's not from here," said Gina. She felt her breath mist against the grass. "It wants to be us. To feel what we feel, like some sick experiment."

The image of her Gran's grey eyes and tough smile made something ache deep within her.

"Bring back the green world. Please?"

Something whirred and ticked under her. One second it was cloaking darkness, the next it was summer day.

"Aw, how sweet," buzzed the Toni-thing from somewhere unseen. "Shame she isn't here to see what you've become."

Gina rose to her feet. "How do I switch you off?"

"Do you want to meet it? I'll introduce you right quick. He's ever so quiet, though."

The tree closest to her morphed. It turned into something like black, oily plastic, making a sound like a thick tongue rolling in a saliva-filled mouth. A slender shape towered over her. It was black all over, though Gina knew somehow it was grey and metallic beneath. Her legs almost buckled when the monster's eyes lit up. Two rectangles of violent green light shone where its eyes should've been. Four identical squares buzzed as its mouth.

Toni's whispery voice echoed in her mind. "He likes to play. Night time, light time is just the best. It's such a scream."

"Sadie was right," said Gina. "It's an alien, landed here to toy with us."

The creature raised a slow hand, pointing a clawed finger at her chest. Its attention made worms skitter about inside her stomach. The air between them tasted of cold silver.

"Oh, lucky you," said Toni. "He wants to show you something."

"I think I've seen enough already, thanks."

"Nonsense. We're just getting started."

Gina pulled her gaze from the impossible being and ran into the trees.

"Sadie?" she called. "Sadie, where are you?"

"Ow, good idea," said Toni. "Get Sadie involved. Really knows how to use her tongue, that one. Let's get the Trio back together, shall we?"

A rustling sounded from behind her. Gina stumbled towards it. She felt the skin tighten at her temples. It was as if she was one thing away from her brain deciding to go bye-bye.

The noise was Sadie. She stumbled forward, slaloming like a drunkard, mumbling under her breath. Gina ran to her, held her by the shoulders. A line of spit ran down her chin. No matter how she shook her, Sadie wouldn't look her in the eye.

"Stay with me, Sadie. Please? Come on."

"I hate this," said Sadie, vacant eyed, staring at the grass. "But we have to, don't we?"

"Snap out of it."

"She'll understand, eventually. I can't stand to be the one to break her heart." A tear tracked its way down Sadie's eye, running alongside her nose. "Poor Gina."

"W-What?"

The wind sighed over her. The trees shook violently, shedding their leaves, making a sound that drowned her thoughts. She slapped her hands over her ears and closed her eyes.

A taint of lavender hit her nose.

She wasn't in the forest. She stood in the doorway of Sadie's small apartment. Toni sat on a couch, legs folded beneath her, wringing the frayed ends of her cardigan, focusing on the motion, getting lost in it.

"Toni?" Gina stepped forward, hitting an invisible barrier. It wouldn't let her through. "Toni?"

Sadie entered, kneeling on both knees in front of Toni, taking her hands.

"I can't stand to break her heart like this, but it's for the best. I can't go on like this."

"Aye, it sucks eggs," said Toni. "How did we let it get to this?"

"All I know is that I love you and the world is tasteless without you here with me. I need you, Toni. I've always loved you. Driven me nuts over the years."

"Driven you nuts." said Toni, a sour laugh escaping her. "Got that effect on people, don't I?"

"Hey. Hey, look at me. Gina will get over it. I promise. We'll stick together. We'll make it through. I know it's tough, but I love you. We're doing the right thing."

"We need to tell her together. Explain ourselves. Own up to it."

Sadie chewed the inside of her cheek and shook her head. Then she darted forward and planted a kiss on Toni's lips. They curled into each other, leaning into it.

"Like two pieces of a puzzle that are meant to be," said Gina, watching with her palm against the invisible barrier. "Why didn't you tell me? Why didn't I see?"

When she closed her eyes, two tears fell down her face. The smell of lavender was replaced by a musty, engine smell. When she opened her eyes, she saw her hand held against the bark of a tree.

Sadie gasped behind her. Blood spouted from a slash across her neck. She sat down, clutching at the blood. It painted her hands crimson. Gina watched as the life flowed out of her friend. The trickle of blood continued even though Sadie was gone, sitting with her legs splayed like a discarded doll.

"I need to know why," said Gina.

The booming voice that came back made her brain want to implode. It buzzed around her blood. "We don't care for your kind."

"Go fu—"

Something yanked at her head, throwing her up into the air. Wind soared by her face as she zoomed up. She crashed through the leaves that hid the sun. She sheltered her eyes, expecting blinding light, but it was full dark above the forest. Cold, green stars twinkled in a black sky.

She reached the top of her trajectory. Her stomach gave a sickening lurch as she slowed, then begun her fall.

The trees raked her on the way down, cutting into her. Hot pain gushed from dozens of wounds as she careened toward the ground. Bones jarred and crunched when she wrapped around a thick branch. She continued to fall, breaking bones, losing blood all the way down.

One branch sent her into a spin. She cartwheeled above the green world, before landing awkwardly on her head. Her neck popped as she stared at the peaceful leaves swaying above.

·········

Gina slowly cracked open another cocoon and moved her way through the trees, searching for Sadie. She found her, yanked her free. They walked side by side without aim, without reason. Gina's head drooped forward as if too heavy for her own neck.

How many times had it been now? Ten? Twenty? A hundred? Each death hurt more than the last. Each took her sanity, piece by piece.

Sadie trundled on, her face gaunt and lined. She looked like a worn desert traveller in search of water.

The sun above the trees made the air humid and unnatural, like someone shone a UV lamp on them from high above. Sweat dripped off her chin as they stumbled on.

Something flapped in the distance. The sound made Gina flinch, expecting fresh torture. It flapped again. Then it cawed. A magpie hopped along a narrow branch ahead of them.

"I love a lassie with a magpie tattoo on her shoulder," said Gina, her voice dry and painful.

She looked at her friend, hoping that the hardy, vivacious Sadie she'd known was still inside somewhere. Her eyes were deadened, like they saw nothing.

They walked closer to the creature and its spectacular white tail. As she neared, she expected it to zip along like a machine, like everything else manufactured in this forest. It cawed again, a noise so sweet and real Gina felt her eyes prickling.

"How did you get in here, wee birdie?" said Gina. "Get out before it gets you."

It flapped from the branch and swooped down to the forest floor. It scampered along the ground, then turned and stared at Gina with intelligent eyes.

"Lead the way, my friend."

Gina had to haul Sadie by the arm as they followed the magpie.

Soon, the scent of purple heather stung her nose, making her want to sneeze. They walked along a thin, unmarked path, up an incline. The magpie waited, urging them on. Gina stopped. Air flowed over her. Scottish air. Not the fumigated kind created by the forest. It was dizzying. She grabbed Sadie and hustled forward, toward the fresh smells and the guiding magpie.

The entrance.

It stood before them, leading up and out of this evil place.

"Come on, Sadie, hurry."

She put Sadie's arm around her shoulders and dragged her forward. The way out loomed larger, only ten paces away, when the forest awakened. Branches came to life like floating snakes all around them. The magpie took flight, aiming itself at the outside world. A thin branch lassoed around the bird, catching it mid-flight. White, black and blue-tinted feathers exploded as the bird was squashed. Gina could almost taste the iron of the bird's blood as she passed its tangled ruin.

"Sadie, help me," screamed Gina as she hauled her friend toward freedom. "We can get out of here. Come on!"

Small branches zipped forward, joining together. The marvellous sunlight of the outside world was dimmed as the forest weaved a barrier over the entrance.

She could ditch Sadie here. Dart for the exit. Make her way out. To freedom.

"To Toni..."

The heart-wrenching image of Sadie and Toni kissing on their couch came to her. Sadie was the one who could make Toni happy.

She took Sadie's arm from her shoulder and shoved her forward. Darkness came for the forest as the wires zipped over the way out. Gina knew Sadie wasn't going to make it. Sadie got her foot caught and fell to the dry ground.

"No!"

Gina threw herself at the interlacing branches. They caught her like a spider's web, wrapping their way over her, twisting, burning her skin.

Distracted by its fresh catch, the branches left Sadie alone.

"Sadie!" screamed Gina. "Get your arse up and get Toni."

Sadie shook herself awake, drawing to her feet. She blinked.

"Go!" yelled Gina.

Sadie opened her mouth to speak, closed it, then turned and bolted up the incline.

The forest raged.

Sadie had escaped.

The branches coiling around Gina strengthened, tugging her limbs in separate directions. Her muscles ached, then split open. She yelled out in pain, in triumph.

The forest's anguish rumbled through her as it instructed the wires to tear her limbs off, one by one.

·· • • • • • • · ·

Born again, Gina walked through the forest.

She saw ghost images of all the ways she'd died since she got here. The thing had tortured her before, but it was just getting started. The death it agonised from her worsened since she'd helped Sadie make her escape.

With every memory of Toni, she felt the forest pull back from her. Gina savoured its frustration.

An image of Toni and Sadie huddled together on the couch came to her. They were broken, but mendable. She'd given them life.

"You'll never take that from me," she said to the green world.

TIME'S SHADOWY TIDE

Padraig drowned once more in heavy silence that smothered the kitchen as he ate breakfast with his parents. He watched Dad spoon slow, languid circles in the depths of his porridge still to take a single bite – his essence was being dragged out to sea a little more each day. Padraig crammed cereal into his mouth, chomping as fast as he could to battle the lump in his throat.

Mum absently hummed about going on a summer holiday. A question bubbled inside him, rising to the surface. It was a question he'd needed to ask for weeks, but it was just too heavy for him to find the words for it.

"What's up with your mopey face?" said Mum. "Once these clouds move it's gonna be a cracker of a day. Can't you feel it?"

Padraig let his spoon drop. It made a little *clink* against the chipped bowl. Despite taking a deep breath, tears pricked his eyes. "You gonna tell me what's really up with Dad yet?"

"Don't go looking like your eyes are gonna puke rivers. He'll be back to work in no time." She tugged at her pink earlobe. "Be just fine."

"Is that what the doctor said?"

"All he needs is some rest and he'll be right as rain."

Padraig looked at his dad. Around his slack jaw, grey shone through his stubble. He used to look so vibrant, so full of life. His zest was what kept Padraig going when things got tough. "He's getting worse…"

"Know what we need?" She turned her dreamy eyes to the overcast morning, combing her fingers through her frazzled blonde hair. "An escape from this dour Scottish autumn. Go somewhere we can, what's the word… recuperate."

Dad stared into the middle of the table like it laid all the truths of the world before him, but he just didn't know how to put the pieces together.

Just three more years of high school then he'd be on his way to becoming a marine biologist, uncovering the mysteries of the deep, unexplored oceans. That had been his dream for as long as he could remember – a passion he shared with his father.

·····•·•····

Dad sleepwalked every night until Mum eventually coaxed him back to bed with a gentle stream of whispers.

His slippers would shuffle along the carpet, the sound reaching Padraig as he lay sleepless, wrung-out from a day's worth of worrying. Tonight, Dad paced back and forth with purpose. The sound of hearty laughter floated to Padraig as he clutched at his pillow.

He wiped at his wet cheek, then slid out of bed. He passed his desk that was littered with figures of turtles, whales, sea urchins, and jellyfish. Their toy-plastic smell filled his nose as he stepped to the closed door.

He placed an ear against it. Dad's excited voice travelled through the old wood as if from underwater. "Woah, look at that big thing. That one's called a stingray."

Padraig opened the door and peeked out. His old man was transfixed by something on the ceiling. "Oh, oh, look." He pointed up at some unseen thing moving above. "Shark! See its pointy teeth?"

Dad looked down at his side as if talking to a kid. When he comically *clacked* his teeth together three times, the memory emerged. Padraig recited the words at the same time as his dad. "'Chomp, chomp, chomp. Good job we're in this tunnel, or we'd be a shark's lunch.'"

A familiar brilliance shone in the big man's eyes as he gazed up at the fish that swam above that aquarium tunnel from so long ago. It was like his mind had carried him back in time.

Padraig's nerves swam all over the place when Dad loped over to him. "Look at him, Marie, just look at him." It took a second to realise he thought he was speaking to his mum. "He's got a fire in his eyes I've never seen before."

Dad's smile grew into a hearty chuckle as he looked at the younger version of Padraig that Padraig himself couldn't see.

"I'll buy him one of those shark tooth necklace things," said Dad. "Do you think he'll grow up to be, like, a marine biologist or something? Man, that would make me proud."

Padraig put his hand inside his pyjama top and took out the necklace, clasping it in his palm. The tooth's sharp edges had smoothed away over time. He only ever took it off to get showered.

"Careful, wee guy. Watch where you're going." His father's long legs bolted and turned a corner in the tunnel – one that didn't exist here in the hall. His skull *thunked* off the wall. He crumpled sideways in an unmoving heap on the floor.

Padraig ran and knelt beside him. "You alright?"

Dad jerked his head around the hall like a fish in a new tank. "Who are you?"

"It's me, Dad. P-Padraig."

"My wee lad's only three, you lying shite. What have you done to me?"

"Dad, I—"

Calloused hands clamped around Padraig's throat. He struggled at the vice-like grip, pressure building behind his eyes. Dad flipped him over, knocking his head off the floor. He clawed at his dad's hands, staring into his glassy eyes. Rings of violet light shone in his pupils.

"If you've hurt my boy," said Dad, "I'll rip your head clean off your shoulders."

The edges of Padraig's vision fizzled with light. The blood in his face grew taut, his muscles turning to soggy bread.

A gooey, translucent substance slowly covered his dad's eyes, making him look like some deep-sea creature. His iris's pulsed brilliant violet rings through the alien eyelids, burning into his weakening vision.

A trickle of blood slid down the side of Dad's face from where he'd smacked the wall. Padraig blinked, the last of his energy fading. Tentacles plumed from the gash on his dad's forehead. They flowered from the cut. Light shone through stitches on the tentacles as if they were made of tiny bandages. He saw this with such vivid clarity as his chest thundered for air.

"What you playing at?" Mum shouted. She yanked Dad's head back, forcing him to let go his iron grip. The fight fell out of him, and he lay in a heap, dazed and confused. Padraig sucked in breath, unable to get enough, thinking he was going to pass out with the rush of oxygen. He tasted the sharp scent of antiseptic on the air as he stood with his hands on his knees.

"Go to bed, wee guy." She helped his father to his feet who stared up at the ceiling, longing to see the sharks and stingrays of the past.

·····•·····

"It's alright, you can come in and get your breakfast," Mum called from the kitchen. "Your old man's not sprouted tentacles."

He crept into the room. His dad sat in the corner, his mouth working up and down but no words coming out. The glazed over cast to his eyes told Padraig his father's mind was drifting on some distant shore. When his dad lifted an empty spoon to his lips, taking a bite of imaginary food, something deep inside Padraig ached so hard he had to squeeze his eyes shut.

"Mum?" said Padraig. "You can't go on telling me he's alright. Look at him…"

"Just take it easy. He's fine, alright?" Her rising voice bounced around the kitchen. "He's fine."

"Fine? Fine? He nearly throttled the life out of me last night. Tell me the truth!" He slapped the table, making spoons and glasses rattle.

Her hair flew to the side as she flicked her attention to the world outside the window. "Some sun will do us the world of good. We'll book a holiday. Get some sun into your old man. That'll spruce him right up. We'll—"

"Stop." Padraig balled his fists, pressing them into his eyes. "Tell me straight. Is he dying?"

"What? No." She laughed like he'd said the most ridiculous thing in the world. "He's on the up. You'll see."

Padraig rubbed his sunken, weary eyes and stood. "He's gonna die, and there's not a damn thing we can do except watch him be dragged away piece by piece."

"He's just a little piqued, is all."

He blubbered the rest out in one long, hitching torrent. "It's not fair. It's like something's sucking him away from the inside. Look at him. Why won't you look at him? Mum?"

Her chair creaked as she stood. She wrapped her arms around him, stroking the back of his hair. "Ssshh, now. We'll get through. I know it's hard, but—"

"I need to hear you say it. Admit it."

She took in a deep breath, her nose nestling against the crown of his head. "You go get ready for school."

· · • • • • • · ·

Later that evening, he stared at the purpling sky outside the kitchen window.

He'd skipped school, then came straight home and hid in his room until his stomach demanded he eat.

Atop the kitchen counter, he found a note with his mum's frantic handwriting.

Out to shop. Back soon. x.

He ate a quick sandwich and hurried back to his room. A loud crash thundered from within his parent's bedroom. He halted mid-step, warring within himself before he walked back to the door. He shoved the door open. "Dad?"

Padraig stood in the doorway, holding his breath. Dad sat cross-legged on the floor, his back against their bed, a large plastic box opened in his lap – a first aid box.

"Dad, what you doing?"

Wet, slurping smacks made him feel like little crabs tapped their way up his spine.

Dad wound bandages round and round one hand. He held that hand above his stubbled, open mouth, lowering the bandages down his gullet like spaghetti.

Padraig tiptoed closer, noticing empty bandage boxes scattered across the floor.

"Dad, are you alright?"

Dad's neck *cricked* as his head jerked in Padraig's direction. The slimy film covered his eyes again. The end of a bandage dangled from his mouth. The cloth scratched against stubble, wriggling until he slurped it up. He swallowed hard, and the bandage was gone.

Padraig stepped back. "You're eating them?"

Neon eyes pulsed at him. His father tore open another pack of bandages, and wound it round his hand in slow circles, never taking his violet gaze from Padraig. When his dad blinked, his eyes made a sucking sound, like wellies squelching in mud.

"If you don't get out my house, I'm gonna phone the cops."

"Dad, it's me." Padraig's stepped back.

"Cheeky wee bastard. I'll show you not to lie to your elders." His dad straightened to his full height in one smooth motion. He took a step forward, a bandage drooping from his mouth.

Padraig clutched at his necklace, holding it in his palm. The indent of the shark's tooth dug into his skin. "I'll do anything. Just tell me how to fix it. Please?"

Dad blinked, his eyes returned to normal, leaving a confused old man staring down at him.

"Go away," said his dad, turning his back on him. "I can't let you see me like this."

"D—"

"Whatever's happening to me, I can't control it. Go!" His dad's voice lowered to a whisper. "Please, just go."

·· • • • • • • ··

Later that night, they ate in stony silence. Padraig stuffed hot shepherd's pie into his mouth to keep the rising tide of his emotions at bay. Dad could barely sit up straight. Mum kept having to lean over and push him upright. Each time she did, she left bone-white marks on his skin that refused to return to normal.

"Do you think his… illness makes him do things he shouldn't be able to?" said Padraig.

Mum let out a pained, hefty sigh. "What you prattling on about?"

"Like, when his eyes go all fiery and violet. The bandages… One came out of his skull the other day, healing a cut on his head. Did you not see it?"

She placed an elbow on the table, closed her eyes, and squeezed the bridge of her nose, her fingernails biting, leaving small crescents on her skin. "Do you not think it's hard enough without you making up this crap?"

"I'm not—"

She slammed her palm on the table, making the cutlery hop and clatter. "He hasn't been eating bandages, he isn't trying to kill you, and his eyes don't go all violet! He's just a wee bit delirious, but he's getting better, right?"

"Wake up, Mum. He's not well, he's gonna d—"

The sound of her slap echoed in the small kitchen. She'd never struck him before. He stood, ran a hand along the hot skin on his cheek and ran to his bedroom, slamming the door behind him.

Tears streamed down both his cheeks. His face felt all spongy and sensitive as he wiped them away. He looked out the window, seeing the large moon shine a brilliant silver in the still and cloudless night sky.

A splintering crash came from the hall. Mum let out a house vibrating screech, then nothing but dark, weighty silence.

At the bottom of his bedroom door, a singular beam of thin light was interrupted. Two shadows cut across that light. The door creaked slowly open. Dad stood, fixing Padraig with a vacant stare. His father cast a long shadow into the room.

Padraig stood. "What you done to Mum?"

A wet, sucking noise made Padraig's skin tremble. Two violet orbs shone from his dad's eyes as he lumbered forward. Blood dripped from his nose, falling off his chin, pattering onto the carpet.

"D—"

Two rough hands grabbed Padraig's throat. They fell onto the bed. Warm blood dripped onto Padraig's face as he beat at Dad's strong arms.

He reached for his bedside table, picking up the first thing he could find, and smacked his dad with a heavy stapler.

The hands loosened. Padraig shoved with all his might, surprised at how light his dad had become. He used to be an immovable rock, but Padraig sent him flying across the room.

Dad moaned as he lay crumpled in the doorway, clutching his head. Padraig crept forward. Small bandages wound their way around his dad's scalp, stopping the blood flow.

Padraig's legs turned into ice. His dad groaned as he stepped on a creaky floorboard, coming back to life. He summoned his strength, knelt, then leapt over the figure blocking the doorway. A hand clamped his shin mid-air. The breath blew out of him as he crashed to the floor.

Padraig shook the hand off and scurried back on his hands. Dad crawled after him. Padraig got to his feet and hauled the door closed. His dad's arm shot out, lodging itself between the door and the frame. Padraig pulled on the door handle with all his young might, but the arm remained stuck. It clawed at the air trying to grab him.

He placed a foot on the wall and leaned back with all his weight. The door closed. He fell back, thumping against the wall opposite his room.

The streetlight spilled through a window, showing his dad's severed hand. It lay palm up. Its skin was yellow and dead.

His bedroom door burst open. Two violet eyes shone at him from the darkness.

Dad held up his injured arm, shorn midway between wrist and elbow. It wasn't blood that oozed from the wound – loose bandages hung from the stump like his old man was made of them.

Padraig let out a breathless wail as the bandages came to life. They slithered out his dad's arm, tasting the air.

He sprinted down the hall, stopping at his parent's room. Mum lay face down among wooden splinters. Blood seeped into the carpet in a crimson circle around her head. She moaned, let out a heavy sigh, and rolled over as if caught in a dream.

Dad followed. A river of bandages streamed from his arm, climbing over the wall.

Padraig raced through to the kitchen, picking up his phone from the counter, cursing himself for leaving it on charge overnight. His shaking thumbs hit the wrong numbers as a bandage whipped toward him, coiling around the phone. It tugged it away and smashed it off the floor, shattering it into useless fragments.

He raked through the kitchen drawers, trying to find something sharp to defend himself with. He snatched a pair of blood red scissors as his dad shuffled his way into the kitchen, bandages hovering in the air around him as if each one smelled prey.

Padraig held the scissors out, his hand and voice trembling. "Don't do this, Dad."

Dad lurched closer.

"Please."

Another slow, shambling step.

"I'm begging."

A bandage shot out. Padraig snipped it with the scissors. Another wrapped its way around his leg. He cut that one, too. He cut the never-ending yellow bandages that snaked through the air until a mound of them lay around his feet.

Dad charged him, lowering his shoulder, wrapping him up in his arms. They both tumbled to the floor. A sickening *crunch* sounded as his dad's head smacked the washing machine. Padraig pushed him off and fled to the living room.

He ran his fingers along the black rope of his necklace, feeling the weight of a thousand fathoms bearing down on him as he thought about what to do next.

He looked back into the kitchen. His eyes went dry, his brain strained at the image he saw.

Bandages rose in the air, hauling his dad's unconscious body up with them. Padraig thought of a lionfish with its spines swimming in the water, ready to strike. His dad's head shot up.

Violet circles glared, bursting with an awful light that burned into him. It made him bend forward and clutch at his stomach.

Bandages shot at him all at once. He snipped at them, willing his burning muscles to move faster. One lassoed his stomach and yanked so tight he nearly blacked out. He snipped it, but all hope fled when a bandage coiled around the scissors and whipped them away.

"Don't let the sickness win, Dad." He scrambled back, bumping into a dark corner, wringing the top of his t-shirt.

Dad walked to the middle of the living room, stretching both arms out to the side. Writhing bandages poured from his stump and from holes that opened in the skin like portholes along his other arm. It looked like a deep-sea creature of nightmare, its tentacle-like bandages swimming through the air, reaching from one end of the room to the other.

There was no escape. Neon violet eyes flared above a mad, ravenous smile he'd never seen on his dad's face. The thing that his father had become awaited his next move.

Padraig closed his eyes, clutched at his necklace, and puffed out his chest. "If killing me will give you the energy to keep on living, then go on. Take me. Take me!"

Bandages wound through the air, wrapping their slow way around each of his limbs. They carried him off the ground, and he was drawn close enough to feel searing, seething breath roll over his face.

"Before you kill me," said Padraig, "I want you to have this."

He wriggled a hand free and gave a sharp tug on his necklace, snapping the black rope, placing the lonely shark's tooth in the palm of his dad's fever-hot hand.

"It isn't your fault. You're not to blame. Y-you were the best dad. I just wanted you to know that before…"

The violet lights in Dad's eyes stuttered, then faded. A single tear fell from his dad's eye. Padraig fell, released from the bandages.

His father dropped to the floor, tucking his arms and legs in at his sides. "Trap me under the couch. Quick! I don't think I can hold it back for long."

Padraig dragged one end of the couch and lay it on top of his dad. He stacked the TV and its unit and the coffee table on top to pin him underneath. Only his head showed.

Dad's voice came in strained gasps. "Can fight it back if I… If I hold on to the necklace." He turned his head, exposing a neck of loose, leathery skin. "Cut me open. Yank it all out."

Padraig picked up the scissors and knelt beside him. "What? Dad, I can't—"

"You have to. Can't be like this anymore…"

Padraig's hands trembled as he pressed the scissors against his dad's neck. "No, Dad. No, I can't." He lowered the scissors.

"I'm not in control. Understand? It's eating me up. You have to do it."

Padraig lifted the scissors in both hands above that neck – the neck he used to wrap his arms around everyday. He couldn't remember the last time he'd hugged his dad. The guilt made his insides churn.

"Do it," his dad begged. "I don't know what I'll do if you don't stop me."

He took in a sharp breath, squeezed the grips of the scissors and brought them down, slicing into skin that parted with a sound like ripping paper. No blood spurted from the gaping wound. He wiped the tears that ran down the bridge of his nose, then stuck a hand inside. Roll after roll of moist, warm bandages came away in his grip. He kept pulling on them, thinking he was performing the world's most vile magic trick as the deep smell of antiseptic hit his nose. He added more and more bandages to the pile beside his father's head.

His dad's voice was a shallow croak. "All I really want is to go see the fish with you one last time. To see that way your eyes light up when a shark swims over us."

Padraig yanked on the bandage in his hand and finally found its end. "We can both go."

The couch shook as his old man was assailed by a fit of harsh, racking coughs. When he spoke again, his voice was smaller, somehow. "Can you get this thing off me?"

Padraig pounced to his feet, merrily kicking the pile of bandages aside like he trod in a pile of autumn leaves.

The surge of hope running through his veins froze when he moved the couch. He could hardly recognise the diminished skeleton on the floor. His dad's chest heaved up and down with each wet, uneven breath.

"That bad, aye?" said Dad in a loud whisper. "Sit. I've not got long."

"Dad?" Padraig wrapped his arms around him, unable to control the sobs that exploded from deep within. He cried into his dad's shoulder, feeling unshaven bristles scratch the top of his head.

"You're the man of the house now. Promise you'll look after your mum?"

"I… I promise." Padraig's voice trembled as the tears ran down his chin. "I'm sorry, Dad. This shouldn't be happening. It's not right. If only I—"

"Hush now. You're not to blame." It was like he couldn't get any air into his lungs. After a few seconds of what looked to Padraig like a man drowning on land, his dad took in a sharp gasp of air, his purple face settling back to red. "Listen to me, my boy. You've made me prouder than you can ever imagine."

Padraig felt a withered hand gently clasp his own. He hadn't known it was possible to cry so hard. It was as if each tear, each hitching breath pricked his heart.

"Dad, don't go. Stay? Please? We need you. I need you. Dad?" He gulped. "Dad?"

He clutched at his father, crying and shouting all his anguish into his unmoving chest.

Padraig traced a hand over his dad's forehead.

He closed his father's unseeing eyes.

THE COMPETITION

Alistair held his breath as he tucked his lavender-coloured shirt into his jeans, scraping his knuckles on the tight waistband. Electric nerves jived on the floor of his empty stomach. Tonight, for the first time in forever, it was just the two of them. He slapped his stomach, choosing to ignore how soft and free it wobbled.

"Get a load of that belly," said Alistair. "Mona? Did you get me preggers? Mona?"

His wife of six years sat at the edge of their bed, fiddling with one of the diamond earrings he'd bought her years ago. When he gave her those earrings, she'd broke down in soft tears. Now, she poked them around her palm like an unwanted vegetable. She sighed and lifted one to her ear.

Just looking at her struck him as dumb as an intern on their first coffee run. She reminded him of starlets in black and white films. A classic beauty, gazing out the window, waiting for some Italian hunk to whisk her away on some grand adventure.

His reflection showed he was morphing into the shape of a bowling pin. He turned, squinting as the last of the day's sun burned pink through the half-shut blinds.

"We should make it quick," said Mona, jabbing the other earring in. "Don't want Darla at your mum's for too long."

"Thought she was staying over."

"She's not ready. Told you that."

"I was hoping…"

Mona stared down at the floor. With her black dress on, she looked as if she was about to bury a loved one instead of going on their first date in twenty months. He fumbled with the button on his collar, his nose crinkling at the lavishly sprayed, woody aftershave he'd piled on.

All he wanted to do was place a hand on her shoulder. Pull her close. Kiss the spot behind her ear that made her giggle and squirm in on herself. They'd drifted so far apart that she barely looked at him anymore.

Yesterday, they'd strolled around Balekerin with Darla skittering about their legs. The sharp, blazing sun felt more like mid-summer in some Greek hotbed than the east coast of Scotland.

As they walked by a rusty outside gym, red roses blossomed on Mona's cheeks. He saw how she zoned in on two young chaps working out. How she fixated on their abs that shone like oily chocolate bars in the sun.

The ghosts of flirty, giggly memories assailed him as he fiddled with a silver cufflink. It wasn't so long ago they'd get ready for a night out and never actually make it out the door.

"What?" said Mona, looking up at him for the first time. "What is it?"

He opened his mouth to speak when a fluttering shape landed on the windowsill. Through the gaps in the blinds, two bottomless, black eyes stared back at him. The sun lit the magpie's back, shimmering up its midnight blue tail feather.

Can you help me win her over again, my wee hopping friend? Alistair thought. He closed his eyes and wished he could be everything his wife wanted.

His heart thudded in his ears as the thing let out a shrill *caw*. The noise rode up his spine. Mona flinched and covered a hand over her chest as the magpie flew away with a sound like someone rifling through an ancient, dusty book.

"Damn bird." Alistair coughed and looked down at his wife. Her olive skin seemed to eat up the last of the sun's light. "You look like a dream. Sorry, ehm, never mind. Guess we should get going."

· · · ● · ● · · ·

Grit pricked at Alistair's eyes and mouth as a dust storm cycloned around him. The soupy nature of a dream settled over him as he let himself be guided by its script. All his life, he'd been able to tell whenever he dreamed, although usually he'd dream of his wife hitting on some guy at a bar while he sat helpless in the corner, insane with jealousy.

His foot slipped forward, jerking him out of his thoughts. Scree tumbled down the edge of a cliff. The sun's foreign heat pierced his skin as he leaned over, looking into a vast nothing-ness.

"This is a new one, Alistair buddy," said Alistair. "This is the part where you wake up."

"Or not," said a man behind him.

Alistair spun. The wind and the dust settled, showing him the flat, circular plateau. The view reminded him of the time he and Mona had ridden a helicopter over the Grand Canyon on their honeymoon. He flexed his hand, almost able to feel how hard she'd gripped onto him as they giggled through the entire ride.

Baked concrete rose up his nostrils as he stepped toward the newcomer. Dust sparked from under his boots as he came to a halt a few feet from the figure. "Welcome to my dream, I guess."

"Our dream."

Alistair wrung the collar of his top as the man turned to face him. It was him. He stared at himself. At the same worn jowls. The same X-Men jammies. The same gut. The same tired eyes.

"God, I really am getting tubby," said Alistair.

"Charming," said Other Alistair.

"Right, this is all a bit weird. How do I get off?"

The Other held out both hands, palms up. "What if I told you we can save things with Mona?"

Alistair breathed out a mirthless chuckle. The air tasted thick with chalk. "And how are you gonna do that, exactly? If you really are me, you'll know how things are. Work's absolutely mental. Spreadsheets don't look after themselves, you know? Wee Darla's up every night crashing on our bed. We're shattered and I can only watch as I turn into Flabby McTabby. How can you possibly save things, oh, magic, other version of me? Go on. Do share."

"I can give you both time and joy. That's what we want, isn't it? Let's be honest, when was the last time Mona actually saw you? I'm here to save us both. You made a wish."

"What? Wait… That magpie?"

Other Alistair nodded.

"Next time, I'll wish for a billion quid."

"Think that would keep her?" The Other came closer and placed a firm, cold hand on his shoulder. "You're losing this fight. They're slipping away."

"They?"

"Aye. Think about it. Mona will get bored. She'll trot off with some hunk and before you can say conditional formatting, we'll be reduced to weekend daddy. Shoved to the side. Batchelor bowling pin."

"Darla…"

"Fight, damn it. We can do this. Together." Other Alistair let go of his shoulder. Although they were the same height, it seemed the Other held himself taller.

"How do we fix it?" said Alistair.

· · · · ● · · ● · · · ·

A few days later, Alistair ploughed through an inbox of shouty emails as his suited co-workers out-flapped themselves over the minutest of details. By the time he left, his brain felt like it had been ground through a meat mincer.

He tasted the heady scent of summer rain and set his hand on the front door handle, willing himself into dad mode. A magpie spread its glimmering wings, landing atop the shaky streetlight just outside his home. It hopped around and turned its shining eyes down on him. The taste of the dusty dream landscape filled his mouth as he gulped and opened the door.

"Daddy, Daddy, Daddy." Darla ran into his leg face first.

"Woah there, sugar plum."

Alistair scooped her up. Her tumbling brown hair tickled his nose. The muggy scent of summer sweat and kiddie shampoo hit him as he was struck dumb by how big she was getting. Their wee girl, dancing her way into a proper kid.

"Make cookie," said Darla, wrapping her arms around his neck. "No cookie for Dad. Big, big, belly. Nom, nom, nom."

After their dinner-time, bath-time routine, Darla cozied up to him as he performed her favourite book. He knew the words by heart, acting it out in his funniest voices, getting lost in the story where the magic doggy stands before the black wishing tree and—

"Shhh, you dafty," said Mona, tiptoeing over. "She's zonked."

"Oh," said Alistair, placing the book on the empty space on the couch beside him.

The smile that played up Mona's face creased the dimple on her cheek. It turned his innards to mush. Coconutty perfume swam around him as she leaned in and kissed Darla on her forehead. "Night-night, my wee cherub."

He felt like Superdad when he lay Darla on her small bed and she didn't stir herself awake again.

After a day of dealing with passive-aggressive suit dwellers, he'd normally be wrung out, ready to collapse onto the couch with an easy book. Instead, he jiggled around the kitchen, humming a tune to himself as he scrubbed the dishes.

"Hey, hey. Not seen those moves for a while." Mona set a used coffee mug on the counter. "Shaking and shimmying like you're ready for a night on the bricks."

"Feel like dancing, is all."

"Well, if doing the dishes makes you this happy, knock yourself out."

Her teasing tone made him wiggle all the more. She let out a little snort of a laugh, then leaned in and grabbed his butt. The spiky tips of her manicured nails made him jump forward, thrusting against the sink.

"Good form as well, if I don't say so myself," said Mona.

The sharp lemony tang of the dishwater floated up to him as he batted his forehead with the back of his hand. "I'm feeling good. Better than I have for a while, actually."

"I can see that. You sneaking in some cheeky gym visits between all that cell formulating?"

When she laid her hand on his arm, he couldn't resist the urge to tense his bicep. To his surprise, a muscle appeared. Mona's fingers traced their slow way up and down it. The sigh that escaped her set electricity dancing up his neck.

He took his pink hands from the water and dabbed them dry on a towel. "So... Darla still sleeping?"

"Aye," said Mona, a sly smile at the corner of her mouth.

He placed his hand on her toned lower back, expecting her to move away, but she stayed where she was, gazing up at him, waiting.

"What about, ehm," said Alistair. "How about we… You know?"

"Alistair Connelly, you beast." Mona's eyes sparkled with a playfulness he'd forgotten she had. "Legs are still jelly from last night. Where'd you learn those new moves?"

"What?"

"Just you calm it, stallion. Tell you what," she leaned in close. Her hot breath sizzled his skin behind his ear. "If you get princess lollipop to stay in her own bed again, then I'll do that thing that makes you sing for days."

He almost buckled at the knees. "I got Darla back to sleep?"

She leaned back, squinting up at him. "Dunno how, but you've put her back to sleep these last two nights. Pulling out the daddy skills. And other skills, too, might I add. Where you getting the energy from?"

"Wait. We had sex?"

"Sex? Sex is what married couples do." Her fingertips danced along his forearm. "What you've been doing to me is something… different."

· · • • • • • • · ·

Mona denied his advances the following few days, preferring to wait on his 'midnight wolf' side coming out. Her dancing, cat-like eyes held the promise of animal passion that revved him up until he couldn't think straight. He couldn't remember anything of their love making, yet he daydreamed of it constantly, so much so it had him walking crooked at his work.

When he came home to an empty house for his lunch, he planted a camera between the shadowy space of a bookshelf, pointing it at their bed.

"Let's see what midnight wolves we can catch," said Alistair as he helped himself to an extra-large lunch.

After bath time the next evening, he sat on the edge of their bed and brought up the feed from the camera on his phone. A dirty tingle raced up his spine at the thought of spying on his wife. On the fuzzy night-vision screen, the silver glare of his pupils reeked of desperation. The phone showed the time as 23:12. He watched as he tossed and turned in the bed, jittery as a cornered rat, while Mona drifted off, looking every bit the peaceful angel.

He watched the time drift toward midnight, cringing inside as he saw how needy he was for her. Eventually, he'd given up, closed his eyes and drifted to sleep. He stared at the vast space between husband and wife as their breathing became deeper. A cold sweat broke out on his forehead as Mona kicked the covers, one long, smooth leg showing in the camera's staticky feed.

Alistair chuckled. "Dunno what you thought you'd find, my ol—"

On the screen, he sprung awake as if his spine were a perfectly oiled hinge. In the pale blues of the camera's vision, he caught a sly smile riding up his own face as he tipped the camera a wink. The plastic of the phone creaked in his hands. He trembled as he watched himself turn that leering smile on his wife.

"Don't," said Alistair. "You son of a bitch, leave her alone."

From the phone, Darla's cry pierced his ears. He watched the screen as Mona went to sit up, but Alistair placed a hand on her shoulder and shushed her back to sleep.

Is this what the Other Alistair in his dream meant? Somehow replacing him, using his body to take care of their child and romp with his wife while he was switched off, dead to the world?

His eyes ached as he watched himself slip out of bed and out of shot. He tipped his ear to the phone. Harsh sounds spiked out of the speaker as the Other went into Darla's room, hushing his daughter, comforting her.

He resisted the urge to shout into the phone, to warn Mona that it wasn't him as if it were playing out live.

All Mona's extra squeezes and stolen kisses had been for the Other Alistair, while he went on starving. He listened as the Other sang a muffled song to his daughter, cooing her back to sleep in a way that he'd never been able to before.

"What you got there, camper?" said Mona, stepping into the bedroom.

Alistair fumbled the phone. It landed face up on the bed, showing her sleeping. He turned it face down as his heart thumped in his ears.

"Are you watching porn? Thought you'd be empty after last night. Jeez, Louise! Need me to try harder next time, sailor?"

She craned her neck into the hall, listening as Darla played with her toys in the next room. He hadn't even heard them come up the stairs.

The bed creaked as she sat next to him. Her cool thigh against his thin work trousers made jitters crash around inside him.

"It's alright, you know." Mona leaned in, trying to see the phone. "What kinda porn you into?"

"It's not. I just… Ha, how could I possibly after last night's events?" He slid the phone into his pocket and stood. "It's just a… a… surprise. Aye, that's it. Secret."

She leaned back on the bed, eyeing him up and down. It wasn't fair. He was the one who had to deal with the stress of riding a desk all day long, busting his gut for his family, while the Other Alistair got to play.

"Where you going, stud?" said Mona.

"Gonna check on wee cheeky face. Get her off to bed." His voice came out as squealy as an excited teenager. "Maybe if I get her to sleep, I could come back, and we could… you know, snuggle?"

"Possibly."

He marched through to Darla's pink palace. If it wasn't pink or dusted with unicorns, she simply didn't want it. The last of the sun dazzled through the large window, lighting on Darla, who played with her dolls in her bed.

"Come on, my wee fluff ball," said Alistair. "Time to go night-night. Quickly, please."

He kissed her cheek, drew the unicorn covers over her. A drift of her watermelon bath lotion sang in his nostrils as he gazed down on her.

"Thanks for being a good girl today," he said.

"Song, Daddy. Song."

"Song? No, no. It's not singing time. It's sleepy time."

"Do the song."

"Time to close your eyes and sleep, sweet pea."

"Song." Darla's voice turned scowly. "Do song, now."

"I don't know what you mean, sweetie. What song?"

"Berry song. You big fibs. Bush berry song. Come on, Dad. Please?"

"I've not got the faintest—"

Darla sucked in a deep breath, her cheeks blooming red. "Sing. The. Song!"

Mona bolted through. "What the flip is going on in here? You alright, sweetie?"

Darla sobbed between each word. "Dad. Not. Do. Berry. Song. Daddy bad!"

"Darling, ssshh," said Alistair. "No need to get so upset. I—"

"If you're not gonna do her song, just go downstairs," said Mona. "Hope you can be bothered enough to do it later, though. Only thing that settles her through the night."

"Hate you, Daddy," said Darla. "No do song. No love you no more."

He marched down the stairs on the verge of tears. Everything he'd worked so hard for, everything he'd dreamed about since he met Mona, was falling to pieces.

"No," he said as he walked into the kitchen. "It's him who's picking up the pieces. The Other one. That sneaky prick. He's the one singing his shitty songs and smooching it up with *my* wife."

Cold soothed his skin when he reached into the fridge and popped open a can of Red Bull. He glugged half of it down in one go, savouring the fizzy burn as it scratched his throat. The caffeine crashed its way through him.

"I won't let you have them," he said, finishing the can.

·········

Two days and countless caffeine-laced products later, reality became rather thin. It felt like he hadn't blinked in forever. He'd paced the same path up and down the living room so much his ankles ached. Least he was getting his steps in, he mused.

The swish-swoosh shuffle of socks on the carpet sent him into a trance. Each time his head drooped, he jerked awake, not able to tell what day it was, or why he stood staring at the triangular patterns on the wallpaper till they swirled about before him.

The early morning light fuzzed through the window. Darla and Mona continued to sleep upstairs without him. The rejection still roared fierce within his blood.

Each time Darla had woken up through the night, he'd raced to her room, desperate to soothe her back to sleep. Instead, he'd lost his cool, shouting at her when she'd begged for the song. He made something up, but that only made things worse.

"Take yourself down to the couch if you're gonna be like that," said Mona, taking Darla through to their bed to settle her down.

"Not letting you in," he muttered, his head hanging forward as he paced like his neck muscles were about to give up. "Nope, nope, nope. Not letting you in. Won't, won't, won't."

Sleep weighed on him like a bag of rocks. As he turned, his brain took a second to reorient itself, almost throwing him off-balance like he'd spent the night on the shots. Only shots he'd had were espressos.

Whenever he felt sleep's claws digging in, he jammed a knuckle into his eye, or pinched his skin until it screamed at him. He refused to succumb. Refused to let the Other in.

What difference was there between himself and the Other? He could sneak up there right now, take Darla back to her bed, then slide next to Mona and get a bit of the midnight wolf action she giggled so much about.

A falling sensation shocked through him. His chin hit his chest, and he flinched awake, holding onto the wall as his legs turned to confused jelly. When he chuckled to himself, the taste of sunbaked sand rode strong in his nostrils.

A black shape blurred in the corner of his vision. The magpie's harsh *caw* burst into his mind, making him slap his hands over his ears.

"Get a grip of yourself, you fat loser," said Alistair. "Go see that fine wife of yours. See if she'll give us a cuddle."

Excitement surged in his blood as he walked out into the hall, past the countless family pictures of days spent outside with his family.

The Other stood at the top of the stairs.

"No," said Alistair, hot pain burning up the centre of his forehead. He rubbed at it, blinking up at the shadowy image of himself. "You're in the dust. You can't be here. You belong in the dust. I'm the awake one now. It's my time."

"And how long do you think you can keep this up, eh?" said the Other, placing his foot on the first step.

"Y–You're not welcome. Get back. Don't you dare come down here. We don't need you here."

Midway down the steps, Other Alistair placed his hands on his hips and glared down at him. "Don't need me? You sure about that? I know all the songs. I know all the moves. I love them too much, now, for you to take them away from me."

"You stay away from them. You stay away from my wee girl."

"*Our* wee girl."

"What?"

The Other charged forward and crashed his foot into Alistair's chest, sending him tumbling to the floor. Alistair clutched at his side as he stared up at the ceiling. His eyes refused to focus as he blinked through the pain.

"You heard me," the Other said as he hopped down the rest of the stairs. "They were never really yours. You don't deserve them. You think it's easy getting to watch you have all the fun with Darla? And what do I get, eh? Half an hour through the night as I hum her back to sleep." A cold smile leered its way up the Other's face. "That wife of ours sure appreciates it though. Wild cat, that one. You've had your time. I'm coming through, and you can't stop me."

Alistair got to his feet, backing away from the imposing version of him who seemed to stand surer than he ever had.

"What are you?" said Alistair. "I take back my wish. I–I'll work harder. I can do it. I know I can make them happy again."

"No need. I'm already here."

"Stop. I—"

The Other shot forward and cracked his face with an open-palmed slap. Purple dots crashed about in his vision as he bounced off the wall. His tired, aching muscles moved like sludge as he held his arms up in defence.

"They'll know," said Alistair. "They'll know it's not me."

"All the better. You've had your time."

Alistair charged, willing his fists to do some damage for the first time in his life. His punches landed, but none phased the Other, who walked through his attack as if he were a kid throwing a hissy fit.

The Other side-stepped one of his lunging attempts and stuck his foot out. The wind whooshed out of Alistair as he hit the floor, sternum first. The Other flipped him over and knelt over him.

"Don't," pleaded Alistair. "I—"

Fingers like iron gripped his throat, cutting off his breath. He stared up into familiar eyes that held a mocking taint of violence he'd never seen before.

The world pulsed around him. He slapped uselessly at the Other, feeling as if his eyeballs would pop out of their sockets.

"You never did have any fight in you," said the Other, a playful glee in his eyes. "Pathetic. You don't know how lucky you were, do you?"

Alistair spluttered and kicked his feet, trying to gain any leverage to buck the Other off and stop the darkness gathering at the edges of his vision.

The Other chuckled, then released him. For a second, Alistair thought he saw something like fear cross the features of the Other as he gazed up the stairs.

Now's your chance, thought Alistair. *Show him you won't give up. Fight.*

He tried to suck in a deep, glorious breath.

He tried to stand.

Nothing.

He lay in a heap at the bottom of the stairs, darkness drifting about his vision like a black blizzard. The only part he was able to move were his eyeballs.

His skin prickled all over like the sun shone on him. He felt as if he'd float up and through the ceiling at any moment, he was that light, that airy.

He tried again to sit up. Nothing happened.

When he looked at his side, an icy chill ran through him.

His side was dissolving into the carpet.

He was crumbling away.

Crumbling into sand, into nothingness.

No! Don't! his mind roared as the darkness took hold.

A floorboard creaked as the Other took the first step up the stairs, toward his family.

"*Here we go round the mulberry bush, the mulberry bush, the mulberry bush.*"

THE FRESH BLOOD OF BIRDS

"That a Rolex?" said Raheem, his face lit behind a monitor on his desk. His hand hovered over the button that would let me deeper into Broadshade prison. "You get a bonus every time you put a murderer back on the street?"

A reflection of my sunken eyes and crumpled suit ghosted back at me when I leaned close to the Perspex window that separated us.

"Just doing my job. You know how it is." I hated how spineless I sounded. When I cleared my throat, the noise careened off the thick stone walls. "Why you always gotta ride me?"

"Gotta do something, Johnny boy, otherwise I'd just be sitting here dreaming about the good life, you know? Who you in for?"

The fake Rolex made a metal *clink* when I rested my hand on the high countertop. Tracie had blown her top at the watch's price tag. Took us back into the overdraft. She didn't understand that nobody hired a tatty-looking lawyer.

"Ulric." A smile fish-hooked my cheek at the sight of Raheem's eyebrows shooting up.

"No shit?"

"Why's that such a surprise?"

"You're a small fish kinda guy. Thought he was Donoghue's case? His ugly mug was all over the papers during the trial. Could hardly keep the smile from the slimy bastard's face. Lawyers. You're all the same."

"Well, maybe I'm making my way up. Let me through, man. Been a long night as it is."

Raheem's brown eyes gazed at a spot on the yellowed wall. "Even the lifers stay shot of that one."

A barrel-chested guard escorted me into the bowels of the prison, walking like a beer keg on stilts. The corridors seemed to get smaller the farther we walked.

Welcome to Broadshade was scratched into a wall like it had been clawed there by a feral beast. Between its red walls, Broadshade held the worst criminals in Fife and the whole of Scotland.

The guard's rubber shoes squealed as he halted before a large door. He fiddled with a ring of keys. "Moved him after the thing with those birds."

"Birds?"

Despite the guard's size, his eyes gleamed with the fear of a lost school kid. "Snatched birds from his window and ate them. Should've seen the mess. The smell the dead crow left behind was like burned rubber. We let him wilt in a windowless cell now. Least he deserves after all he did."

It felt as if cactus barbs jabbed my gullet. I gulped the feeling down. "He ate a crow?"

He unlocked the door and rested his hand on the handle. "Crows. Magpies. Seagulls. It's like they're attracted to him or something." The guard stood straighter. "Right, you know the routine. I've cuffed him to the table. I'll be here on the other side of this door. Don't let yourself get too close to him. Shout if you need me."

"I doubt that's necessary."

"Shout if you need me."

I took a long breath in through my nose, tasting the dust and a faint trace of piss.

This was it. My ticket to the big leagues. My foot in the door. A chance summons from a notorious killer could see me in the papers if I played it right. Build up my name. And I'd make sure they saw me. Wear my Rolex, get a new suit. Couldn't afford it, but I'd find the money somehow. Can't have them seeing me scruffy in my big moment.

My daddy is just the best, I heard my wee Cordelia say one golden afternoon when I made it in time to pick her up from primary school. *He makes sure the bad guys stay in the jail forever. They ain't ever getting out when he's on a case.*

My shoulder muscles collapsed like my soul just gave in. One day, she'd know the truth of it. Lawyers skew things for their own ends. Your job is to mush black and white together until it becomes a grey, confused smudge. Then you pray for the verdict you worked for, no matter how shifty you know your client is.

"Won't blame you if you change your mind," said the hulking guard. "That poor bairn..."

A mist of cold rattled through my bones when I stepped into the over-bright room. The sharp glare of the fluorescent lights stung my eyes after the dim light from the corridor. The room tasted of sweat and metal.

And there he was, hunched over, his long strands of hair pawing at the table. He looked smaller than he did on the telly. They portrayed him as a tall, gothic gentleman who wouldn't think twice about ripping out your heart. He looked up. The silver of his eyes froze me to the spot.

I coughed and wiped some imaginary dust from my Rolex. The scrape of the metal chair as I took it out was like getting jabbed in the ear with a screw.

I wriggled into the plastic seat and stared at Ulric's pointy, regal nose instead of his dead-fish eyes. "You gonna spew your guts about the missing ones? There's more, isn't there?"

Ulric chuckled. The sound set my bowels quivering.

"Straight for the headline results," he said. "Eye on the prize, have you? I admire those with mighty aims." He waved his thin, smooth hand before him in an arch as if painting a headline. "*Hero lawyer makes Ulric talk. More victims revealed.* Do I have the right of it, Mr. McKenzie?"

It was an effort to stay seated. Part of me was crawling away from the man who'd committed murder on a level I'd never seen before. Even the way he talked made my shoulders tingle. His accent was a mixture of what sounded to me like Russian, German and possibly Romanian all jumbled together. Part of the mystique the papers lurched onto was that no one knew where Ulric came from.

I muffled a sickly burp that rose up my gullet. None of that mattered. This man could become a client – treat him like one. It didn't matter what any of them did, and most of the time I avoided finding out, but I'd never been face-to-face with someone who'd cracked the spine of a child and—

Pain lanced behind my ear. I'd dug a fingernail into my skin, bursting me out of my red thoughts.

"If you're not willing to spill," I said, "then why did you ask me here?"

The smile faded from those silver eyes. "I need out."

"Out?" The word came out as a chuff of laughter. "Out? Kidding me, right? Out. The red walls of Broadshade are your forever home. Don't care how much money you got, no lawyer getting you out this place."

Ulric worked his jaw. The sound of grating teeth filled the space, itching something in the center of my skull. The look in his eye was so panicked, so lost, an apology bubbled out my mouth. "Look, I didn't—"

"They can't take my window away," he slapped the table with an open palm. The chains attached to his wrists clattered. "They can't take the sky."

Ulric looked down at his palms. Harsh light bounced off the metal surface of the table and handcuffs, making me wish I'd popped some headache pills before I'd stepped into the unknown.

"Snatching birdies and eating them is probably not gonna do you any favors."

I opened my mouth to continue when the wind sighed through the prison. Even from this windowless room, it barrelled down the corridors like a long heartbroken wail. Could only imagine how that ghostly noise cut through the dreams of the most hardened criminal. The sound still sent electric ants swarming up my spine.

When it died away, I asked, "Why'd you ask me here?"

His eyes settled on my tie. I resisted the urge to straighten it.

"Can a man of your means really afford that suit?" he said.

"Rocking that prison gear, there. Really brings out the color of your cold, dead eyes."

"So quick to anger, Johnny. You'll end up doing something you regret."

I took in a sharp breath and looked away from his coy, expectant gaze. "Why don't we start again? You asked for me specifically, and you say you wish to leave this place. Why would they even consider it, given what you've done? And what do you think I can help you with, exactly?"

"I have revelations to make."

My tie seemed to tighten around my neck. "And you want to use these... revelations to deal? You think singing is gonna get you the Hilton upgrade? Get you some Kobe beef prepared every night by Swedish models, that it?"

"Such a charm artist, you are Johnny. Wife of yours must love that." Ulric smacked his lips like he'd just finished a nice meal. "Help me and it can be the start of everything for you. No more buying knock-off watches. No more recycling your one good suit. You and your family could live the good life. Remove debt's hammer from over your heads. Be the big deal you were born to be."

"The big deal..."

He was having me on. Once they were chained, people would say anything to improve their conditions. In here, guys who harmed kids or women got battered in the showers until they gave in and stopped washing themselves. And Ulric had been guilty on both scores.

Papers still ran stories about him, though, despite the trial being open and shut. The enigma of him still rang through the pubs. Whenever he killed, he left such a mess behind that the media started whipping up a craze, saying he was supernatural. And in all the pictures of the trial, that bastard Mark Donoghue quirked a greasy smile for the cameras while shepherding his client into the courthouse. Prick got all the good cases.

"All right. Say I am willing to go along with whatever the hell this is. What would you have me do?"

"How about I tell you my truth. From the beginning. Then we can both decide what can be done about my," he raised his hands, bringing the silver chains to a clinking halt, "situation."

A flash of light bounded off the face of my watch. It was far too fucking late for a round of *This Is Your Life*.

"Don't be so hasty," said Ulric. "I can make you the next big thing. A made man. And I keep my promises, I assure you."

"Make it quick."

"Yes. Can't have the wife accusing you of visiting another streetwalker."

"How did you—"

"Settle your blood. Lend me your ears and I will bring you the stars."

Heat reddened up my face. I'd spent a few quid on prostitutes in my life. Tracie was more upset about how much it cost rather than the act itself. She'd checked out of our relationship a long time ago. I guess we both had.

"Bring me the stars, aye? Go on, then," I said, crossing my arms.

"Keep an open mind. No one knows what I'm about to tell you." Ulric rolled his shoulders. The dry *crick-crack* of his bones made my neck muscles tense up.

"I'm much older than I look," he continued, staring past me at the closed door. "My family have always been special. Unique. You see, we're all born with certain... abilities. Small things, but special, nonetheless. Oh, how vital we were."

Sadness clouded his smooth features. "I'd shown no such talent by the time I was ten. No matter how I tried, I seemed the first of our family to be born normal.

"They took me to the coast, far from our homeland. They locked me inside a stone building that hung over steep cliffs. The sounds of the crashing sea and the salt air was all I had to keep me going. That and the sight of the sky through a small hole in the wall like a window. The sky became my world. How I screamed for my parents. They left me. There in the dark. Weeks I went with nowhere to go but out the window to my death.

"That's when the crow came. Trip trapping along the window ledge as if giving me a final performance."

I unfolded my arms and leaned forward. Memories of my granddad locking me in his musty house for days at a time flooded over me. I hadn't thought about that place in years. The house would be empty of food, of everything. People laughed about being hungry, about being starving. They don't know what true hunger is. Try finding the last can of mushrooms hidden in the back of a mouldy cupboard but being unable to find anything to open them while your stomach and your brain scream at you. I still can't eat mushrooms to this day.

"You know how it feels to go hungry," he said.

"I do."

"You understand what I did next."

"You ate the bird."

The man nodded his head. The way he ran his hand over his mouth told me he could still taste it.

"More came," he continued. "That window brought me the world. Bird by bird, I got my strength back. And then the most wonderful thing happened. It felt as if I rode a current of rainbow colored air. Something surged within me. I used it. I used that power to smash through the barred door.

"Different birds give me different powers, you see. Crows give me a burst of strength. Robins let me see what's in a person's true heart. Magpies... Well, let's not go there.

"I harnessed my power, testing it out wherever I went, following the long road home. My family was shocked to see me. I killed them. All of them. I am the last of my people. And I will rot inside these walls."

A mirthless chuckle burbled out of me. "You think a sob story will somehow reverse what you did?"

"I don't think you're paying attention. I'm giving you a lifeline. A way out of your own miserable stew."

I slapped the table. "What about the boy, eh? Wee Daniel. You think you can swan out of here like it never happened? How could you slice him and leave him like that?"

A shiver raged through me. The crime scene photos were worse than any horror film I'd ever clapped my eyes on. Daniel with the braids in his hair had been in Cordelia's class. A right wee character, he was. Even joked about them marrying one day.

I settled back, nearly sliding off the plastic seat. Getting worked up wasn't going to get me anywhere.

"So," I said, "you've been eating birds to what? Get your powers back? They won't put you back in a cell with a window. The best I can—"

"You have to make them!"

His burst of raw emotion made my back straighten.

"I need out," said Ulric, hunching forward like a junkie scratching for a fix. "Please help me. I'll do anything."

"Things you did, you ain't ever getting out. Even if I did have any clout around here."

Ulric clawed at his arm. The sound of his long nails biting into his skin gnawed at my brain.

"I was rich beyond wildest dreams," said Ulric. "Had everything. And it was never enough. That was my crucial mistake. Hear me well, Mr. McKenzie. Help me out of here, and I'll give you everything you ever desired. Money. Power. Status." A slow smile widened up his face. "Women. Oh, yes. I can make them all scream your name. I can make you the force you were born to be. Face it. You've always felt something was missing – like you were born for greatness, but the rich boys won't make way for the likes of you. Join me."

I gulped the shard of ice that had lodged in my throat. "H-How?"

"Just help me out of these and I'll do the rest." He held up his restrained hands.

Could it be done? Slipping him past Raheem would be easy. Lazy bastard barely paid attention unless he was giving you shit. I turned and looked at the closed door. I'd need to wrestle the key to Ulric's cuffs from the hulk of a guard.

"I can help you kill him," said Ulric. "Those birds I ate before they took my window away – I've stored their power. That's how it works. I drank of their fresh, sweet blood, and their souls fly within me. But I need help. Don't we all at some point in our lives? Be my angel, and I will be your savior."

Was I actually thinking about it? Thinking of the women with their lingering touches around my neck? About the flashy cars and interviews? Nothing for me in this shitty town but shoddy cases. If I turned Ulric in, revealing the fact that he had these powers and knew more than he was letting on about other murders, that prick Donoghue would snatch the limelight back faster than a heart attack.

A giddiness settled over me. I could do it. Take out the guard. Run like the clappers, right into my idea of heaven.

I'd never see wee Cordelia's face again, I knew. Or hear my wife's sweet voice in the rare moments she wasn't mad at me.

"I can't," I heard myself say.

"That's rather disappointing. I quite thought you were the one."

"I'm sorry." The sweat under my fake watch itched. "Sorry? What am I saying sorry to you for? You're a monster."

Ulric shivered all over, his skin warping as if he sat before a heat haze. His skin crackled as spiked ridges popped out along his arms, pressing through his clothes.

"Are you sure you can't be persuaded?" said Ulric, looking at me with his sad, silver eyes. "Final answer?"

"W–What are you?"

"Little Cordelia, with the pink unicorn pajamas, sleeping with her mumma-bear, cuddling into her back because she's crying. And why does she cry? Crying again because her daddy is far away, spending all his time with the bad people."

I shot up to my feet and pointed a finger in his face. "You leave my family alone, you got that? I'll kill you in your evil face right now if—argh!"

With a blur of speed, he sunk his teeth into my neck. The pain exploded, lighting up my spine. I toppled to the cold, dirt-streaked floor, staring up at Ulric, clutching at the hot blood oozing out my throat. His eyes rolled in ecstasy. Brown spines grew out his back. He morphed into a creature of nightmare. He grunted, then lifted his arms. The chain snapped in two. The monster was free.

"All right in there?" The guard banged on the door.

I opened my mouth to yell for help, but the blood clogged up my words.

Ulric kneeled beside me, a touch of sadness in his dilated moon eyes. Broken chains hung from each manacle, scraping along the floor.

"Y-Y-Y—" I struggled, red and purple flashes dancing in the corners of my vision.

"Yes, Johnny. It's not just birds that give me power. Such a shame. I could've made you a star, if you had only helped me. Now, I take your essence and escape this place. See the sky again."

He stroked my cheek. His frigid hand made a chill burrow into my chest.

"Bye, bye, Johnny. Rest now."

The creature shouldered the door open. My eyelids drooped, sweet sleep begging me to stay still.

Before the darkness closed in, I heard the sound of claws slashing the guard into shreds.

Mister Sleep

Julia twisted the frayed fabric on her sleeve, rolling it between her fingers, praying the invite to this sleepover wouldn't be her last.

"Don't be a raging weirdo," she whispered to herself.

Jonnie sat at her side, studying her, a smile tugging his lush lips. Heat swam up her neck as she fought the urge to grab him by his lick-able chin – stupid hormones were flying all over the shop.

The four of them sat in Connie's bedroom as if a board game was in the middle of the floor. Connie was Jonnie's twin sister. Julia could still taste the blackberry, chemical tang of hairspray that Connie used to plaster her black hair to her scalp. The room had silver picture frames on every surface with Connie, Jonnie, and their happy, picture-frame family. Julia's house had no such photos.

This part of Balekerin seemed miles from the crumbling street where Julia lived. Her mum hadn't even opened her eyes when she told her she was staying over.

"Aw, gingersnap. That you got actual friends now, aye?" was all she'd said. No *be careful*, or *make sure you aren't drinking*, or *watch out for that murderer*.

To her shock, the parents left them in the house on their own. They all giggled and made yuck noises as they watched Connie and Jonnie's dad fondle her mum out the door to the pub for some 'mummy daddy time.'

When amber streetlight from the large window hit Connie's face, Julia noticed just how much she looked like Jonnie. A vision of drawing her in for a long kiss made her mouth go dry. Stupid hormones.

The snap of chewing gum brought her out of the fantasy. Darla sat on her left, chomping away, staring out the window. Whenever she deemed a conversation interesting enough to partake, her speech came out slurred and nonsensical. Julia's mum sounded like that whenever she took her sleeping pills.

Jonnie sat on her right, unable to stop tapping his thighs, like a drumbeat cycled eternally in his mind. She wanted to take those fingers and show them a beat he'd never forget.

"Stop," she whispered, closing her eyes, pressing her thumbs into her temples.

Connie sat directly across from her, squinting at her like a queen ready to whip her subjects.

Julia focused on the details she noticed in her friends, feeling her heart rate calm the heck down. She kept her observations to herself. She often got into trouble for being a 'noticer'.

"Proper mad your folks leaving us with a killer pure roaming about," said Darla.

"No one knows what really happened," said Jonnie.

"Cops are covering up the truth, according to my dad who—"

"I heard," Connie butted in, "that the murderer broke in through an upstairs window and tried putting them all to sleep. When they didn't obey, he killed them. One by one."

"No way," said Jonnie. "He's just a run-of-the-mill psycho who splatted that poor family up the wall. Smashed their heads like conkers."

"Talked to Chuck, the homeless outside the shop," said Darla, staring into nothingness. "Said they saw the man who did it. Said he was a proper monster, likes. Drives a tiny car he can barely fit inside. Had a ladder strapped on its roof. Mental."

"I heard," said Connie, ignoring Darla's sigh, "he climbs that ladder and cradles whoever he can find, shaking them until their brains rattle in their skull. And when they don't fall asleep—" Connie slapped her hands together, making them all flinch, "he chokes the life from them."

They all looked at each other then burst out laughing. Julia joined in, trying to shut out the grainy image in the paper of the killer's victims.

"They call him Mister Sleep," said Julia.

She wished she could take it back. She had no idea where it came from.

"That's exactly what they call him," said Connie, a smile slowly rising up her thin face. "Mister Sleep."

"*Mister Sleep, climbs your house,*" Darla sang, "*He's as quiet as a mouse. Going to bounce you off to sleep.*"

"*And your soul is his to keep,*" finished Connie.

"Stop," said Julia.

"Aw diddums. Why?"

"That family died."

"And?"

"Could have been one of us."

Connie snorted like a riled horse. "If it is us, Jonnie should be fine. Only guy I know who can fall asleep standing up."

"I love my sleep, so I do," said Jonnie, sitting straighter. "Don't need no Mister Sleep to help me, no sir, I—"

A car door clapped shut on the quiet street. Julia felt her soul trying to escape through her skin. They stared about at each other, unmoving, barely seeming to breathe.

"L–L–Ladder," said Jonnie, pointing.

Something wooden clonked off the window. The top of a ladder jangled against the glass. Julia crept over, peering over the windowsill. A small blue car was parked squint outside Connie's house. Thumping vibrations tickled the soles of her feet.

She inched closer, looking down. A man sprung up the ladder. Her first thought was that it was a gargoyle come to life. When he looked up, she stumbled backwards, hitting Connie's bed. She'd caught a glimpse of an ashen face with red circles painted around fevered eyes.

"Run." Julia stepped away from the bed, towards the door, her legs almost buckling beneath her. "Run!"

"No," said Connie. "We stick together."

"What? That's stu—"

The window crashed in. Shards of glass skittered across the room. Jonnie grabbed Julia by the elbows, holding her close, using his back to shield her. She'd lain awake in bed on countless nights, dreaming of being as close as this.

A smell like sour apples came from Jonnie as his breath raced. She watched his glassy pupils as he slowly lifted his chin, tracking the killer as he stood.

"I-It's him," hissed Jonnie. "It's Mister Sleep."

She turned. Darla and Connie backed into her, shuffling away from the towering man. Mister Sleep stood in front of the bedroom door, blocking the way out. His shoulders were massive, meaty things. His bare arms were pale trunks. A butcher's apron hung from the oily folds of his thick neck. The air between them tasted of hot iron and spice. His eyes were the worst part. It was as if he hadn't blinked for years.

"Didn't you hear me?" said Mister Sleep, slow and patient. "It's nighty-night time. Let's try again."

Connie shook beside her. "Gotta get out."

"No!" said Julia.

Connie sprinted forward, trying to dodge her way around Mister Sleep. He side-stepped then rose one of his knees into her stomach. Connie's head hit the wall and she crumbled to the floor. She groaned, then wrestled her phone from her pocket.

"Put away the toys, you wee rascal," said Mister Sleep, leaning over Connie. "It's time. To go. To sleep."

"You're a monster," said Connie, frantically thumbing the screen on her phone. "I-I'm calling the police."

The giant of a man leaned back, staring at the ceiling, breathing in deeply through his nose. He closed his manic eyes and blew out a long, exasperated breath. "Why won't you just go to sleep? Come on. Nighty-night time."

When Mister Sleep opened his eyes, Julia felt as if bugs were tapping their way along every part of her skin. Those eyes seemed to be seeing something else entirely.

He scooped up Connie like she weighed nothing, setting her across his wide abdomen. Her head rested on his shoulder as he hushed sweet noises into her face. "Hush, my dear boy, hush."

"Let go!" Connie slapped at his trunk-like arms, but it was futile.

"Please stop." Julia pressed her fingers into her jaw, thinking about how she could sneak around them. She'd left her phone in the kitchen downstairs. The night billowed cold tendrils through the broken window.

The giant bounced Connie so much her breaths became ragged and shallow. He paced the corner of the bedroom like a prisoner in his cell. Julia stepped forward, but Jonnie grabbed her wrist.

"Put me down," screamed Connie. "I can't die. Not me. Help!"

The demeanour of Mister Sleep snapped. He stopped bouncing her, leaned over. When he hissed in her face, Julia saw how yellowed his teeth were. "Why won't you just sleep, you wee shit? Mummy and me need some space. Sleep! Why won't you sleep? Just fucking sleep!"

The muscles up his arms tensed like some rigid mountain landscape. He straightened his arms, batting her into the air, then he shoved the sole of his boot into her abdomen. The force of the thudding kick made the back of her skull hit the wall. Mister Sleep kicked her and kicked her, speaking in time to each blow. "Go. To. Sleep. Now. Go. To. Sleep. Now."

Darla, Jonnie, and Julia huddled together. Darla let out a yelp each time the man's boot thudded Connie's head. The sound her skull made on the carpeted floor made Julia's insides curl up. She placed a hand over her mouth.

Mister Sleep stopped. His shoulders heaved. He wheezed in air like he'd just sprinted a mile uphill. Shiny blood trickled from the discarded thing at his feet.

"W-We made you real," said Darla, standing straight. Her voice was an awed sigh. "You're an actual thing?"

Mister Sleep turned to face them. The streetlight shone in through the smashed window, lighting up the shades of red around his eyes. He turned his slow attention on Darla, tilting his bulbous head.

"*Mister Sleep, climbs your house,*" Darla started singing and took a step forward.

"Nope." Julia tugged on Darla's hand.

"*He's as quiet as a mouse. Going to bounce you off to sleep. And your soul is his to keep.*"

"Darla?" said Jonnie, backing himself against a wall.

"It's not sing song time," said Mister Sleep. "It's nighty-night time. Come on. Let's try again, wee man."

In a blur, he shot forward, wrapping Darla up in his arms. He cradled her and turned his back, making cute chuffing and cooing noises at Darla.

"Window," said Julia, pushing Jonnie in the back. "Quick."

"I—" Jonnie stared down at the mangled ruin of his sister. "She was the better one. I can't..."

"Go!"

Julia shoved him again and he stumbled forward. She followed, placing her feet carefully around the sharp glass. Darla seemed almost peaceful in Mister Sleep's arms, staring up at him with widening eyes.

"He's nearly done it," said Julia.

"What?" hissed Jonnie, almost at the windowsill with its teeth of ragged glass. "We need to go."

"Wait."

"Wait? You nuts?"

At the sound of Jonnie's words, Darla craned her neck, looking at them. Her lips sounded a silent *help*.

"Just close your eyes," groaned Mister Sleep, his shoulders sagging. "Why do you have to be like this? What's it gonna take? Don't you trust me, Nolan? If you go to sleep, I'll buy you some cake. Let's try this thing again."

Mister Sleep shook Darla, cradling her, humming a lilting, awful tune as he strode back and forth and back and forth.

"Stay still, Darla," said Julia, not daring to move. "Please stay still."

"I'm going," whispered Jonnie. He knelt as if about to throw his leg over the windowpane. He buckled instead, letting out a pained whelp and tumbled to the floor. Light reflected off the thin shard sticking out the sole of his foot. Julia yanked it free, and Jonnie let out a pained wheeze.

"Don't leave me here," said Darla, whimpering. "Don't."

Mister Sleep stomped to a standstill, threw his head back and sighed up at the ceiling. "You just like testing me, eh? I got news for you, pal. It's nighty-night time."

Julia gasped when Mister Sleep dropped Darla. She tasted the sweat and fear and blood on the air as she waited for him to stomp Darla to death. Instead, he grabbed both her ankles and swung her into the air. He swung her behind him, raising her up like an axe, then brought her down with all his might. Her head crunched on the floor.

"Go," implored Jonnie.

"Not without you."

"No time. Go!"

Mister Sleep swivelled around. His fevered gaze lit up with anger when he noticed Jonnie. A line of drool dripped off his chin. "So, you're just flat out refusing to sleep? You're tearing me apart, wee dude. I'm begging you, please go to sleep. Why won't you go to sleep?" The hitch in the desperate voice made Julia stop before throwing her leg over the sill.

"Please?" continued Mister Sleep. "If you love me at all, just close your eyes. What did I ever do to you?"

Julia knelt beside Jonnie and squeezed his shaking hand. "When he comes, go to sleep. Hear me? Close your eyes. It's the only way."

"W-What? I—"

Mister Sleep careened forward, knocking Julia into a bedside cabinet. Ornaments and silver photo frames wobbled. Something told her to bolt, to flee out the window to safety, but she couldn't bring herself to abandon the boy she'd fancied for years.

"You have to sleep," she said, tugging at her hair, watching Mister Sleep carry Jonnie into the shadowy corner.

"There, there, wee man," said Mister Sleep, stepping over the still forms of Darla and Connie. "Hush now. Daddy's got you."

Julia looked down at her hands. Her jammies were stained with glistening blood. Movement caught her eye. A man walked by the house, yanking his dog by its chain, not letting it stop to sniff anything.

In the corner of the bedroom, Mister Sleep bounced Jonnie across his arms, humming sweetly. She resisted the urge to yell for help, to interrupt the spell. She hurled a photo frame. It smashed on the concrete below. The man outside only shot her daggers when she waved her arms, hoping the panic and the blood would make him call the cops. He only jerked the chain and walked on down the silent street.

"Ssshh, ssshh," whispered Mister Sleep with warmth in his voice. "There we go. Good boy."

Cradled in his arms, Jonnie's head drooped back. He had an angelic, peaceful look on his face. Mister Sleep tiptoed towards Connie's bed, holding Jonnie with such care that Julia fought away the jealous feeling.

Julia winced as she stepped back, making two pieces of glass tinkle together. He didn't notice. It was as if she weren't there. She held her breath.

"I did it," whispered Mister Sleep, standing straight. His eyes filled with tears. "We did it, wee man. Together." Mister Sleep looked at his hands covered in drying blood then down at his overalls. "What's going on?" He looked at the sleeping boy on the bed. "Nolan? Why are you so big? W-Where are we?"

Mister Sleep stood, rotating his large hands out in front of him. Julia tried her best to breathe in shallow breaths, to be silent. She aimed a prayer at Jonnie to not wake up, not to snap Mister Sleep from whatever illusion that seemed to be keeping him calm. She had a sudden, gut-swirling urge to go over and kiss Jonnie then as he lay on the bed.

"No... What did I do?" said Mister Sleep, his hand shaking as he brought it up to his mouth. "What did I do?"

Julia almost leapt out of her skin as he turned his attention on her. Some intelligence seemed to light his eyes. They weren't as fever bright as before.

"I got him to sleep, didn't I? I'm a good dad, right?"

Looking into the child-like quality of fear in those eyes, she moved forward, palms up.

"He's sleeping now," said Julia. "E-Everything will be okay."

A sob wrenched out of him. Julia felt the floorboards protest as he fell to his knees and sobbed. She hesitated, then walked slowly over.

He talked at his bloody hands in his lap. "My baby. My wee Nolan. I... I remember now. They took me away for what happened. What I did. White walls. Too bright. Pills every hour. He... He wouldn't sleep. I got so angry with him. One night, after hours of pacing, I snapped. Something just... slipped inside my head, you know? Gone bye-byes. I rocked him. I rocked him hard. Too hard. I... I..."

Julia set her hand on his broad shoulder. The heat that rolled off his skin felt like it had the power to burn her palm. "It's alright. We—"

He turned and buried his head in her stomach, wrapping her up in a fierce embrace as if she were the only thing solid in his world. He sobbed into her stomach, clutching at her t-shirt. She ignored the brown-red stains that washed off on the fabric and concentrated on Jonnie's shallow breaths.

"He's forever asleep, now," said Mister Sleep. "I sent my Nolan to sleep. My God, what did I do? What did I do?"

She hushed him, took his arms from around her waist, then slowly knelt beside him, offering her lap. She gulped as his reddened eyes met her.

"You've been through a lot," she said, surprised at the calm, soothing tone that came out of her. "Have a wee lie down."

His cheeks streamed with tears. He wiped them with the back of his hand, smudging a line of snot up his face. "It. Was. Me. I. Killed. Him. I—"

"Ssshh. Lie down. Go on, now." She stroked his matted, oily hair when she guided his large head onto her lap.

She sucked in her own sobs as she looked at the carnage he'd left. The silvery attention of Darla and Connie's dead eyes glared at her.

"You rest now. Have a sleep," she said, resting her chin on his shoulder.

"Is my Nolan really dead?"

"Ssshh. Everything's going to be fine."

KEEP YOUR HEAD DOWN

They sent me to the shop to buy the jackets for the jacket potatoes. That's when I knew it was going to be a rough first day. In the shop, the look the lassie behind the till gave me could've melted enamel off a bathtub. Stood there in my butcher's overalls like a proper bell-end with a queue tailing behind me, all guffawing and pointing knobby fingers at me as realisation of the prank dawned.

The door chirped its robotic *beep, beep* as I stormed out of there. The sun beamed down on Balekerin high street, almost shimmering off the grey stone. The pressure in my gums promised blood as I grit my teeth, keeping my head down on my way back to Denny's butchery.

A hazing – that's what they call it. Only to be expected, really. Reserved for anyone starting a new job. They'll all be eating out my hand soon. Work hard. Make yourself known. Not gonna be the whipping boy for any length of time. Gotta get on in life. Make your mark.

I squeezed myself back into the shop, getting elbows and rough comments about skipping the queue before they noticed the blue apron. They parted like the red sea to let me through as if I was Mr. Denny himself.

With the blood eventually cooling down my face, draining down my neck, I made my way behind the counter. The sweet, watery smell of fresh meat collided with the sprinkling of bleach and lemony cleaning products. Glass counters reflected the sun and the large fluorescent lights above, aching a space behind my eyes I didn't know existed until today.

The team of butchers and servers crawled over each other like a mob of ants, barging, giving each other the odd punch in the side. If it weren't for the customers, there would've been a brawl.

I looked at the clock on the wall above my station. It wasn't even ten o'clock yet.

The crowd were so desperate to get in and get served, shouting their orders over the counter. They were like a horde of ravenous zombies. Their eyes... Dunno if it was a trick of the light, but they all seemed to shine silver, reeking of desperation. I stood there, fidgeting with the knot on my apron behind my back, trying to fight away the image of falling into that crowd and being torn limb from limb.

Beep, beep, the door dinged as it opened. Its constant noise as the customers piled in tweezed at something in the centre of my brain.

"There he is, though," said George, my manager, standing next to me. "Where's the jackets, Aiden? Poor potatoes will have to go in the bin now."

"Ha, bloody ha," I said. "Got me good. Won't get me again, though."

"Wanna fucking bet? Jackets, that's what I'll call you from now on. Hey, Jackets, look over there."

He pointed to something on the pock-marked ceiling. As I stared, he drilled me with a kidney punch. I folded over, wheezing out pain. The guy was at least twice my seventeen years, and about twice as big, too.

"Listen," he whispered as he leaned in, "you sound like a nice enough lad. Just you keep your head down. Smart arses don't survive long."

I tried to spit anger, but it came out in a constipated wheeze. "Prick."

He turned, rage slipping off his face. "Mrs. Robinson. Nice to see you, my love. Interest you in the best sausages Scotland has to offer?"

Beep, beep. Beep, beep. Beep, beep. The door went non-stop. It made me want to take the thing off the top of the door and stick it through the mincer.

Keep your head down. Aye, right. That's what my old man said before I left the house this morning, too. Bless the old guy and his proud brown eyes. Don't care what they all say. I'm not one to wait around. Not gonna die with nothing to show for my hard work. Won't be laying on my death bed, plugged into a machine, *beep, beep, beeping* endlessly, waiting for—

"Oi, Jackets," said George, snapping me out of it. "Slice this fucker up for me. Thin as your hopes and dreams."

My job was to slice ham all day. George flung a thick, slippy piece of pork at me. The meat slicer looked like a jigsaw a carpenter would use to saw through large pieces of wood.

Despite its gnarly teeth looking as if they'd split through my finger bones, I was only given a two second showing of how the thing worked before they opened the doors and pandemonium started.

By the time the hour crawled to noon, my forearms ached. My temples dripped with sweat. Sweat that landed on the ham more often than not. When I asked George for a lunch break, he almost dropped a handful of orange sausages.

Those were the award-winning ones. Stretched translucent skin showed the almost pumpkin coloured meat within. Only the senior butchers like George were allowed to run down to the cellar where they prepped the meat. A coded door made sure I couldn't peek at the secret ingredients that had the customers practically frothing at the ears, dancing on the spot while they waited to be served like junkies outside the pharmacy on a Tuesday morning.

George had told me all about the last boy that dropped a packet of those sausages. Fired on the spot, but not before they took him downstairs to the fridges and beat him senseless until he could barely walk. Hadn't shown his face around here since. There were a lot of stories like that.

My side groaned in pain. I could feel the bruises already forming. I swear, if someone chopped me in the ribs again when I wasn't expecting it, I'd be spitting blood by the end of the day. Gotta go along to get along, as they say. At least to start. Until I could show them what I'm made of.

In they came. *Beep, beep. Beep, beep.* On and on, like the whole of Balekerin stumbled through those doors.

I got myself into a rhythm, ignoring the hunger pangs that pulled my mood down to the sticky floor. The vibrations of the meat slicer rumbled through my palms as I pushed pork through it, turning it into floppy slices.

The air in the shop changed.

The butchers and red-faced servers all went quiet. Chins drooped to chests as if someone had placed a heavy weight on their heads.

The reason for the sudden hush sauntered out from the back. Mr. Denny himself. His apron was as crisp as mine had looked that morning. Not a red spot on it, while the almondy stench of caked blood wafted up to me every time I moved.

Sun-tanned like he lived in Greece, waving like a politician, he walked forward. Something about his movements seemed awfully practised. Robotic, even.

He was allowed to swim in the adulation that came his way. The creator of the sausages that had everyone in Scotland crawling in like maggots to get a taste.

I set the pork on the tray. My gloves slapped against my wrists as I took them off.

"Don't do it, Jackets," said George, the piss-taking note gone from his voice. "Honestly. Don't even."

Bertie, an old, crumpled butcher stared down at a chop of beef on the counter, barely blinking as he sliced at it with precise movements of a small knife. His voice was a smoker's whisper. "Keep your head down. Always and always. The blood is real. Beep, beep, beep. Don't you lose your head like those other boys. Couldn't listen. They never listen. Will you listen?"

Mr. Denny waltzed from behind the counter and into the waiting crowd, shaking hands. If there was a fresh baby in the shop, he'd probably have kissed the thing.

"Warning you," said George, following my gaze. "Put yourself in front of the big man there, and your career will be cut short."

"You happy enough doing what you're doing there, aye? No big plans for the future."

"Calm yourself, Jackets. I've had dumps longer than you've worked here."

An image of my dad came to my mind. How burst he looked after each day at work in the factory. How he sat on his big seat in our sparse living room with barely anything to show for the elbow grease.

"Need to make your mark to get ahead," I said. "Need to—"

George burst forward and smacked me so hard in the belly I folded over, knees crumpling. My face hit the bleach-laden floor, leaving me with a taste in my mouth like swimming pool.

When I bounced back to my feet, ready to throw a punch of my own, the look in George's eyes stopped me. I'd expected them to shine with malice like they'd done all day, but there was a note of sadness in them that made my fist fall against my leg.

He only nodded at the slicer, and I took my designated spot. Mr. Denny swanned through the crowd and out the door, taking my opportunity with him.

"You the new fellow, young lad?" said a reedy voice.

A cave-creature like man with glasses so thick I couldn't see his eyeballs leaned over the glass counter. He was all arm and bowed back, his spine bumping over the contours of his jacket. A green line of mucus snailed down his nose, almost touching his upper lip.

"Got a tongue in that shiny gob?" he said.

"A-Aye." Couldn't take my eyes from the globulous trail being made. "New, aye. Started this morning. Aye."

"They giving you a hard time?"

"Let's just say I've earned my nickname already."

The man slapped his thigh as if it was the funniest joke ever told. "He he, doesn't take them long, eh? You got a nice set of stones on you laddie?"

"Excuse me?"

"Most young chaps burst out of here crying and bawling like they miss their mumsies. Can't take the heat."

Beep, beep. Beep, beep. More crowd flooded in.

"Can you take the heat, hmm?" the creep continued. "Most of the young team that worked here before you haven't been seen since."

George coughed into a balled fist, shooting me a look that said *why you talking to the customers, Jackets?*

"Better get to my station," I said, backing away. "You need anything? I can ask one of the—"

"No, no. Just checking out the new meat." He licked his lips with a wet, lizard sound. His tongue attached itself to the pale snotters like a spiderweb. Soon, there was a line of gloop from nostril to lower lip, vibrating like a guitar string. He just let it hang there, not touching it.

That line of bogies haunted my mind when I got home that night. Went straight to the fridge, opened a can of Fosters and shoved half the can of lager into my face. The harshness of it scratched the back of my throat as I gulped and gulped. Jesus. What a day.

Ribs ached like fuck. Eyes throbbed like I'd been at a Daft Punk concert for twelve hours straight. Seen more punishment and abuse in that shift than I'd seen at school an entire year.

"Ah, you survived," said Dad, lounging on his big seat in the living room, eyes almost drooping shut. He stared at the blank TV as if it was too much of an effort to find the remote. "Good shift?"

I rested the back of my head against the wall. "Was alright, I suppose. Not top of the food chain. Yet."

"Och, enough of that pish. Always gotta be skipping ahead of yourself. Need to learn the value of an honest buck. It's all your salmon t-shirt wearing, eyebrow weirdo generation. Don't know that it's all about the graft."

"Out grafted most of the old bags in there today. Burst couches, all of them."

"They'll burst your coupon for you if you're not careful. Bunch of hard nuts in there, so I heard."

I almost told him that it felt like they'd bruised my organs. Instead, I gulped the rest of the can of lager. When I crumpled it up in my hand, the tinny noise was loud in our small, two bedroom council flat.

"That your advice?" I said. "Work myself to the knuckles and hope I get seen one day? Nah, fuck that shit in the tailpipe.

Gonna walk right up to the big dog tomorrow and put myself on his scoresheet."

"Your mum, she'd—"

"Don't you bring her into this." My voice cracked off the low ceiling. "Don't."

The next breath I took in had a wavery quality to it. I held it in, not trusting myself to speak straight.

He looked so old. So shrunken. He was a giant in my thoughts and memories. I'd done zero good by him these last few years. Not chipping in. Blaming him for not being man enough, not working hard enough when I could see plain how he gnawed himself to the bone with his double, triple shifts. He looked like a man whose heart was about to pack in and that he'd welcome it. Looked that way ever since my mum beeped her life away. All those machines, doing sweet fuck all to help. *Beep, beep, beeeee—*

"Make my mark," I barked out. "Have to. Don't you see? I can't be like her. Can't whittle myself away for a company that doesn't give a flying fuck, only to get to the age where you might wanna start enjoying life, and for life to pull the rug. I can't... All that hard work for nothing."

"Quite sure she wouldn't put it like that. Quite sure she'd say she would rather be here. Money or no money."

The queue the next day was unbelievable. Saturday and it looked like we had Oasis or Stereophonics headlining at lunchtime. Queue snaked around the two other butcher's shops, who were empty and desperate.

A butcher I hadn't seen before unlocked the door and let me in. As I snuck past him, a couple of tidy lassies from the queue looked me over like I was a boss. That's right, babes. I'll be leading this thing in no time. Make my mark. Just you wait and see. Taste all my treats and creations by the time I'm boss man. Piece of me in every one of you, my—

"Jackets," roared George, popping up from behind the counter. "Nice of you to show up. Shift started at seven."

I covered my semi with my pathetic lunchbox, pushing the thoughts of summer lassies and their sly smiles out my mind.

"Seven? Eh?" I said, sounding every bit the squeaky douchebag.

"Oh, that's right," he said, menace in his eyes, "didn't tell you, did I? Like I did it on purpose or something. Oh, well. Late again, Jackets and I'll report you to the big guy."

"Woah, hey, no, no. Don't. Was hoping to have a word with him today. Can't have him knowing I was late."

"What did I tell you about keeping that thick head of yours down? Drop it and do your work and maybe I won't slap you about. As much. And they say I'm not a good manager. Ha."

Shoppers swarmed the shop like a Black Friday sale, leaning against the glass counter so much I thought it would crash in on itself.

Slice, slice, slice went the machine as I fed it pig guts all morning long. Sweat stuck my t-shirt to my back. The customers waved their shaky hands over the counters, trying to claw at the servers for their fix.

If yesterday was manic, today was mania. Lost count of the serving lassies who whizzed past me in tears. The butchers wiping their injuries on their aprons, too busy to stop the bleeding. We all tripped over each other like soldiers in a trench.

"The blood is real," said Bertie, staring at his thin hands like they were someone else's.

I walked over and put a hand on his shoulder. "You alright there, big guy?" I had to talk loud to be heard over the tumult. "If it was me running this place, I'd look after you, bud. Make sure everyone was kept alright."

He turned his milky eyes on me. "W-Who are you?"

"I... I'm Aiden. You know? Jackets."

"When do we shut?"

"Got, like, seven hours left."

"Is that all? Aw, man. I tells my Katie I need to be here so much to bring in the pennies, you know? Hates me, so she does. She hates me. Hates my blood. I hate me, too. Kept my head down, though. Always kept my head down."

I pressed his shoulder and tried to guide him round the back to have a seat, get a drink of water, but he shrugged me off. He went back to his place at the side of the counter, kneading mince with his skeletal fingers. The sloshing, purple worm sound of it made a shudder ripple up my spine.

Back at the slicer, spots started pricking at the sides of my vision. Breaths came up short like I'd just run a marathon. Uniform was suddenly tight about the neck. Blood gathered about my cheeks. Strange sensation ran up and down my arms.

I stumbled towards the double doors that led to the back area, side-stepping a donkey kick from George. Back here was even worse. It was as if a boat-load of Vikings had landed at a village and chased the locals about with cleavers and meat hooks. The crazed look in every workers' eyes made me slink away to a corner.

As I turned my back on them, I collided into someone's aftershave-laden chest.

"Watch it, you ar—" I gulped, looking up at the figure. "Mr. Denny. I–I'm so sorry. Didn't see you there."

Fuck, fuck, fuck. Fucked it now. Slam into my boss on day two. Idiot boy. Should've just kept your head down and—

"It's Aiden, right?" he said, his white, white smile breaking like dawn over a field. "Or do you prefer Jackets?" He leaned in closer. "Only the very best ones get a name in the first couple of days. The worst go straight in the bin. And we see a lot of those. Takes a certain kind of man to work in here. Think you got what it takes?"

I stood as straight as I could, doing my best not to puff my chest out. "Aye. I mean, yes sir. Ready to take on any challenge. Ready to make my mark."

White and blue blurs zipped around us as if we stood in our own time zone. I felt the air of my co-workers as they whizzed by, but it was only Mr. Denny and I that mattered.

"I like my boys to have a certain set of guts to them," he said. "We're a close-knit family here. Every one as important as the last. Well, except the ones who barely last a day. Their contribution won't be forgotten, no matter how short lived it was."

He leaned over and patted me on the back with a hand as big as a paddle. Nearly burst the air from my lungs.

"Best keep your head down. Get on with it. Leave the running of the place to us."

There it was again. Keep your head down. I felt a vein throb in my temple when he uttered it. He pivoted on the heel of his shiny shoes and started walking away, the workers zipping past automatically giving him space.

I stared down at the floor. The smell of the place filled my lungs as I tried to steady my breaths. That smell. It was more brown than red. It caked everything. The lining in your nostrils, the roof of your mouth until everything tasted black pudding, fried scab metallic.

"Mr. Denny?" I called after him. He paused and looked over his shoulder at me. "I get what you're saying about getting on with it. But sir, I can take on more. I promise. I'm not like those other boys that vanished off the face of the Earth."

His back still turned to me, I caught the rise of a smile in his eye. "Oh, really? And what makes you any different?"

"I know what it's like to go hungry."

He chuckled a stately chuckle. "About here, we all know what it's like to go... hungry. Maybe in five years you can take Bertie's station when he pops his clogs."

"Five years?" Almost choked on the words. Five years of constant abuse and silver eyed customers for maybe an extra quid an hour?

Mr. Denny's shoes clopped on the shiny, yellow-tooth coloured floor that had once been white.

"I can do it," I shouted after him. "Whatever to help this company succeed. You tell me, and it's done. Anything."

A moonlight gleam was in his eyes like a hawk staring down its prey. "Shop's shut tomorrow, but you come on down. Let you directly see the contribution you can make. How about that?"

Despite feeling like my soul and my body had been hit by a train, I was buzzing by the time I got home that night. A special meeting with the big boss himself. I was well and truly on my way. Those bastards that gave me sly digs will be sucking my managerial dick in no time.

"Dad, you alright there?" I said as I took a seat on his armrest.

Snores clicked out his open mouth. This close, I could see from the lines in his face just how worn he was. Hadn't seen him smile since Mum went. In the hospital, waiting, waiting, waiting. Mum with her tubes, wires and heavy smile saying not to make a fuss. *Beep, beep. Beep, beep.*

"I'll make you proud, Mum," I said. "Do my bit for the family."

The world felt like it had hit the pause button as I sauntered down to the shop early the next morning. Sunday. No junkies in the alcoves of shops. No customers queuing anywhere. Even the wind was hardly there. Mozzies buzzed around my head in lazy squares like I was a piece of spoiled meat.

Mr. Denny waited in the shadowed doorway for me, looking every bit like he should be smoking a cigar, his hair greasy as a gangster's.

"Good morning, Mr. Denny," I said. "What special stuff you got to show me, then?"

"You really don't stop, do you?"

"Not until we're relaxing, me and my dad with pints in our hands, watching as Mu..."

"Yes?" he said, leaning closer.

The image of Mum with her toes in the sand, face up to the sun, cut a dagger through me as I waited on him unlocking the doors. It was almost a physical pain, harder than any blow George and the other crazy arseholes who worked here had landed in the last two days.

"Doesn't matter." I ducked under his arm and into the empty shop.

It smelled as if the place had been lathered with every cleaning product known to the human race, yet the coppery, almondy taste of meat was an undertone that would never leave.

"Weird without all the pressing bodies, eh?" said Mr. Denny, shooting past me and behind the counter.

"Aye," I said, a lump gathering inside my throat. "Like a sweaty church in here."

He turned, an amused smile across his sun-wrinkled face. "A church, you say? No one called it that before. But I suppose we do provide a service for the good of the community."

"How so?"

He cleared his throat and examined the ceiling. "We produce what the people want. What the people need."

"The stuff that keeps the other butcher shops empty as a finished crisp packet."

"Indeed. They are jealous of our traditions. The secret ingredients of our produce have been passed down through my family for generations. Centuries. All through Europe they brought it."

He turned his attention on me. My back straightened. My insides wobbled like they were about to fall out my arse. Keep it together, man. Don't do anything weird. You're here to make your mark.

"Want to see how it's done?" he asked.

"You mean…"

"I can see you'll do whatever it takes to help us succeed. Your team mates, they're set in their ways. They don't care about you. I'll take you down into the workings and share what only a few trusted people have ever seen. Unless, that is, you just wanna keep your head down and get on with the job?"

Big gulp. It felt as if ice was packed tight in my veins. The shiny points of his teeth when he smiled were more silver than white.

"No, sir," I said, standing outside the locked door with its green-lit keypad. "Let's do this thing. I won't tell anyone what I see. Promise."

For a flash, the corners of his eyes crunched up like he'd just been told his puppy had been run over. It melted away, then he tipped me a wink. He pushed the buttons without making any effort to conceal the code. *Beep, beep, beep, beep.* 1-5-6-7.

A rush of cold air covered me like a mist, hitting me with the crisp taste of ice and things frozen. There was an undernote of sweetness to the air as we stepped into the cave-like dark, being enveloped into a large space. As my eyes adjusted, I saw the two doors to the freezers on the far wall.

"Here's where all the meat is prepped." He pointed to the rows and rows of silver tabletops with racks of knifes at each one. Mr.

Denny flicked a switch and my eyes screamed at me when the lights came on.

I stood there, blinking like an absolute fud for what felt like a whole minute.

"A good man is hard to find. Someone who is true to the cause knows how to keep secrets. You've got something like that in you. Worth your weight, you are."

Something about the way his eyes crawled up my legs made me want to shit and run. I didn't know what to expect. Was he going to come closer and try to punch me, or try to stick his tongue down my throat?

"In there is where the most important insertion happens," he said.

"E-Excuse me?"

"Freezers. Where we keep the goods. Let me show you."

He made his way over to another heavy door. As I got closer, I could feel the cold radiating off it. The sensation made me go green all over. Must've been the nerves. This was really it. I was on my way. Being trusted with all the secrets.

Mr. Denny punched in another code, then set his forehead against the silver freezer door as if breathing it in. "Once I open this door, ain't no turning back. You're mine for the rest of your days, got that? And you'll make the most important contribution to our success here. That will not be forgotten. You'll be part of the family. Part of the success that keeps the punters coming back and back for more. Always back for more."

"Oh, hell yeah. Let's do it."

"Yes, indeed."

The heavy door scraped along the metal floor. The noise made something squirm about between my ears.

I walked past him, into the curling mist of the freezer.

As my eyes adjusted, something heavy knocked into me, sending me onto my knees. It was a slab of meat, hung from a hook.

The laugh that escaped me sounded like a giggling school girl. The noise bounced around the space, doubling, tripling in volume.

The meat swayed. The metal of the hook creaked like an old swing at a play park.

"Keep it together, man," I told myself.

I pictured my mum in her death bed. Her skin had turned porcelain white at the end. Her eyes focused on nothing, gone inside. I wondered what she'd say to me, seeing me in the bowels of the operation, making a mark in such a short time. Stuck it out longer than most of the young guns that came through the doors of Denny's only to disappear.

I looked up. The meat rotated slowly in front of me, pale and waxy looking. When I sniffed in, the sweetness of it was dulled, numbed by the misty cold in my nostrils. That cold tried to nip at my bones.

My eyes felt as if they'd creak out my eye sockets.

A gasped exhalation died white around my face.

What had bumped into me was not dead cow.

It was human.

My eyes grew wide, stinging in the icy cold.

Rows and rows of human bodies extended to the end of the freezer. They all didn't have heads or feet or hands. All primed, hung, ready for the butcher block.

"Now you understand," said Mr. Denny behind me. He was outlined by the bright light from the room outside.

"T-The boys before me... The ones who worked here who everyone said just disappeared."

"Some poked their noses in where it shouldn't be poked. You young ones don't know how to work hard and show up day after day. Expect everyone to throw you a bone just because you want something bad enough."

"The customers. They go crazy for it. They're... They're eating human meat. You sick bastard. Let me out. I—"

I went to lunge forward, but my boot scraped to a stop on the icy floor. Mr. Denny looked like a glowing shadow. Something evil with only a void for insides. One hand slowly rose from his side. It was the outline of a gnarly meat hook. I could just make out the silver-toothed smile that wormed its way up his face.

"You're crazy. Let me out," I said. "W-Wait. This is another joke, eh? Like the jackets for the potatoes. Ha, ha. Got me good again. Mr. Denny? Y-You can let me out now. Mr. Denny?"

Before my brain could tell my numbing limbs to dart forward, to fight, he slammed the door closed. Darkness crawled all over me as I slapped uselessly at the door.

Mr. Denny's voice was muffled through the thick steel. "Should've kept your head down."

FOR ALWAYS

The blade of the knife flashed silver when Melissa took it out the soapy water. Running the sponge up and down it, she marvelled at how well the black handle fit in her hand. The water had been so hot that it left the skin on the back of her hands red and taut. She didn't pay this any attention, only stared at her blurry, ghostly reflection as it danced across the metal.

"Kids are away," said Scott, clomping his way into the kitchen. "Man, that school bus is utter chaos. Honey cake, you alright? Oh, you like the new knives I got you? Nice, eh? Fella said they'd cut right through a thought they're that sharp. Zing, just like that."

Just like your shrill, annoying voice, she thought, forcing herself to let out a smiley, agreeable sound.

"Didn't have to buy them," she said. "Old ones worked just fine."

"Och, nothing but the best for my sweetest cherry doll."

Even his terms of endearment made her spine squirm about like it wanted to burrow its way out the top of her skull.

"You okay?" he said, plonking himself down into a seat at the small table.

Twenty years now. Twenty years of the same routine. They'd chat meaningless blah-blahs before he crawled out of the house, ready for another day at the office. And her, stuck here with her Monday task list. Dishes, shopping, pick up new clothes for the bairns, try not to die too much inside, dinner.

She stared out the window at the long stretch of grass now unused. It was a place where swing sets and paddling pools once reigned. Whenever she went out to hang the washing, she'd close her eyes and hear the ghosts of their kids' laughter. Once so high, so merry, delightful. Now they uttered nothing but grunts, their attention stuck in their phones. Did they even know she existed?

She pushed the knife back under the water. Metal whined as she scored the sink bowl with the blade. She tightened her grip around the handle and punched her hand forward three, four times. The *tap, tap, tap, tap* sound had her husband looking up from his phone. She felt his worried stare burn the inches between her shoulder blades.

How many hours, days, weeks of time had she spent here, doing slow dishes while Scott fannied about trying to talk to her? Trying to pretend he cared.

His chair scraped the floor. She tensed up, staring down into the moving water and the bubbles that wobbled about. The citrusy smell of the washing up liquid spiralled up to her as she prayed for him not to wrap his sausage hands around her waist.

He planted a kiss on the back of her head. A sudden urge to bury the new knife in his gut flared within her. She wanted to watch him squirm on the floor with his insides on the outside. Watch him bleed and—

"You coming down with old lady fever or something?" said Scott. "Feeling a bit on the tropical side, aye?"

"I... I'm sorry, I just..."

Just thought about sticking your husband and leaving him on the kitchen floor to bleed out, she thought. *You sick old hag.*

"I don't know what came over me there," she said, speaking over her shoulder. "Sorry."

He squeezed both her arms, then let go. Her bare arms cooled as he turned and took his seat back at the table.

"You ever think about how we used to be?" he said. "Back in the day. Just two ripe tomatoes. Man, I'd do anything to go back to that. All young. Knees like springs. All the firecracker fun we used to have when we... you know. Know what I mean? Honestly, I'd do anything to go back. Anything."

She turned. A line of bubble water splatted next to her foot. "Anything? You mean that?"

The hangdog expression on his stubbled face melted a lump inside her chest. She tried to cross her arms, stopped when she noticed the knife still clutched in her hand. It'd slice right through her wrist if she wasn't careful. Right on through like red butter.

"My mum will pick up the bairns after school," he said. "Have them overnight, so we don't have to worry about them. They're taken care of. You know Mark and Macy, they'd live there if given half the chance."

Yes. Yes, they would, she thought. *They wouldn't miss us at all.*

"What's going through that head of yours, Melissa? Looks like you're chewing a crowd of wasps. Open up, cookie lumps."

Open up? I'll open you up, you miserable—

"Sorry, sorry." Melissa felt as if a current was running all through her blood stream. She couldn't keep still. Her fingers itched. "Some wicked thoughts shooting around my head for some reason. Do... Do you really think about us? About those times when we first got together? It was that long ago."

"Sometimes." He glanced down at his twiddling thumbs. "Most times."

Melissa turned back to the sink, staring out at the grey boredom of the sky. "They say when you die, you go back to the time when you were happiest. Is that the time you'd pick if you died?"

"I'd relive the hell out of those whole couple of years. Summers seemed to last longer back then."

"I-I'd go back to those days, too. Oh, that sounds horrible. Shouldn't we be saying that we'd spend the time with the kids when they were little?"

"Imagine that when we die, we'd still have all our memories of the kids. It's just that we'd be back to living our best life."

"Our best life..."

Her mind leapt back to days strolling along beaches with nowhere to be, Scott's hand clutched in hers, smiles forever on their faces. Back to the Himalayas when they went trekking, losing and finding themselves again. Back to nights filled with surprise and pleasure.

The glare from the outside sparkled along the blade, bringing her back from the smells of mountain, sun-baked beach, tequila.

"Oh, did I tell you this one?" said Scott, excitement bouncing into his voice. "Office have done us a right solid. Get this. If I kick the bucket, the family will get ten times my salary on death. Well good, eh? Means if anything ever happened to you and me, then the sprogs will be all set. For a good bit, at least. Isn't that great? Almost makes dying a good proposition, ha."

"A good proposition."

What was he trying to say? There was a longing in his eyes she'd never seen before. Like something inside him yelled, screamed at her. He seemed as trapped as a hamster in a small cage. They'd both fought the same daily cycle, not knowing how to claw their way out of it.

The air tasted dry on her tongue, as if she stood on some alien moon. She stared down at her hands. They looked like someone else's. The hand holding the knife seemed metres from her thin, emaciated wrist. "You bought me the knives for a reason."

"What's that now, dearie buns?" he said, scratching at his grey stubble.

Melissa closed her eyes. She remembered how supple her skin was when she'd first laid eyes on Scott. They'd gotten 'fixed' one day after school. Those nights were full of aftershave-laced kisses and love bites. When every day was unplanned heaven.

"Y-You're right, babes," said Melissa. "This is the way. The only way."

She walked over to her husband, placed a hand on his shoulder, guided him up. He towered over her. She always had to stand on tiptoe to give him a smooch on the lips. A cold chill ripped through her gut. She couldn't remember the last time she'd kissed those lips with anything that was more than cursory.

"Close your eyes," she said.

He did.

"We're on the beach. We've had a few drinks. Skin's a bit pink from being out all day. You've just been riding on one of those donkeys. Remember that day?"

"About broke my skull when that thing bucked me off."

She leaned in close. She swore the taste of that beer they'd drank that bright August afternoon was on his breath.

"We could be like that for always," she said.

"If only."

"This is what you wanted. The kids won't miss us. I–It's okay."

"What?"

"Ah, ah. No peeking."

Melissa shuffled her feet apart in something like a fighter's stance. The ropey muscles in her forearm stood out as she clutched the knife.

In and out. Easy as pie. And then me.

"Let's go back there, Scott. Let's go back. For always."

ON DREAM-WINGS FLOAT

The first thing Hogan McIntyre noticed when he set foot in the dusty shop was the vibrations that rumbled up his calves. It felt as if a train barrelled its way beneath him. It made him feel dizzy, off-balance, wavy. He tried to blink the sensation away, leaning on a metal shelf to stop from falling over.

"Kester?" he called to the empty aisle in front of him. "I seen you dash in here. Quit playing, you wee fud."

His muscles had gone weak when he couldn't find his brother among the busy crowd of Christmas shoppers on Pitlair high street. All the bad things that could happen to a six-year-old boy flew through his mind. Dragged to his death and splashed all over the front pages of every paper in Scotland.

He'd have to go home and tell Mum he was the worst big brother ever. Watch her fall apart at the news Kester was gone, kidnapped. She'd shake her head in that heart-splitting way she had that always said *You're no good, Hogan. You're no good at all.*

The chill of the dark winter day evaporated from him as he looked about the quiet shop. The sweat that built inside his puffy jacket made his skin stick to the nylon inside.

"I'll wring your neck, Kester. Kester?"

He was sure he'd seen a flash of red trainers dart up the piss-soaked alleyway and into this shop. It was a shop he'd never set eyes on before. Words and symbols that didn't make any sense were spray painted all over the front of it, windows and all.

Three aisles stood tall before him, filled with disorderly knick-knacks. Shelves were stacked with old toys that had a coating of dust like they'd been sitting that way for decades. He could taste their moth-ball scent as he moved forward.

A small figure darted across the aisle at the top of the shop near the shadowy counter. Its red shoes were blurs.

"Get your scrawny arse here, now," said Hogan. "Never coming with me again if you're just gonna leave me high and dry." Hogan's off-white trainers squealed on the linoleum floor as he approached Kester who stood still, gazing up at a shelf almost twice his height. "Kester? You alright?"

"I want it," Kester whispered. "I need it, I want it, I need it."

He mumbled the same phrase over and over. The desperate sound of it tugged at something deep within Hogan. Before they fell asleep in their shared bedroom, they spent each night listing the things they'd buy, the things they'd do if they had all the money in the world. Supercars. Private jets. Record labels. Owning football clubs. Then the penny would drop, and Kester would fall into a deep sulk. It was stupid to feel guilty about it, Hogan knew. Stupid to fill their heads with lavish thoughts while they'd have to wake up the next morning and piece together a breakfast from empty cupboards.

Looking at his little brother and his mop of raven black hair, Hogan would have given anything to be able to splash the cash. Give Kester all the things he dreamed of having.

"I want it, I need it," Kester mumbled, his mouth barely moving. It was like he wanted to take the purple supercar down from the shelf and lick the thing.

Hogan opened his mouth to speak and clicked it shut. Again, that feeling rumbled below him. He was on an alien spaceship, crashing through space. The ship pitched and yawed beneath his feet, the Gs tugging at his gut until he felt all green in the belly. The sleek, black ship was like an arrow, darting past the stars. Something was wrong. Voices sharp and panicked crackled in his ears, though he couldn't make out what they were saying. Smoke billowed from the ship as it spun toward a blue-white marble. Earth. He was on an alien spaceship crashing to Earth and—

"Help you, little ones?"

The wavery voice came from behind the counter. The sound jerked Hogan out of his vision so fast that he pressed his lips together, making sure he didn't sprinkle his lunch all over the shopkeeper's floor.

"Where'd you come from?" asked Hogan. "Weren't standing there a wee second ago."

The old man studied him. He was stooped over like the arms he folded behind his back weighed a tonne. A set of wireframe glasses on his long nose reflected light. It made him look like he had coins for eyes. When he cocked his head to the side, surveying them both, Hogan thought the sharp, stilted way he moved was more crow than human.

"Help you, little ones?" the man repeated in exactly the same cadence.

"No. We were just—"

"Treasure!" said Kester. "It's a cave filled with treasures I haven't ever seen my whole entire life. I-I've needed a TVR Speed 12 forever, and it's right there. Look, Hog. All purple and swirly. Could look at that all the day. Imagine driving that thing. Woah."

When Kester fixed his pale green eyes on him, his heart beat a little harder in his chest. He wanted nothing more than to say yes. To buy it for him and spend the rest of the day zooming it around the carpet of their small bedroom.

Hogan cleared his throat. "You know we can't. I don't have any—"

"You didn't even look at the price. Look at the price. We can to get it."

"Unless you brought some coin, we're not leaving here with anything. Well, you'll leave with my foot up your arse if you run away from me again. Buy a dog lead with my Christmas money. If we get any."

"The price, the price!"

"Yes," said the shopkeeper behind the darkened counter, "look at the price, why don't you?"

Hogan could feel himself getting sized up. Like a cold swath of light started from the floor and slowly beamed its way up his body. He squinted at the little white tag on string woven through the spoke of the racecar's wheel. "You yanking me?"

"The price is what you pay."

"Not when it's zero."

"We can take it?" Kester squashed his excited face between two balled up fists. "Can we?"

"What's the deal?" Hogan put his hand on Kester's shoulder. "You running some kind of paedo trap in here or something?"

"When I'm older," said Kester, "I'm gonna buy myself one of those. A real one. Bet you can go super fast whoosh mega in one of those. It'll be my Sunday car."

"That right, aye?" Hogan felt something like a burst of static tug at his face, his hair. "Forget it. We're quitting this wasteland."

The old man shuffled closer to them, leaning both hands on the counter. He cocked his head so far to the side that Hogan almost shouted out at him to stop it. The singular crack of the shopkeeper's neck bones was a dry, almost scratchy sound.

"It is not a wasteland," the shopkeeper said. "Look around, Hogan. You can have all you ever wanted here."

"C-Come on, Kester. We're out."

"We're taking it!" Kester squealed. He bounced up and slapped the side of the box the muscular looking supercar was in. He did it a couple more times and managed to bat it down to himself, catching it in outstretched arms before it hit him on his head.

"The young man has made his mind up," said the shopkeeper. "You like going fast?"

"You best believe it, mister. Dream it every night when I'm in my bed."

"You ever had the dreams of riding so fast your stomach nearly bleeds? Boys like you have all the power. All the life ahead. Bring that over here. Let me ring that up for you."

The car looked massive in Kester's small arms. He started waddling over. Hogan set a hand on his shoulder.

Kester glared up at him. "Don't ruin this one, Hog. Please?"

Hogan did his best to level an icy glare at the old man as they stepped to the counter. The smell of something ancient and rusted hit him, making him crinkle his nose.

"And you," the shopkeeper said. "Let me look at you. Ah, a flyer. Someone who longs to be in the places where men were never meant to be. Conquer the sky. You were born to soar."

"How?" said Hogan. "Just... How?"

"Hey, mister," said Kester. "You really know your stuff, eh? Hog says he wants to be a pilot. Won't tell any of his high school friends, though. They'll laugh and giggle and fart at him about it. But I say he can do it. Right, Hog? Tell him. Tell him your dreams."

"Suppose it's true, aye. What's it to you and your stupid weirdo shop?"

"I can bring your dreams to life. Anything in your blood's desire, you can experience. I can make it sing from you."

"What a load of pish," said Hogan. "Thanks for the free car. But we're offski."

"You're talking about magic, eh?" said Kester.

"We're leaving before we get dragged through to his secret back room where kids never return."

"It's like you want to be a grown-up. Fun died up in you a long time ago, Hog. It's all sad."

The shrill sound of his brother's protest spiked his heart like something physical. He was right. Dad had left an awfully long time ago. He buggered off and left Hogan to be the 'man of the house'. When Mum got super-sad, she always said how sorry she was for Hogan having to grow up quicker than he should've. How he was a star for looking after Kester in the way he had. He'd skipped part of his own childhood to look after his brother while Mum went to work two, sometimes three, jobs.

"I can assure the both of you this magic does exist," said the shopkeeper. "I've seen it. We brought it from the far away. How about we... no. No, forget it."

"What?" Kester burst forward, setting his hands on the counter. "What, mister? What?"

"Are you really special boys?"

"Quit being a wee donut, Kester," said Hogan. "You're one move away from me dragging you out by the hair, likes."

"Mum thinks I'm special," said Kester. "Says we're both her wee soldiers. Always telling us how we put on a brave face. Particularly at Christmas. We don't get much at Christmas. I'll be thankful for a warm meal and—"

"Och, away with it, you wee blether," said Hogan. "Don't listen to him."

Silence filled the grey shop. Hogan thought he should be able to hear some passerby from the world outside, but nothing.

When he looked at the windows, they were covered in some kind of grey-black paint. It made him feel as if he were in an underground tomb. A pressure built up that he could feel in the lobes of his ears.

The old man leaned down, looking at something on his side of the counter. He clucked his tongue, a sound that made Hogan blink his eyes each time the wetness of it reached him.

"A supercar is all well and great," the shopkeeper said. "You're free to take it. But I have something that's much better. Ah, ha. There you are, you little devil."

He lifted something and placed it on the counter next to the supercar. It looked like a brick that had been melted somehow. Like its edges had been smooshed by a giant hand. Its surface was charred like someone had tried to set fire to it over and over. Hogan squinted at it. Tendrils of thin smoke leaked out small, square holes. A faint green light glowed from those holes. The light moved about, like some glowing firefly buzzed around inside, trapped.

Kester reached up a hand to touch it. Hogan darted forward and slapped the small hand away. "Don't you touch it. Don't."

"Ow." Kester ran his hand over the reddened mark. "That hurt."

"Sorry. I didn't mean to. It's just…"

"Fear not, small ones. You are close, aren't you? Good brothers. I understand how hard it can be when you're on your own, fending for yourselves. This—" he gestured with an open palm at the block, "can fix everything. This artifact will give you everything your heart desires. Turn your dreams into reality."

"If that's the case," said Hogan, "why are you giving it away?"

Something like a smile rose up the man's face. "My time with it has come to an end. I have tasted all this world has to offer. I have lived. Trust me, I have lived. Now it's your turn. Take it." He lifted the object, held it toward them. His forearms trembled with its weight. "You need to accept it. Say it. Say you accept it."

"No. No, we—"

"We accept." Kester grabbed the artifact. "Me and my dummy brother here. We accept a million times over."

Kester held it close. It fuzzed dark green light over his pale face, his big eyes. When he breathed in, it was like smoke fingered its way up his nose.

"All you need to do is dream near it," said the shopkeeper. "Close your little eyes and dream. And then you'll see. You'll feel every part of it in your bones. Go home and dream, boys. Dream away."

········

The artifact made a stony *thunk* as Kester set it atop a bedside table that was sandwiched in the thin space between their two beds. The thought of having the thing so close to his head while they slept gave Hogan a chill.

"It's not gonna work," said Hogan. "Old geezer just yanking our chain. Probably wanted to yank something else if you let him. Paedo."

Hogan hugged himself by the elbows, trying to rub some heat into his arms. It was so cold he felt his teeth wanting to chatter. The moonlight streamed in through the condensation licked window. That light hit the lumpy artifact. The green-blue patches reminded him of sunken ships on the ocean floor. It was misshapen like it had been melted and smooshed together. He'd touched it once. Its surface was slick and rough at the same time. It irritated his skin so much it was still red and itchy.

Kester's legs dangled off the side of the bed. He set his palms on his thighs, eyes fixed on the artifact as if expecting it to sprout faeries. "It has to work. It has to."

Hogan's belly gave a loud rumble that he felt in his throat. It was five o'clock, usually dinner time, but there was no way he was stepping out the room with their mum and her partner Gerry roaring and knocking things over. Money. Always about money. He caught snippets of the argument that spilled from the living room in their small, two-bedroom home.

"Stop spending our money on useless shite," his mum yelled. "That's the bairns' Christmas."

"I've told you once, I've told you a million times. A man needs to look the part. They'll never take me serious if I look like a cheapo. I couldn't give two hairy dumps about the pair of them anyways."

Kester let out a meek cough into a balled-up fist. He leaned over so far he looked like he'd topple onto the floor. "How does it work?"

His little brother was an expert in pretending the fights didn't happen. He swept it away, never asking about it.

Hogan rested his elbow on his knee and stared at his brother. "I dunno. This is your gig, remember."

"Nut-ut. We're in this together, bro. You accepted it, too."

"Did I?"

When Hogan breathed in, he could taste the black damp that coiled itself in the corners of the room. The moonlight shone its colours into the bedroom. The only other source of light was the artifact. It glowed like some green candle flickered inside.

"Go home and dream, boys," said Kester. "Dream away."

"Dream away."

It had been what the creepy old man had said. Right before Hogan grabbed the artifact thing and dragged Kester out of there. The walk home had been frigid and silent. He rubbed the palm of his hand. It was like the artifact had left him with an ice-burn.

What to do now? March through the living room? Tell Gerry to shut his oily lips and leave them alone? Scone him over the head with a plate or two. Show him what Hogan McIntyre was made of. The man of the house, by all rights. He looked down at his thin fists. Thirteen-years-old and not a muscle on his arms. He'd be about as useless as a chocolate egg in a fire.

His bedsprings creaked as he shoved himself back on his pillow, staring up at the ceiling. The bed was so damp it felt almost wet. Anger cycloned in his blood, making him grit his teeth. Peace.

He needed peace.

He needed the sky.

He closed his eyes.

In his mind, he was in a fighter jet – *his* fighter jet. A black thing that darted through the sky at his command. It pitched and yawed at his behest. It burst through the clouds as he went up and up. The creaking plastic of the control stick felt real through his thin leather gloves. The roar of the engine rumbled through his palms as a smile almost split his face in two. The world whooshed by beneath him.

He pushed the controls forward and felt his stomach pitch as he pointed the sleek, shiny nose at the Earth. Before he pulverised himself into a burning ball of metal, he pulled up, levelling, twisting the jet through an enormous orange hoop. Crowds waved their banners in a stadium below. He imagined them screaming his name as he rushed on by.

"Hog?" Kester's squealy voice blasted through his headset in his helmet. "I'm in the dream with you. I'm here, Hog. This feels pure ace. Woohoo! Do a barrel-roll, Hog. Come on, come on."

The craft twitched as Hogan turned his head. There he was, strapped into the seat behind him. Kester pumping his little fists, hands up as if riding a rollercoaster. He'd never thought of having his brother here with him. These flights were for him. He and the sky.

"At your command, oh brother of mine," said Hogan.

He jerked the control to the side, making the jet spin in the air all the way round. Hogan's insides felt like a loaded washing machine about to burst apart. The blood in his face rushed forward.

He levelled the plane out, laughing at the joyous screams Kester made.

"Is this real?" said Hogan, turning one gloved hand over in front of his face. "I… I can feel everything. The way the helmet is pressuring my head. The Gs tugging at my gut."

"Doesn't it feel amazing? It's the artifact doing it. The shop-keeper said—"

Hogan opened his eyes. He blinked as his vision adjusted from searing blue sky to murky bedroom. Back in the damp. Back on the ground. Back to where his mum and Gerry continued their fight in the hall.

"Holy amazeballs," said Kester, sitting up in his bed. "You fly smooth as an eagle. That was the best!"

"You… You felt that? Like, actually felt it?"

"You pulled me in. Into your dream. I was there."

Hogan eyed the artifact. It glowed a bright green – the green of alien worlds and radiation sickness. "That was no dream."

"What was it, then?"

"I… I dunno."

Kester shuffled out of his covers. He rested his elbows on his knees, holding his head in his hands. He fixed Hogan with a look that should only be reserved for heroes.

"I think it was a daydream shared," said Kester, "where you, the dreamer, pulled me through. Isn't that the coolest?"

"Feels like Mike Tyson's been hammering my stomach."

"That's all those G forcey things. I feel that way too, although might be cause I'm hungers."

Hogan couldn't take his eyes from the artifact. A green heart seemed to pulse from inside, making it look as if it were vibrating with each sickly beat. He squinted at it. The air above it shimmered like a heat haze.

"My turn, my turn," said Kester, throwing himself back on his pillow. "Lie back, bro. I'll take you for a spin."

"We… We shouldn't."

"Och, you ruin everything. Spoily sport. Lie down and let me take us for a drive."

Hogan watched as his brother's breathing slowed. He half expected little pig snores to come from his wee mouth. He looked so young, then. So wrapped up in his dreams.

He lay back down on his pillow, closed his eyes.

The roaring blast of the supercar's engine had him gasping for air. His lungs couldn't take in a full breath. His chest was compressed by the harness of the racing car. The engine rumbled his backside until he felt it in his teeth.

Kester wrestled with a massive steering wheel in the driver's seat beside him. The car had somehow been built with his small frame in mind. Kester jammed the gearstick forward while spinning the wheel with his other hand, gliding the car around a corner. Hogan's stomach was close friends with his heart by the time the car straightened again.

Beyond the sparkling purple bonnet of the TVR Speed 12, Hogan recognised the scenery. They were on the racetrack at the Monaco Grand Prix. They shot out of a tunnel. Power yachts covered the water under a bright blue sky. As the sun beat its way into the car, Hogan could feel its warmth light up his arm. It was a dry, almost tropical heat that he'd never experienced before. They'd never stepped foot on a plane. How could his body know this heat?

"I'm alive!" roared Kester, so loud in his helmet it burst through Hogan's thoughts. "I'm alive, I'm alive, watch me drive."

As Kester whipped them around a zig-zag bend, then onto a straight next to a roaring stadium, Hogan wondered how this could be possible. How could his little brother know how to drive like a pro? It was their dreams. Maybe it was only their imaginings of how a car should be driven, how a plane should be flown.

"It's wonderful," said Hogan. "How? Just... how?"

"It's the artifact," said Kester, his voice strained as he wrestled the wheel. "We could go anywhere. Be anything."

Horns blared as they reached the finish line. Hogan's stomach gave another lurch. He slapped a hand against the almost searing hot plastic as Kester spun them round and round. The thick and cloying smoke attacked his nostrils as Kester finished his donuts. The fumes covered the view of the perfect world outside.

Hogan sat up in bed. He spluttered on the taste of it as if it had all happened right here in their bedroom. His eyes were smoke-stung and watery. Against the opposite wall, Kester stirred awake, sitting up on an elbow.

"I could spend forever like that," said Kester.

Hogan lay a hand against his chest. His heart *thud-thudded* against his palm. His forearm was turning pink, like he'd been out in the summer sun for too long without sun cream. "It can't..."

"What a ruuuusshh!" squealed Kester.

When his little brother sat up and shoved his covers to the side, he noticed the beads of sweat on his forehead. The skin on his face had taken on a yellow, sickish colour like he was coming down with a bad flu.

Hogan opened his mouth to ask if he was okay, but the yelling made him stop. The fight had moved to the hall, meaning their mother was slowly pushing Gerry out. Next would be a tipping over of something, some curse words flying around and then a slammed front door. Then it would be over again until tomorrow.

"At the price it was going for," Gerry screamed, "I couldn't afford not to buy it! You stupid, stupid bi—"

"Let me try again," said Hogan, leaping back onto his pillow. "Lie down, Kester. Come on. Let's go on a trip."

He closed his eyes and willed himself to daydream. It was like moving through a static space. His skin prickled as he phased from the world of his bedroom to the beaming sunshine day he imagined.

"Niiice," said Kester, appearing at his side. "You flying that thing, aye? Super rich style."

Hogan breathed in the scent of hot tarmac. Behind him, a huge airplane waited. The top of it was hazy in the sun. He winced as he set a hand on the hot metal railing of the stairway that led up to the open door. Inside was all deep red woods that looked more fancy office than aircraft. A private jet of his very own.

"We're waiting on one more passenger before we get going," said Hogan, gesturing for Kester to hop on.

"Who?"

"Mum."

"But—"

Kester stopped as they both eyed the figure coming at them from the runway. It appeared as if from nowhere. Their mum cut a slim figure, clutching onto the broad brim of her hat.

Hogan thought there was something like an old-school Hollywood look about her. She could've made it anywhere, but instead Pitlair had held her down. It was hard to say just how much she'd given up to raise the both of them. How many nights she juggled jobs, kept enough food on the table so they didn't starve, clothes on their backs, toys at Christmas.

Hogan stepped forward and coughed into a balled up fist. It felt like his knees were going to give in. "Always said you deserved the world, Mum. How about we go see it, eh? Just the three of us. The way it was always meant to be."

"Mum's funny," said Kester, standing behind Hogan.

He was right. Mum was funny. Her walk was more of a wobble, like a toddler taking first steps. The scent of silver metal clawed at him as he shuffled back. He set his hands out to the side to shield Kester.

"Mum?" said Hogan. "That you?"

"Monnneeeeyyy." The way the thing hissed made Hogan think it had a black serpent's tongue that would lash their skin if it got too close. Under the brim of its hat, two black marble eyes glared. "Alllll the monnnneeeeyyy."

"Argh!" Kester yelped.

Hogan closed his eyes tight and willed himself out of the dream. Again, that staticky feeling crawled over his skin, like he'd just walked through a doorway covered in spiderweb.

"What was that?" said Hogan, lungs heaving as he worked the fright from his chest.

"That wasn't Mum."

"Aye, no kidding? Stupid arse. I know it wasn't her."

Kester sat up, hugged his knees close to his chest. "That wasn't Mum."

The house was silent. They'd missed the grand finale. Hogan held his breath, listening. Sounded like their mum was in the kitchen. She'd be picking up, cleaning, mumbling to herself about the state she'd let herself become. Always was too hard on herself, no matter how much Hogan told her she should stop, that she was the best mum ever.

"M-Maybe it doesn't work for grown-ups," said Kester. "We made the deal, remember? Don't wanna see that Mummy again. Never ever, ever again."

"Kester?"

His little brother tucked his head into his knees and sobbed. He hadn't called their mum *Mummy* in years. Not since he'd wobbled about learning how to put one foot in front of the other. The shambling, stick-insect gait of the creature in their daydream made Hogan shiver from the underside of his toes all the way up his neck.

"No," said Hogan, "let's not try that one again."

"I think grown-ups don't have that part in them anymore. The part that dreams. I think it dies." Kester levelled a sullen, tear-streaked smile at him. "You're losing that part of you, too. Soon it won't work for you."

"What are you on about?"

"You'll leave me. You already want to be on your own. Can't stand to dream like we used to. You say it's stupid. And you'll leave."

"Would you shut it with the dumb talk? Not going any-where."

Kester humphed, threw himself back on his bed and hauled the covers over his small frame. He looked away from Hogan, toward the moony light that trickled through the droplets of moisture on both sides of the window.

Hogan wanted to go over, place a hand on his shoulder. When he looked down at his hand, he saw it was still shaking.

On the bedside table between their two beds, the artifact glowed strong. A skeletal line of mist coiled in the air, reaching over the space above Kester like a gathering storm.

·· • • •· • • •· ··

"Gerry's just trying to do the best for all of us," said Mum. "Can't expect you to understand that."

"I understand plenty." Hogan's jaw was so tense it almost ached. He had to fight to push the words out his mouth. "Needs to do one. He's no good."

They both sat on the couch in the living room. Hogan sat upright, elbows on knees, trying to catch his mum's eye, but she refused to meet it. She kept on staring into her steaming mug of hot chocolate.

Every morning, he'd wait until the coast was clear, come through and make her a mug of hot chocolate and then they'd start their day. Kester would normally be about them, jumping and running about like a ball of energy. Since they'd come back with the artifact three days ago, he'd hardly left their bedroom.

When Mum spoke, her voice was paper thin, like she was holding back tears. "Your step-father's just trying to make ends meet in his own special way."

"Mum, he wouldn't be able to make ends meet if you gave him a suitcase full of crisp twenties. He'd blow it on necklaces or new trainers. And he is *not* my step-father. What is it, Mum? What's wrong?"

"He took your gran's necklace. You know the one. Topaz. As blue as the sea is in drawings. Just up and took it. Only thing my mum ever left me. And what did he get? Eighty quid. Eighty quid he's already blown, mind you." She traced a finger around the rim of the mug, her eyes glassy and vacant. "Might as well have flushed it down the toilet."

Pain flared in Hogan's gums as he clenched his teeth together. "He's a leech, Mum. Get shot of him. It's starting to weigh on Kester. I can tell. Like he can smell how scared I get when you fight."

A gentle smile touched her lips. "Had some fever on him earlier. Wee hot potato."

He and Kester had spent most of the last three days and nights floating away on dream-wings, their fantasies getting larger and larger. He eyed the open door. Even being this far away was difficult. He could feel the fantasies tugging at him, begging him to experience things no one on Earth could possibly imagine. Kester had woken with a fever yesterday. Sweat had glistened on his forehead as he begged Hogan to come drive with him.

"He's pretending he owns a formula one racing team, and he's the driver. On his seventh world championship, I believe."

"Ha, that's him. Dreams so big his head will explode one of these days." His mum tapped at the mug with her fingernail, making a *ding, ding, ding* sound. "Promise me something, Hogan. Promise me when you grow up, you won't splash away whatever money you get. Save it. Be sensible. Have a plan. Money can never make you happy."

"That's not right. If we had the dosh, you wouldn't have to break yourself working. You could be happy. Let me buy you a wee island in the sun. Go there any time you want. Get mint choc chip ice creams on a beach only we could walk on. Where the sun is bigger, and the moon is a silver penny in the starry sky. We'd jet you there any time you want. We—"

"Starting to sound like Kester with all that dream chat."

"I… I'm sorry. Been spending too much time with the wee snot bag. Rubs off on you, I guess."

"You're really worried about him, eh? Bless your socks. He'll burn off whatever's going on inside him. Just hope he's straight for Christmas." His mother let out a hefty sigh. It made the air between them smell like sour chocolate. "Christmas."

Hogan gently closed the bedroom door behind him. The damp of the room seemed to hit his chest first and then mist over his skin like a fine rain. Kester huddled underneath his blanket, shivering, sweating.

The artifact glowed a green so strong it was almost lime. It pulsated like a living thing.

"Finally," said Kester. "Get in on this one with me."

Hogan stayed at the door. His feet felt as if they were encased in lead. Kester's pupils were as large as moons. These imaginings, these dream wings, were all Kester cared about since they'd come back from that shop.

"Let's fly, bro," said Kester. "Let's fly."

The thing pulsed its awful, offbeat rhythm, spilling its alien light over the wall. He should bin it, he knew. It took something from them both, leaving them hollow.

"Where we off to?" said Hogan, jumping onto his bed.

"Fly us between the stars."

· · · • · • • • · ·

The stars whooshed past the large, bubble-like dome like flakes of snow in a storm. They mesmerised Hogan as he played with the controls, feeling the rumble of the spaceship between his palms. Green dials phased their light over him in the cockpit. His brother was at his side in another seat, strapped in, a buzzy look in his eyes. That look urged Hogan to zoom-zoom on through space, past asteroids, comets and their blazing trails, impossible planets. There was no horizon he couldn't reach. The universe was his.

Beep, beep, be-beep, urged the controls all around him. Red warning lights flooded the flight deck.

"Ah, farts. Kester?" he yelled over the din of alarm. "Kester?"

Kester cocked his head at him, his bright eyes full of fright. His little mouth was flapping, yelling something that Hogan couldn't hear. Two lines of tears streaked down his face.

"Can't hear you. Hold on. I'll bring us out."

Hogan closed his eyes. He concentrated on his breathing, reaching inside, willing the dream sequence to end and for them to reappear in their bedroom. His gut lurched when the prickly skin feeling never came.

He opened his eyes. They were still on the spaceship. The alarms buzzed and chittered, a new one joining the fray every second.

"Kester, hang on, I'll—"

His brother cried uncontrollably. Proper toddler tears. Then he faded away. Just ghosted out right in front of him, leaving Hogan on the speeding ship on his own.

He reached again for the plug, for the escape hatch in his mind.

"I can make it sing from you."

It was the shopkeeper. He stood in front of the viewing window. He was stooped, arms folded behind his back.

"You…" said Hogan. "You set us up. This thing is killing us."

"And yet, here you are enjoying the flames of dream."

"How do I stop it?"

"Stop it? Stop it?" Awful green light began to show in the man's eyes, beaming out from behind his glasses. "Why would you want to do that?"

"Should never have accepted that thing from you. You sicko."

"He belongs to the dream world, now. It has him. Heart and soul."

Hogan unclipped his harness and marched toward the man who glowed green. The ship almost sent him tumbling, but he kept his balance, holding a hand over his eyes to stop the sick light burning into his vision. "Let us go. I–I'll do anything. Please."

"The artifact needs an owner. A willing soul to partake in the dream kingdom."

"You can't do this. Let us go, you old—"

The inside of the man's mouth buzzed with green light. It showed rows of rotten teeth that looked like black tombstones.

"You're right, we are old," said the shopkeeper. "Older than you can ever guess."

"What?"

He felt the explosion in his ears before the world around him dismantled. The ship came apart, splitting into black fragments. Hogan covered his head. His feet had left the floor. Zero G made him float among the wreckage.

When he removed his arms from his head, he saw the ship was a kaleidoscope of pieces floating in all directions. The man was nowhere to be seen. He hoped he'd been pulverised, destroyed by the ship.

His lungs begged for breath. There was no air. He floated in space without a suit. The pressure behind his eyeballs rose until it felt like they'd pop right out of his skull. His nose, his mouth tried to gulp in oxygen. He clawed at the building panic in his throat.

Something laughed nearby. It was a mimicry of a human laugh, deep and rumbling, something electric about it. Hogan batted at the space, swam himself around. Three figures floated in front of him. They were as sleek and black as the ship had been. The only reason he knew they were there was that they blotted out the stars and the ship fragments. That and the awful shades of light that blared from their eyes and mouths. Each had what looked like empty squares where their eyes should be. Those holes spat out light. Their mouths were a row of four squares that pulsed.

Hogan clawed at his throat. His vision fizzled around the edges as he took in the impossible sight. Each alien figure emitted its own light from its eyes and mouth. One was murder red. One was alien-ocean blue. One was the same sick green light that pulsed from the artifact.

The green one reached a thin, too-long hand out and grabbed his forearm. Hogan's world ignited with pain. It flared up his arm, into his chest, burning him up.

He launched himself up from his bed, falling on the floor. When he thumped his chest on the carpet, he sucked in sweet, wonderful, dusty air. He dragged it into his lungs, sure he was going to pass out from taking too much in at once. He let the acidic spit run down his chin as he concentrated on his hammering heart, his pulsating vision.

A slimy laugh burbled its way out of him. He tried to push himself up, but his arms wobbled, collapsed. His chest slapped the carpet again, and a chuckle whooshed out of him. Stomach muscles tensed, the laughter ascended, made it difficult to breathe again. He fought against it, but it was no use. Giggles forced their way from him, streaming tears down his face.

He felt helium balloon light in the head when he rose to his feet. As he straightened, he could feel his brain wanting to keep going, up, up, and up.

"Away in the clouds with you," he said, laughter spewing out his mouth again, folding him over. "S-Stop. I-I can't."

The joyous feeling fled him. He stood with his arms by his sides, blood turning ice cold.

A figure stood at the bottom of Kester's bed while he continued to sleep. One of the aliens. The one with the blaring green light inside. He imagined the creature's body was just a casing for that unholy light. A tendril of smoke weaved its way from Kester's sleeping, sweaty form, sucked through the four gaps in its face where its mouth was.

"Leave him al—"

When Hogan stepped forward, the thing vanished. The shadows in the corner of the room shifted about. He looked out at the night. Christmas decorations blinked on and off around a lamppost. That light had made the shadows shift and his mind had added the rest, that was it. Fresh from nightmare his brain created the being.

Hogan ran a hand through his hair. A smell like an unwashed dog came down to him as he did so and he removed his hand, squirming up his face.

"No…"

On his forearm, three lines of burn marks gave out a red heat.

Fierce wind tugged, howled at Hogan as he made his way to the high street. The blocky artifact weighed down one side of his puffy jacket. The silver taste of the zip was on his tongue as he did his best to hide his face from the prickling sleet.

It was the worst kind of weather outside. Mum had sparked with joy at the sight of the dashing snow, picturing a perfect, greeting card Christmas. The snow had turned to sleet, the wind turned sideways, making it hard to walk the grey-black slush. His calves ached by the time he made it to the land of zombie Christmas shoppers.

Anger buzzed about him. How could he let Kester fall for such a ploy? Nothing in this world ever came for free, he knew that. The world of fancy flying and rich lifestyle was so far away from real life. The image of the shopkeeper and his vibrant green eyes made a shiver splinter its way down to his gut.

"Hope you do returns, you crony old bastard," he muttered to himself. "Gonna return this thing upside your mushy head."

The wind pushed at him, becoming more powerful as it barrelled down the length of the straight high street. It was as if it screamed at him. *You're an awful man of the house. Turn back. Let it eat you. You can't protect him.*

"Shut up," he said, covering his ears.

The dragging wind died away as he turned up the shady alleyway. The stench of piss and spilled apple cider was strong. He straightened, patted some of the snow from his jacket and walked to the shop.

It wasn't there.

Five lengths of wood were nailed across the entrance. The windows were greyed out, making it impossible to see inside. He leaned on one of the wooden bars. It looked old, weather-worn, splintered. A skittish fear danced along the back of his neck. In this part of Scotland, he'd long come to know any semi-hidden thing could only last so long without being graffitied. Everything had to be marked. Drawn on.

Longannet remembers.

Mon the Hoops – Paul McStay forever!

"Paul McStay…"

He traced the old writing. It had been scrawled in white paint but now looked like old seagull shit. Paul McStay had been a Celtic legend back in the day. Way back in the day. In the days when CR Smith was emblazoned as the club's sponsor.

When he leaned in closer, he could almost taste the sun-worn quality of the wood.

Petey5 + Pauline 4eva IDST 06/05/98

"What the actual…" he said, covering his mouth.

He took the artifact out. It beat a slow, pendulous rhythm in his palm like something inside rocked. The green glow built like a small explosion and then it died away again, leaving a vaporous cloud that tasted of bleeding batteries.

Its sharp edges jabbed him in the side as he shoved it back in his coat. He needed rid of it. It needed to be gone. He couldn't stand the wet, rattling sound his brother made when he coughed.

Panic flooded his veins. He marched back toward the high street and the howling wind. The slush plopped and slipped under him as he made his way to an overflowing rubbish bin. Shoppers slalomed around him as if scared to touch him.

"Get gone, you demon fuck."

Rubbish crinkled when he shoved the artifact in the bin. He marched down the street, wanting nothing more than to see his mum, see his little brother. The hiding he'd get from Kester for taking away the dream wings would be legendary. It was his job to make sure his brother was okay, and this alien thing was killing him, sucking him dry from the inside out.

His trainers slipped. Pain rocked up his knee. He'd fallen in the slush. The grey coldness clung to his tracksuit bottoms. He batted it off and stared in the direction of the rubbish bin.

"No," he whispered.

A weather-beaten old woman shuffled closer to it, cocking her head as if the thing were whispering at her. This could be someone's wee grannie. Someone loved. Cherished.

Hogan balled his fists and bounced up and down on his toes. The sleek shapes of the alien creatures haunted him. The burn mark on his forearm seemed to light up with pain. He couldn't leave a nice old woman to that fate, could he?

She held it in a shaky hand, transfixed by it. Hogan's chest burst to yell out. Tell her to leave the thing be.

"This is what you wanted," he said to himself.

With a sinking feeling in his chest, he turned and faced into the wind.

The walk back to the house was like trying to shuffle over massive sand dunes. He fell a few times, scraping his knee off the concrete below the slush that reeked of mud and diesel fumes from buses hurtling past.

When he got into the house, he closed the door, relishing the still air, the warmth that wrapped around his torso, the feeling rushing back into his numb face. He told himself over and over that he'd done the right thing for his family. That tough decisions weren't black and white, easy-osey. They were slush grey. And stuck to your heart like the snow that caked his trainers.

His soaking trousers clung to his legs as he walked down the hall, fearing the conversation he'd have to have with Kester. He knew what he'd done would count as a betrayal. Something he might not ever forget. Hogan would be fine with that as long as he knew Kester was alive.

"Ooopf, watch it, you wee prick."

He hadn't watched where he was going, and Gerry barrelled right into him.

"S-Sorry," said Hogan, hating the lame sound of it as soon as it passed his lips. He massaged the centre of his chest where Gerry had knocked into him. He held Gerry's oily stare for a long moment, refusing to be the one to look away. "Nice chain. That what my gran's ring bought you?"

"What you all about? Don't need this shite from you, as well." Gerry ran his thumb along the thick gold chain that looked like it came straight out an Argos catalogue. "You wouldn't understand. Power perceived is power achieved, little man. Got to look the part if you want to make anything of yourself.

Speculate to accumulate, and all that. Need to show them. All the time."

Red fantasies of slamming Gerry's shaven skull against the wall made him scrunch up his eyes, trying to blink the rage away. "Look like Vanilla Ice's cheap nephew."

"What did you just say?"

Hogan held the man's glare. The way his thin lip quivered had Hogan thinking it was going to come to an actual fight. He knew he'd end up getting smashed for pushing Gerry's buttons, but he needed it. Needed to know he wasn't just going to sit around and do nothing.

Hold still. Don't step backward. Keep glaring right on back. He willed his body to stay still and not to skitter away like his blood was singing at him to do.

Gerry made a raspy noise and shook his head. Sour spittle hit Hogan's cheek.

"Whatever," said Gerry, walking past him, "you'll never amount to nothing. Scrawny looking buggers, the pair of you. Hope you catch whatever that sour wee brother of yours has. Choke and die, motherfucker."

Hogan resisted the urge to laugh at the catch-phrase sound of that last one. He watched Gerry stomp down the hall and out the door. Cold wind blitz over him when Gerry slammed the door shut. He let out a stony sigh. It always felt safer with him out of the house.

Hogan set his hand on the door handle to his bedroom. Inside, Kester sneezed, then talked to himself. The words were muffled but there was something stilted in them that set his hair on edge.

He sucked in a breath, let it out through his nose, then entered the room. "Listen, man, I know you're as mad as a box of frogs, but I had to. Hate me all you want. I know you won't unders—"

"Ah, there he is," giggled Kester. "Quick, in the dream seat. Let's go for a ride."

On the bedside table between their two beds, the artifact buzzed its green light.

"But, I…"

"Been missing you, Hog. Not the same doing all the races without you. Better as a tag team. Tag team champions of the world, that's us."

Hogan wiped away the sweat that appeared on his forehead. It felt as if he'd be sick. The dream world tugged at him, begged him come fly.

"Hurry up," begged Kester. "Got something to show you."

He could smell the stench of sweat and snot hanging about his little brother. Like it was a cloud of moist air.

"I'm losing it," said Hogan. "Like, full on losing it."

"It doesn't matter. Come dream with me."

·· • • • • • • ··

They'd spent the night dream-soaring until they both crashed into sleep. The next morning was grey. One day closer to Christmas, but Hogan couldn't remember exactly how many days. Normally the countdown would be on, well and proper.

Kester hadn't mentioned it since they brought the alien artifact home.

One minute Hogan felt as if he were in a sauna, the next he was stuck in a freezer, shivering. The same stench that hung over Kester now hovered over him. The sweaty smell permeated everything, mixing with the damp.

A good brother would've chucked that artifact out of the window. Ran down the street with it, punting it away from Kester even if it came back every time. A good brother wouldn't have got into bed and soared across the bright skies in a dream land.

But how it made his blood sing. How it made Kester chuckle and giggle. Between his coughing and spluttering that was. They were both gripped in the throes of a fever, and Hogan felt dirty on the inside whenever he flew a plane or sat in a racecar.

The alien creature hadn't appeared again, but he could feel its eager presence every time they dropped into their fantasies.

He groaned as he heard the rising voices in the living room. It was a biggie this time. Gerry had taken Mum's bank card, and all but emptied it. Something that sounded like a ceramic mug shattered against the wall, making them both sit up in bed.

"It's alright, Kester. Just you chill back out."

"Mum's not okay. She's not okay."

Gerry's roaring made tension cycle in Hogan's temples. "What? What don't you understand, eh? I'm the man of the house, and I'll spend my money how I want. That's right. Your money is my money. My money is my money. And that's that, baby cakes. Show you how Gerry does. Old bitch."

The shouting gave way to punches, things knocked over, curses and yells. Hogan shot out of bed.

"What are you doing? Hog?"

Hogan marched over and picked up the heavy artifact. It numbed his palm like it was going to leave an ice burn on his skin. "I'm handling it. Don't leave this room."

When he stepped out into the hall, it was as if burglars had tipped everything on its side, looking for money. The sight of his mum on her knees, holding a hand against her bleeding head froze him to the spot.

Gerry grunted, turned, and looked at him. A slow smile slimed its way up his oily face as he jogged toward Hogan, his gold chain flapping about under his chin.

Hogan held the artifact. It glowed violent green, casting the hall in sickly alien light. Gerry stopped in his tracks, smile falling off his face.

"What is—"

"This little gizmo can give you anything you ever dreamed about. That's why me and Kester have been locked away. We've been touring Monaco, Barcelona, America in Kester's collection of supercars. And I've been whizzing us around the globe, among the stars. You should see the way the girls all look at us. Like they want to eat us. And the crowds. They shout our name. Over and over. We're kings. And all thanks to this."

Gerry's eyes took on a childish cast. Like someone being told a story about dragons for the first time. "You... You're yanking my chain, man. Not possible."

"Anything's possible. Believe it. It can give you anything you ever dreamed. All you never had." The thing vibrated in his hand. Its light bounced around the walls, showing the patchy, almost rusty skin of the artifact. "And it can be all yours."

"All mine?"

"Imagine whole worlds knowing your name. Gerry the legend. That's what they'll call you." The image of Gerry being eaten by the creature until he was skin and bone made him feel charged inside. "That's what you deserve, isn't it?"

"Gerry the legend," he repeated, something ghostly in his voice.

"One condition."

"Anything."

"You leave. Take all your shit you bought with our money and be done with us. Take this as a gift and create your legend far away from us. Got it?" It was an effort not to launch the thing at Gerry's skull. He reached out his shaking, rage-filled arm, offering the artifact. "Take it."

"You being real at me, man? It... It can't be true."

An image of the shopkeeper and his coin eyes came to him. *You need to accept it,* he'd said in the shop. *Say it. Say you accept it.*

"Say you accept it. Accept it as a gift from man to man. You have to say you accept it. Or I can keep it. Take it back and you'll never know the feeling of a hundred thousand fans singing your name, and—"

"I accept." Gerry grabbed the thing and held it close to his chest like a new-born baby. "I accept. But if you're yanking me, I'll come back and fuck you up, *capiche*?"

"Leave us. Never set foot in here again."

Gerry didn't look back as he stuffed the artifact into a gym bag and ran out the door.

Hogan knelt next to his sobbing mum. The cut at the side of her eye had already begun to heal. The blood down the side of her face was dried. He set his hand on her shoulder. "He won't be back, Mum. I made sure of it."

······•••····

After Kester realised he was never getting to drive a TVR Speed 12 again, he lashed out with a volley of kicks and slaps until his sobs made him buckle over. Looking at his broken, sweat-sheened brother, he held on to the fact he'd done the right thing. The artifact hadn't reappeared. Gerry accepted it as new owner. Once Kester calmed down, he told him about the aliens. About how they were the reason he felt so miserable. And Kester told him he was just making it all up to make himself feel better. That one stung, but he let it be.

It was Christmas in a couple of days, and Mum was as stressed as ever, trying to put the house back to rights. There seemed to be a lightness about her that Hogan hadn't seen in a long time. He'd helped. He'd really chased Gerry away and fixed everything.

But every time he closed his eyes, his stomach did loop de loops. It was as if the memory of flight roared through him, his body demanding more. For the first time, he started to wonder what steps he could take to become a real pilot. With his mum and Kester behind him, he knew he could do anything.

He'd sent Kester into the garden to build them some snowmen. The snow had fallen hard, turning the muddy slush into a postcard version of their street. Kester stood in the corner of the garden, kicking the snow. A lost boy in a dark winter's day.

Hogan closed the curtains in their room and crouched behind the door in the darkness. His eyes adjusted. A feeling of shivery fear crawled along his skin. He imagined the alien creature being in here with him, opening its eyes, casting sick green everywhere.

The slamming of the front door snapped him out of it. He huddled against the wall, ready for Kester to burst into the room. Cold nerves jittered through him as he waited, the seconds dragging by.

Kester opened the door.

Hogan flicked the light on.

"We've got twenty minutes to race across the Sahara desert. You'll be driving this." Hogan gestured toward an office chair he'd borrowed from their neighbour. He'd spent the last of his money on a plastic steering wheel, complete with gear stick. "In the racing seat, Kester. Let's go."

Kester's mouth hung open as he stared at the racing set up that Hogan had spent all day on. Hogan's stomach felt like someone had fish-hooked it, pulled it toward the floor.

"I… I'm sorry," said Hogan. "It's dumb. I thought—"

"Y-You made this?" A tear dripped down Kester's cheek. "You made this for me? Specials?"

Hogan coughed and puffed out his chest, trying his best to sound official. "Are we racing or not?"

"Y-Yes sir!"

Kester threw himself into the chair. The plastic creaked and complained as Hogan grabbed the backrest and spun it around. On the wall, on a large sheet of paper, he'd drawn a desert landscape. Kester gasped when he saw it, clutching onto the steering wheel.

"You'll have to be faster than everyone else if we're gonna win the desert cup. Ready? Oh, wait. You'll be needing this."

Hogan lifted a cardboard box and slapped it over Kester's head. It had a large hole cut out where its visor should be. Sharp lines and flames drawn in black marker.

He watched his brother trace his fingers over the seat, over the steering wheel. Kester seemed a little life-worn, a little older. He'd been quiet, sullen since they got rid of the alien artifact. It had been too long since he'd seen his little brother smile so freely, a big goofy grin spreading up his face.

"Easy left." Hogan rumbled the backrest, bouncing Kester in the seat. "Medium right. Over jump."

Kester giggled and tried to stay in the seat as he pushed and pulled it this way and that. Their mum opened the door a crack and Hogan saw her slowly peek her head in. Hogan met her eye and tipped her a wink. She whipped out her phone and took a sneaky photo and then gently closed the door.

Kester hadn't noticed. He'd stopped wrestling with the steering wheel.

"What's up? Look, I'm sorry about not being able to take you to the stars anymore, okay. This… This was stupid. It's not the same, is it? Don't know what I was thinking. Sorry."

"Know what?"

"What?"

"There's no where on Earth I'd rather be."

Hogan felt his eyeball twitching as he held Kester's excited gaze. "Well, then. Let's win that cup." He grabbed the back of the chair. "You ready?"

WITH DUST SHALL COVER

1.

John stepped into the consuming dark of the pub, tasting the ghost of cigarette smoke that still hung in the air from decades ago. Whites of eyes jerked up to examine him before dropping back to lonely pints. The straps of his backpack seemed to bite into his shoulders. The soft floor squished under his wet boots as he moved towards the bar. Outside the International, the hammering rain continued to roar.

A man in a dripping anorak sat on a barstool at the short end of the L-shaped bar, nursing a pint of Guinness. His eyes widened when they met John's, then he grabbed his pint, vacated the seat, and shuffled to a shadowy corner.

As if by magic, a golden pint appeared on the bar-top when John sat on the barstool. *His* barstool. He placed the backpack on the floor, resting his foot on it. Even through the thick sole of his boot, a soft vibration hummed up his calf.

"Cheers," he said, lifting his pint to Chuck, the bartender, before taking a long, throat-itching drink.

John said little else as the wiry barman poured pint after pint, a companionable silence resting over them.

He ran a hand over his scalp, the shaved hairs rough on his palm. A stranger stared back at him from the cracked mirror behind the bar. Used to be built for brawling, but now he had the figure of a darts player turned to sag.

He was mid-gulp when a figure appeared at his side, leaning on the bar.

"What's in that bag, pal?"

John slowly set his pint down. "Don't want what I've got, mate."

"Aw, you from Liverpool, aye? Beatles and that. Pure class them, likes."

John shifted in his seat, glaring at a tall man with clawing, red scars on his chin. John's thick accent was the first thing punters noticed. It was a contrast to the mumbling drone that was typical to this dank corner of Fife, Scotland. He was a long way from the melodies of his hometown.

He studied the bloke who scratched nervously at his elbow, leaning in, desperation in his grey eyes. The bag had a way of calling out to lost souls.

"Trust me. Leave it," said John, taking a drink. "Don't want none of it."

"Come on, big guy," said the man, almost hopping from one foot to the other. "Don't hold out on me. I can tell you've got the goods. Can sniff it on you."

John grit his teeth, a promise of a cold sweat needling in his temples. He stared the man in his boyish eyes, wanting nothing more than to scream in his face, tell him to get out of here, get his life together.

He turned, downed his pint, and called to Chuck, "Mind if we…" then nodded at a closed door by the side of the bar.

Chuck ran a towel around the inside of a pint glass, not looking up from the task. "Sure, John. Whatever you gotta do."

The bartender walked over to the other end of the bar as if there was a bad smell.

"Aw, shit hot, man. Name's Graham—"

"No names," said John. "Follow me."

The stool scraped under John when he stood. He hefted the bag over one shoulder, surveyed the quiet pub, then opened the swinging door to a disused back room. They used to host dominos and darts tournaments here every weekend. Dust clung to the old, chequered benches and stools tasting of ash.

"Make sure that door's shut behind you," said John.

"Sure thing, boss," said Graham.

John felt his forearm protest as he set the bag by his feet. Each time he did this, the bag seemed to grow heavier, somehow.

Graham peered through the thin rectangle of glass. John wondered who this rake of a man might have waiting for him at home.

"Last chance," said John. "Walk away."

"God, what kind of dealer are you? Got the dosh, man, relax."

"I don't want your money."

Graham turned. His arms dangled by his side like they'd both been pulled out of their sockets. "Freebie? Awesome, mate. Top class, you are."

John set his hand on the bag. The canvas thrummed with life, irritating his skin. He could tell it had once been army-green, but the colour had frayed from use, leaving it with sand-coloured patches all over like a disease. Burning ozone wafted up to him. How he longed to burn the bag. Be rid of it and all it promised.

"You're not police, are you?" said Graham, taking a step back.

"What? No."

"Why with the dodgy look, then? Feel like you're scraping my soul, or something."

John undid the golden clasp and opened the bag. Neon green tickled his hand. He looked away from its awful light and reached inside. When he touched the item, it felt like ice crackled up his arm. He brought it out, holding it in his hand towards Graham.

"Woah," said Graham, who snatched the three glow-sticks like a greedy toddler.

John rubbed his palm on his jeans, trying to work some warmth back into it. He watched Graham's eyes grow wide as he brought the colourful sticks up to his face.

It didn't matter what the object was, the reaction was always the same. Soon, John was forgotten about. Just a dark shadow in the corner as the bag's magic took its greedy hold.

Graham placed a red glow stick in one hand and held the green and blue ones in the other. "We used to go all night, lads. Life was a rave back then." His head snapped up to look at John like a gun had just gone off. A manic smile climbed the man's face, lit by the soft colours. "Can you hear those tunes? Total banging. We'll always be this young."

John ran his hand along his chin. He eyed the door, wanting nothing more than to rush out of here and into the rain. He waited, chained to the moment.

Graham shuffled on the spot, eyes closed, looking like a drunken daddy-long-legs trying to dance. He raved until beads of sweat sparkled on his face. As his trainers scuffed the uneven floor, the sticks glowed harder. No matter how much he tried to look away, John couldn't help but watch.

The man started to break apart.

Flurries of grey dust plumed into the air around Graham as he danced. The air turned hot and acrid between them. The cloud of dust grew thicker.

A soft noise like someone puffing out a candle sounded in the small room. It was done. Where the dancing man stood was only a mound of grey, powdery dust. Atop the dust, three glow-sticks continued to let out their vibrant colour.

John blew out a long, shaky breath as he stared at the door, making sure no one was watching. The dust was warm and fine, falling through the gaps between his fingers when he scooped up handfuls, shoving as much of the remains into the bag as he could. He stared into the shifting colours of the glow-sticks. A pang of sadness hit his gut. It never got any easier.

He closed the bag and put his arms through both straps. The bag felt lighter, satisfied. When he leaned over and blew the remaining dust from the floor, he could almost taste the nightclub smells of sweat, sticky floors, and smoke machines.

"I told you not to," said John.

· · • • • • • • · ·

2.

Bobby McClanahan sent his fist through a wall. White dust covered his aching hand. He tasted the manufactured quality of the plasterboard as he drew it out and massaged his knuckles. Shame settled over him like a fine mist. He was a man who prided himself on his discipline. Patty, his wife of fifteen years, appeared in the hallway behind him.

"I don't even know who you are anymore," she said.

His arms shook. He closed his eyes, breathing deep. "Discipline," he whispered to himself, clutching for something that wasn't there. "Peace."

He turned to face her. Patty was a pint-sized ball of fury. Over the years, they'd laughed about how they were polar opposites in many ways, but he knew that's what kept them together. She'd provided the spark in his otherwise calm and serene world. She was the loving soul of their family – what was left of it.

Bobby glared at the hangings and photo frames that covered the sterile walls. During the turmoil of the last year, Patty demolished the house, transforming almost every part of it. She'd knocked down walls, turning their semi-detached home into something like an open-plan Hollywood mansion from the nineties, going on a silver, grey, black, and white binge, sucking the life from their family home. There was only one room left with any colour.

"That you a wall puncher now, aye?" said Patty, crossing her arms.

He tried to find the fountain of peace within himself that his sensei taught him when he was a kid. He'd carried that peace most of his life, drawing from it in times of need. The sound his fingers made as he stroked his bushy beard was like dry straw. His fountain had run dry.

"I'm sorry, babe." The air stung the open flap of skin between his knuckles as he stared down at it. "Can't keep on top of all the apologies I owe you. I… I pushed her too hard, Patty. And it's killing me up inside."

He longed to march forward, take her in his arms, feel her tuck her head into his chest like she always did, but some unseen canyon yawned between them. He stayed where he was, staring at a line of blood that seeped out his knuckle.

"What, you think cause you're the man you get to shoulder it all?" she said. "You're really losing it, eh? We all had a part to play. But she was the one who did what she did."

"You can at least say her name."

She sucked in a breath and stared long at the ceiling. He almost stepped back when she marched up to him, but she only took his injured hand in hers and dusted the plaster off. The soft coconut scent of her hair drifted up to him while she turned his hand over. Where would he be without this angel in his corner? All these years and still fussing over him, making sure he was alright.

"Take up the karate again," said Patty, giving his hand a slight squeeze. "No, listen to me. Those kids need you, Bobby. Some of them don't have anything else. I just hope they haven't ended up clapping each other out in class, or who knows what else. And you need it, too."

She dropped his hand and hugged herself with one arm, staring at her furry slippers.

"It's been a year," she said. "Violet's gone, Bobby. She's gone."

At the end of the hall, the night's rain continued to drum against a window. The way the water fell in waves down the glass held his attention. It felt like it'd rained since Violet left that night.

He could still taste the humid note on the air from last August when they'd had their final fight. Over and over again, they argued about the same things. About her coming home in a hazy mess all the time. About her not having any respect for her parents. About how being nineteen was no age to be acting the spoiled, drunken brat. About how anyone could be waiting to snatch her up.

He leaned down and kissed his wife on the forehead. "I can't let her go. She's somewhere. Feel it in my bones. She wouldn't just take off. Something happened, I—"

"Stop," said Patty. "How many times do we have to go round like this, eh? You know loads of bairns go walkies around here. At some point, we have to accept it. Accept that we might never know. It just... feels like I lost both of you that day. I need my husband back, Bobby. Come back to me."

It was in this hallway where Violet had stomped past him that night. She'd turned, vacant-eyed, slurring a venomous, 'See you later,' before clomping off in her garish, yellow heels. She never came back.

"I can't," said Bobby. "She's out there."

He walked past his wife, picked up his coat, and stepped out into the night.

·····•••••··

3.

Warm rain dripped off Bobby's black hair onto the shoulders of his leather jacket. The streets of Balekerin were drenched. He couldn't remember there ever being such a wet summer. He kept his eyes on the ground. After a rough upbringing on the streets of Pitlair, this nice part of Scotland was almost more than he could handle. Nice cars. No dog shit on the ground. No fights or couples screaming at each other all night.

A few streets and wrong turns later, familiar gloom set in. The buildings loomed large and menacing the closer he got to the town's concrete centre. Drunks hid in the alcoves of closed shops away from the waterfall rain.

I don't even know who you are anymore, Patty had said. All he remembered of the last year was hassling cops and doing everything he could to keep alive his dream of finding their daughter.

A bus rumbled towards him, and he stepped closer to the shops, away from the kerb and the shimmering puddle that promised more of a soaking. The cloying scent of diesel smoke hit his nostrils as the bus passed, leaving a muddy tsunami on the pavement behind him.

Movement caught his eye. Under an awning that promised new and used books, someone huddled on the step outside the shop's front door. The kid was young for the homeless life. He fixed his glazed eyes on Bobby, and that's when he recognised him. It was Harold, a boy he used to teach Shotokan.

Harold had been a good student, always there on time, running through katas with the younger kids. He'd struck Bobby as one of the good ones, a disciplined kid who would go places, no question.

Harold's arms shook like it was midwinter when he hugged his knees to his chest. His hair was wild, his eyes wilder. Those eyes narrowed and Bobby looked away, walking on.

Trying to keep the kids off drugs was the challenge for every parent here. He could still feel the cold way his jaw went when he'd found a little plastic baggie in Violet's drawer, tucked behind some old socks. It had been yet another sign of his failure as a father. It drove him to anger, and he became even harsher with her.

He reached the shuttered high street. It had once thrived, been the centre of everything in this town, but was now only rows of charity shops, hairdressers, and old man's pubs.

A sharp ammonia tang flooded him as he stood outside a boarded up Poundstretcher. He took out his phone. Tonight was all about his own investigations. The police hardly bothered with Violet's case anymore. He could see the boredom in PC Berg's eyes every time he cornered her about it. She'd sit at her desk, hunched over a mass of paperwork, while she recited how they'd exhausted all channels, that they'd keep an eye out, that there wasn't anything they could do when a young woman walked off with no suspicious circumstances to point to.

He checked his phone again. Nearly ten o'clock.

Turns out Violet's old chum, Dougie, had been in the International pub right before Violet had disappeared, but that's not what he'd told the cops. Bobby got this after feeding pint after pint to one of the regulars in the dingy pub. The old man with the turkey neck swore on his wife's grave that he'd seen Dougie that night.

It had taken him a while to track down Dougie's number, but when he did, he bought himself a burner phone and text Dougie from it, asking him to confirm if he knew of anyone that 'provided a class-A delivery service.' Dougie had text back with no stealth in his message whatsoever. Just a list of drugs and prices like he was a handyman offering services.

He kept to the shadows when he saw Dougie's lanky reflection from the supermarket's large windows opposite him. Dougie kept his head down, sloshing through puddles.

When he stopped outside the Poundstretcher, Bobby lunged forward and grabbed him by the shoulders, slamming him against the wall.

"Ah, shit," said Dougie, throwing his hands over his face. "Take it, alright? Don't hurt me. I've got practise tomorrow."

The wiry energy seemed to uncoil itself from Bobby's gut at the sight of Dougie caving without a fight. Bobby was supposed to be the one who practised peace. It was something he taught religiously when he ran his dojo.

"Calm down. It's me, Bobby. Violet's dad. Just want a word, that's it." He let go of Dougie's shoulders.

"This again. Already told you, I wasn't there, man."

"Pish."

"Honest."

"You wouldn't know honest if it slapped you across the face like a wet fish."

Dougie lowered his hands slightly, staring over them. "What?"

"Cops might be shite, but I've been asking around. Got someone who swears they saw you in the International when my Violet went missing. Someone who I trust more than you're quivering arse."

"It-It was nothing to do with me, I swear."

The look in Dougie's eyes was the same as it had been all those years ago when he'd asked if Violet was coming out to play. Bobby had smiled at the sincere, forthright way the kid had asked, and even thought this boy might be okay if Violet ended up with him. He stifled a sordid chuckle at how naive he'd been back then. They'd probably hung out at the park getting loaded on White Lightning, meeting their friends for a cheeky spliff or three.

Dougie twisted the toe of his spotless white trainer into the concrete. Fresh hope tumbled about Bobby's gut. It had been the first thing anybody had said that felt like progress in such a long time.

"Out with it," said Bobby.

"I left her."

"Left her where?"

"She was speaking to that big guy. You know, the one from Liverpool or something. Always carries around that bag of his, like the world's biggest school kid."

Bobby had seen the man before. Had even asked him about Violet just after she'd vanished. He could still feel the crawly sensation he got when he just stared at him, not saying a word.

Bobby leaned in close to Dougie, feeling his dry lips pull over his teeth. "If you don't tell me everything that happened, I'll snap every pathetic finger you've got. That's just for starters."

Dougie wouldn't look him in the eye. "They invited me to go through the back. No one talks about it, but that's where he does his deals, you know? No one's that stupid to bring it up. Please understand me, Mr. McClanahan, I begged her to stop, to come away, but she wouldn't have any of it. Nothing was stopping her from scoring that night. She was on a mission. Was kinda scary."

Bobby felt the spray from the rain outside the small space hit the back of his neck. It chilled his skin, and he suppressed a shudder. "Guess I can picture that. Keep going."

"I only sell it, really. Honest. Well, everybody's dabbled around here. Suicide not to. I've always been scared of the hard stuff. Violet... she liked to test the waters. Push it. I begged her not to. Even refused to go with her."

"And then?"

"She left me. Stomped into that back room with that man. Didn't even look back. That's the last I saw of her."

· · · ● · ● · · · ·

4.

The next day, John sat on his stool in the International, downing pint after pint until Chuck called last orders. He was thankful for the quiet night. No one had tapped him on the shoulder. He picked up his bag and headed out into the rain.

The rain had turned from a hammering downpour into a misty drizzle that was almost pleasant. It cooled the redness of his face as he stumbled through cider-soaked alleyways, down cobbled streets to the large black of apartments that was his home.

His steps echoed loud as he entered an underpass. A moth fluttered by his face, lit in the flashing, broken bulbs that ran the length of the tunnel. Graffiti that promised various ends and offers of vitamins B12 and B16 swirled the walls in green and purple.

The rain fell on him again when he reached the other side of the underpass and into a vast, prison-like space. The apartments were jammed into a rectangle with a kid's play zone in its concrete centre. All the doors of the tiny flats overlooked that play zone. Walking through it, he looked up at the three stories of balconies and cracked windows, certain he'd be heckled by his fellow prison mates.

A dog sniffed at the broken metal fence of the play park. The dogs roamed around here without owners like stray cats. He resisted the urge to go over and stroke its flat head, and moved towards the stairs that led him up to his dark abode.

He just wanted to collapse in his bed. Forget about everything. Dream of his beloved hometown, forgetting all the reasons he'd never step foot in his beloved Liverpool again.

Metal groaned beneath him when he set his boot on the first step. At the noise, a group of boys hushed each other on the next level up. A boy, not even a teenager yet, John guessed, leaned his head over the railing. He was joined by another, then a third, who all grinned down at him with promise.

"This our stairs, you dick," said one.

John sighed and continued up the stairs. His heart was heavy when he rounded the staircase, surveying the three kids and the large bottle of Buckfast they passed among themselves. He could taste the sharp, almost medicinal scent of the alcohol.

"Know you'll get herpes sharing that thing around, right lads?" said John.

Two of the boys stepped forward. When he saw the moon-pie eyes, he knew there'd be more than the trading of insults. One clutched at something in the front pocket of his hoodie.

"Move your scrawny arses out my way," said John, "or I'll tell your dad I buggered all of you."

One boy swooped forward, trying to puff up his thin chest. Something silver glinted in his hand. "You an english? Hate those bastards. Go back to where you came from, or I'll score my digits into that bald head of yours."

The boy who'd remained in shadow walked forward. He was taller than the other two, less wild-eyed. He moved with an athlete's grace and grabbed the boy's wrist. The knife made a metal tingling sound as it hit the ground.

"Gonna get us all slaughtered, Terrence, you wee prick," said the tall one, still grabbing the boy's wrist despite him trying to wrestle free. He looked John in the eye as he hauled the flailing kid to the side. "He's just, ehm, kidding about. Not stopping you, big guy. On you go. Tell you what, we'll watch your door for you, how about that?"

"I'll murder the cunt," Terrence said, his voice turning from pretend gangster to spoiled toddler. "Hear what he—"

"You daft?" hissed the leader in Terrence's face. "You know who that is?"

"Cheers, lads," said John, stepping past.

The stairs wobbled under him as he took the next step. The muffled sounds of the three boys arguing drifted up to him. There was only space enough for one person on the long walkway. It was as if they built it with the purpose of creating as many altercation points as possible.

John jangled his keys in his door, opened it, and heard the weight of paper smack his laminate floor. His shadow spilled into the dark. A crisp envelope with perfect, fancy writing made him stop with his hand on the door handle. He imagined the person who sent him these notes sitting at an oak desk, writing with a quill.

The smudgy smell of rain steamed off him as he stared into the dark flat, wanting to be anywhere else but here. He thought he'd gotten away with it tonight. No one invited themselves over at the pub or on the way home. The bag's straps dug into his shoulders.

He slammed the door shut and threw the bag on the floor. Drops of water dotted the envelope. Every now and again, the boss left him targets in this way – like an assassin's calling card. They were always worse than the randoms he seemed to draw naturally to him.

Two burning green eyes flashed in his mind. His boss's eyes always bored into his soul, making him want to puke his guts. A cold sweat clung to him as he picked up the envelope and stepped into the narrow living room.

The first thing he noticed, the first thing he always noticed, was the way the streetlight from the window bounced along the acoustic guitar hanging on his wall. His fingertips itched to play, to strum out its silver sound.

"That was a mighty long time ago, mate," he said and plonked himself down on the sole chair in the room. "Forget it."

He tapped the envelope against the arm of the chair, staring out the window. The way the light came into the flats through the iron railings made it seem like a cage.

Should he try to escape again? It was no use. She always found him. He was her's.

He'd made his deal.

His hand quivered as he tore the envelope open. Its vanilla scent hovered about him as he shimmied the small card out.

Who next? Another young kid would break him, he knew. It was like his soul grew weaker each time a card turned up. There seemed no mercy to the list of victims he'd fed to the bag over the years. He couldn't keep going this way. One day he'd snap, lose his mind entirely.

He held up the card to the light coming in through the window.

Father Brown.

·········

5.

The next day, Bobby felt the sun trying to singe its way through the dense clouds on his way to the police station. PC Berg had called him for the first time in months, making him nearly drop his phone when he answered it. She wouldn't tell him what it was, only insisted he make his way to the station in her icy, no-nonsense tone.

The rain had stopped, and the heat built, making him clammy and irritated, though he wished for some glorious sunshine. Blood thrummed in his ears as he marched.

Patty was at her wit's end, hovering about the house in silence. He'd fixed the wall, plastering over it. He'd always been good at handiwork, and made some money on the side from helping people out. It was nothing compared to the bucks Patty brought in. She was the breadwinner, the one flying around offices, clad in sharp suits. Despite her size, Patty wasn't one to mess with and she took that same fire to work. While she brought in the money, he stayed at home, looking after Violet. In the evenings, he'd help kids with their karate lessons.

Violet had been such a wee chancer when it was just the two of them against the world. Seemed like just yesterday she'd sit on his shoulders, giggling and shouting that she was the tallest giant who'd ever lived. What he wouldn't give to be able to go back and fix it all. Not be so tough, so stern with her. Maybe she'd still be here.

She blossomed into the soul of any party. A right wee madam, willing to do a trick or a song or a dance, always free with her hugs.

A car sloshed through a puddle, sending murky brown water over his trainers. A wet squidgy sock snapped him from his happy memories.

When he got inside the imposing police building, he sat with his hands in his pockets, staring over the desk at a stoic PC Berg. She glowered at him as if he'd been caught ticking school. She shuffled some papers, then shoved them in a tray as if she wanted to set fire to the whole place.

"We're calling off the search," she said.

Bobby leaned forward. The plastic seat creaked under him. "What did you just say? I thought you were bringing me in to talk about something you found or plans to step up the search. And you're giving up, is that it?"

"Mr. McClanahan—"

"Half-arsed search and then, what, sod it? Leave her out in the cold without even trying?"

PC Berg coughed into a balled fist, glaring at him. "The case is still open, but until anything else comes up, I refuse to put any more men on it."

Bobby clenched his fists inside his pockets. He looked away from the police officer, scared of what he'd do next.

"I understand it's difficult—"

"You've no idea, hen," said Bobby.

"—but without any kind of proof that there was any wrong-doing, I really can't waste time. You know how many actual crimes are being committed out there? Desk's overflowing with them. Listen, we've talked a lot over the last year, right? Mind if I lay my honest opinion at your door?"

"Not really."

"From what I hear," she continued regardless, "Violet's out there somewhere island hopping, somewhere on a beach with gorgeous, oily studs catering to her every whim. You ever think that she's somewhere she actually wants to be? Away from here?"

"Away from me, you mean?"

"I never said that. Now, I've got a busy day, Mr. McClanahan. Maybe a private eye in Ibiza, or wherever, might be more suited to your problem. If there's nothing else, then I suggest—"

"You checked all that already. She hasn't left the country."

"There are other ways. Mistakes happen. Truth is, we just don't know."

A rage began to churn its slow way around his stomach. In those first days when Violet hadn't come home, he'd thought the same thing. He was even relieved at the thought she'd only be partying her wee head off. Not his problem anymore. Patty had been the worrier back then, begging him to do more to find her. And she'd been right. Something worse had happened, he felt it in his bones. Maybe if he'd spent more time tracking her down when she first vanished, she'd have made it home. They'd be a family again.

"If it was me," said PC Berg, standing, then leaning over the desk, "I'd move on. Pray she decides to come home. Live your life with that firecracker wife of yours. And don't let me catch you going rogue again."

"If you lot did your job, maybe I wouldn't have to."

"Let me make myself very clear, Mr. McClanahan. If I find out you're going around hassling people again, I'll let you see the inside of a cell for a week. Now, if you don't mind, I'd like to get back to people that I can help."

His mind was a fog of sizzling anger by the time he stepped out of the building and into a downpour. The rain drowned all other noise. He walked aimlessly along a path, searching desperately within himself for some semblance of peace. Something to stop the whirlwind inside his head.

Did she really expect him just to drop it? To move on? To simply pray that his daughter would magically turn up one day?

Why hadn't he told the officer about the new information he'd gotten from Dougie?

"Cause she doesn't want to help anymore," said Bobby. "On my own, now. On my own."

·· • • •• • • • ··

6.

The velvet curtain of the confession booth slithered over John as he stepped through it, taking a seat on the bench inside.

Wood cracked and bowed under him. He rested his bag by his rain-slick trainers. The bag had never felt heavier.

"You carry a burden," said a voice from the other side of the partition.

The soft, purple walls seemed to press in on him. He stared down at his hands and the calloused fingertips that had played guitar all his days. Music had been his way of escaping Mersey-side gang life.

From the pit of his soul, a little boy's scream spiralled. He jammed the balls of his palms into his eyes trying to drown out the image of dusting the ten-year-old. That had been one of the worst ones.

"Yes, Father. I've sinned more than any God can forgive."

John had stood in the closed school across the street, making sure it was Father Brown giving confessions today, and that he was alone. When the Father had pushed the heavy doors open, his rosy, irritated skin looked like he'd been hitting the wine all day.

Father Brown's shadowy outline moved. The sound of fingernails scratching skin was harsh in the small space. "No man is so far gone that the Lord will turn his back. Give yourself over to him. He will take you into his mercy."

"I don't know about that," said John.

He'd already given his soul away. To her. To the boss. To the one who kept him trapped in this place. "It's too late for me."

The scratching got louder, making the hairs at the back of John's ears squirm about.

"I have heard of these… acts you commit," said the priest.

"How?"

"Accent like that, there's only one person it could be. Do not fret, my child. No judgement is cast before you here. You are free to speak. Free to be the real you."

"Free." He tasted the word as if it were the silence of a crowd after he'd hit them with a slow ballad. The hefty feeling right before the applause. "I've killed people."

"Go on."

Fingernails ripped skin. John wanted to scream for the priest to stop. To slam his head through the partition. "I'm not sure how many, Father. I guess you could say I… give them things."

He stared down at the bag. A mist curled from gaps at the top, lit in a pulsating green. Heat hit him in a wave like he sat in an engine room.

"Anything they want," John continued, "I can get. Call it magic. Just like that." He clicked his fingers. "Can you imagine that, Father? Do you believe in magic?"

"I-I believe a miracle is in every soul. That anyone is capable of doing anything. No soul can be lost forever. That's what I believe, aye. That's the real magic."

John's hand hovered over the bag, about to undo the clasp. Mist breathed around his fingers like dry ice. The boss was finding new ways to consign his soul into the furthest depths of hell. Old men, countless hungry teenagers, and now a priest. He longed to stop, to rest, but what difference would it make? There was no way out.

He undid the clasp, reached in, and took out the item. His skin turned in on itself as he brought it up to his face. It was a doll. A girl dressed in cutesy school clothes with big, wondrous eyes. Below a pleated skirt, its private parts were smoothed over.

Heat began to slither its way up his neck. The plastic creaked in his hands. The deal he'd made had ruined his life. Not a day went by when he didn't long to set fire to the bag he was forced to carry. Its gifts always revealed a person's inner-most desires. Those things that could destroy you.

The empty, black eyes of the doll seemed to plead with him. "You don't believe that, Father. About no soul being lost. There are some who deserve to rot." John leaned in closer to the partition, almost able to taste its silver mesh. "Do you really believe everyone should be saved, Father? Even those who dream of innocent kids?"

"Aye," started the priest, his voice a piercing croak. He coughed and started again. "Even those… unsavoury souls."

"I've got something for you, Father."

John's guilt had been replaced by something fiery. The light from the bag pulsated over the walls like some alien heartbeat. He wrapped his fingers around the doll, making a fist, then punched in the partition. The priest on the other side flopped to the floor, hands coming up to his pocked face.

John opened his palm, offering the doll.

"For you, Father," John spat the word. "This what you've always wanted? Little girl on a plate?"

Father Brown shook as he got to his feet, not taking his eyes from the gift. John bet he didn't look at his flock in the same reverent way he did the doll.

"Oh, you're my wee secret, aren't you?" said Father Brown, grabbing the doll. His voice turned hushed and private, and he stroked the doll's hair. "Come, tell me everything. I'll make it alright. I'm a priest. You can trust me."

John came out of his cubicle, eyeing the pews to make sure they were still alone, then entered the priest's room. He barely contained himself from rushing in and stomping his face open.

Father Brown ran a pudgy thumb up the inside of the doll's leg until he got to the smoothed-out space between her legs. He started rubbing. The clean squeak it made seemed to bounce around the walls, piercing John's brain.

The priest began to fade like they all did. The vibrant red of his skin turned to grey as he continued to rub plastic, his thumb a blur.

Just as John thought he couldn't hold himself back from dashing the man's head on the floor, dust began circling its way around them. John turned his head and spat the ashen taste from his mouth.

When he turned back, the remains of the priest rained into a mound of grey ash.

His lip curled over his teeth as he knelt and scooped handfuls of warm dust into the bag.

· · · ● · ● · ● · · ·

7.

That evening, Bobby sat on a stool in the International, sipping his pint of lager tops. He shifted around, not quite able to get comfortable. He felt the stares of the locals crawl over his back.

The barman floated over. His neat moustache and the straight-backed way he held himself was out of place in this dive of a pub.

"Not a big drinker, are you?" said Chuck.

"How can you tell?"

"Been nursing that pint for half an hour. And no one drinks lager tops anymore."

Bobby glanced over his shoulder at the other five patrons who sipped pints at their tables. "I suppose not. Used to think I was too in control for that nonsense. Not that there's anything wrong with anyone taking a drink. I…"

"Calm down, man." When Chuck emptied a drip tray into a sink, the amber sent of lager loomed between them. "Figure if you ain't in here to get trolleyed, you're in here to case my customers about that daughter of yours again."

"I—"

Chuck silenced him with an open palm. "I get it. Just don't go driving them off, alright? Place ain't exactly jumping."

Bobby stared at the marks on his knuckles from where he'd punched through the wall. "Does that guy from Liverpool come in here much? You know, the one with the backpack?"

Chuck dropped the drip tray. Punters chuckled as the plastic noise filled the silence. He bent down and picked it up in one, fluid motion.

"You don't want to be looking for John," said Chuck.

"John?" Bobby felt his heart kick in his chest. "John who? Where can I find him? They say he was here that night."

"I don't know anything about that. Told you before. Now get—"

Bobby reached into his pocket and slammed a photo on the bar. Violet's hazy smile from one of her profile pictures stared up at him. "This is what I'm looking for. They tell me this guy, this John, was one of the last to see her. That was a year ago, man. A year ago. I know something bad happened to her and I need to find out what. It's killing me. Tell me where I can find John, or do I need to tell the cops about him dealing whatever he deals in here?"

"Threats like that'll get you a sore face."

Bobby felt the room go silent, waiting. "I'm begging."

"Aw, man. Don't do that."

Chuck reached over the back of the bar, poured a red liquid into two shot glasses, and set one down before Bobby. Aniseed stung his nostrils as he stared into the thick liquor. Chuck raised his glass, expectantly. Bobby hesitated, raised his own, sniffed it, which was a huge mistake, then clinked glasses with Chuck before they each downed it.

The alcohol burned its way down his gullet. It was a struggle to not shudder all over.

Chuck merely stood, unaffected. "I'll give you some friendly advice. Walk away. You don't want to know what John's about, you hear me?"

"I think you know I can't do that."

"Thought as much."

"Where can I find him?"

"Just hang around here long enough and you're bound to bump into him."

········

8.

The next night, John stared into the frothy dregs of his pint, leaning on the bar that beckoned him to rest his head, to sleep for just a bit. From his spot on his barstool, he heard the mumbling and laughing of customers behind him. Chuck busied himself, keeping away for some reason. The only other sound was the rain thrashing down outside.

The look of ecstasy on the priest's face played over and over in his mind since he'd shared the bag's gift. Dusting an innocent would usually plague his dreams, but he'd felt good about what happened to that pervert. The bag lay at his feet like a coiled hound.

Chuck set a fresh pint on the bar, staring down at him with pitying eyes. The barman looked about, making sure no one was listening, then leaned in closer, telling him about the man searching for him. How he didn't think this man, this Bobby, would let it go.

"Let him come for me then," said John, his thick tongue softening his words. "See what happens."

Earlier, he'd gone so far as to take his guitar from its bracket on his wall. He ran his fingers along its strings, delighting in the soft, strangled notes it made as he did so. He couldn't bring himself to pluck a string. Last time he'd played music had been a long time ago. He didn't have anyone to play for anymore.

He'd headed to the pub to deaden his emotions in lager. Everyone left him alone because everyone always left him alone. Other customers gave him a wide berth when they came to the bar to buy their drinks, and soon there were only a handful of them left in the pub.

The alcohol burned his cheeks red. He sucked in a lungful of air, tasting the wet dog smell the pub always had when punters brought the rain in with them.

Chuck sighed, then he reached for a bottle and poured them both a hefty shot of whisky.

"Breaking out the good stuff, my man," said John.

"Turning into one of my best customers. Adios."

They both took the shot. John coughed into a balled fist and closed his stinging eyes. He could almost feel a chemical sensation run up the back of his neck.

"You gonna be alright, John? Not used to seeing you this plastered."

"You're the only one who's said a single nice thing to me since I moved here. Ain't that the saddest thing?"

"Everybody's kind of afraid of you."

No one had been afraid of him in Liverpool. When he played on Matthew Street, the crowd roared and laughed with him. He was everyone's best friend.

"I'm out," said John. "I-I can't do it anymore. Their faces... You understand me, Chuck? I hope—" he downed a gulp of beer before he went on. "I hope they'll forgive me for giving up. I just… can't anymore."

He slapped the bar-top with both hands. The noise seemed to ricochet around the pub while his balance sorted itself out. He staggered to the door, not caring for the mumbles or stares that followed his progress.

Chuck called to him. "John? Forgot your bag. You hear me? John?"

John turned and glared at him. Guilt fluttered at the top of his stomach at the sight of the barman flinching with such fear. Chuck had been the only one he might consider calling a friend.

"I'll, ehm," said Chuck, "just keep it behind the bar for you, aye?"

"Burn it," said John. "If you can."

The rain pattered against his bald head. He welcomed its cool embrace.

He'd moved his family up here to start a brand-spanking new life, away from all the idiot gangs that roamed the streets. Scotland was no different. The only thing it didn't have was the music.

His fingertips itched as he stumbled towards the entrance of a park and its wet, green smell. Every gig he'd performed was like a struck deal. He would provide the tunes, selecting the right one to fit the mood, and the crowd would give him back their energy and their broad grins. That was the sort of deal he was comfortable making. A deal made with music and love.

Those gigs had set him up nicely. It was easy to find jobs across Scotland. All he had to do was say he'd been a regular at the Cavern Club.

Sally had been in the crowd one night, smiling her angel smile up at him the entire gig until he sang only for her.

"I'll never sing for anyone else again," he said, stottering down a shiny, cobbled incline and into darkness between trees.

It didn't take them long to get married. Sally was from Edinburgh, but they bought a house on the east coast of Fife because that was all they could afford. That home had been filled with music and laughter. It had been the worst mistake of his life.

He collapsed onto a glistening, wet bench. The water crept through his jeans and soon he was soaked through, watching the trees sway, listening to the heavy rain clatter off every surface.

This had been Bonnie's favourite spot.

The flat patch of grass beside the bench was the perfect place to teach her how to ride her bike. He'd been such a wound-up bag of nerves on that day, helping her into her pink kneepads and helmet. She was fearless, and soon she was riding around with her pigtails flapping behind her like streamers.

He closed his eyes, turned his face towards the sky and let the warm rain pelt his face. "Take me back. Please? I just wanna go back."

"Too late for that, hotshot," said a familiar voice beside him. "Dealing a soul is a one-time thing."

John flinched and sat up. The hot beer in his stomach almost rushed out his mouth. His boss, owner of his soul, appeared on the bench next to him.

Her ancient, sing-song voice seemed to vibrate in the base of his spine. She appeared as a spritely young girl, but John knew underneath she was something monstrous and rotten. The rain should've bounced off her gothic, broad-brimmed hat, but it phased through her as if she wasn't there at all. That black hat with its white pattern of stitches looked like something Johnny Cash might wear. Her burning green irises burned into his vision.

"Here," she said, "you forgot this."

She snapped her fingers and the bag appeared at his feet.

Rainwater entered his mouth as he stared at the thing. Slashes of rain darkened the canvas in moments.

"I can't ruin people forever," he said. "It's too much. I can't…"

"Oh, pish-posh, dead nosh. You made me a deal, sweet cakes. Or do I have to remind you what's at stake here?"

"I'm blind out here on my own. That's what's killing me. How am I supposed to know my Bonnie's alright? That Sally's not ripping her own hair out?"

"Fine," she said like a pouty child. The radiant, green-tinged smile that slid up her face made his bowels freeze. "Just can't get the staff these days. D-E-A-T-H, that spells trust. I never once said you couldn't get in touch with them."

"I know."

He ran his hand along his bald head. On a tiny kitchen table he could barely fit under, handwritten letters stood in piles unsent. They contained a million sorrys, a million pleas for forgiveness. He knew he'd never send them.

"It's best they never find out what I've become. What you've made me. You promise they have everything they need?"

"Aye, they are well provided for, you know that. I keep my end of a bargain. When you're in my line of work, you have to... Look, twinkle fingers, they're fine. They have all the money you bargained for and are set up for life. Just like you wanted."

"I wanted to be with them!"

"Well, every deal comes with stipulations. Fine print will get you like that."

Her eyes flared green then disappeared under the brim of her hat as she glared at the bag. Green flames plumed from it. He felt its heat touch his legs.

"Chop, chop," she said. "You be a good collector boy. Or are you thinking about... relinquishing your duties? Need I remind you Bonnie will be the first one to dive her wee hand into that bag if you quit on me? I wonder what gift will be waiting for her, when—"

"Stop. I just needed to know they're alright."

"They're alright. Now stop moping like a pathetic puppy."

All the ecstatic souls he'd help perish over the years since he'd made his deal with this demon-child flashed through his mind. Each one took more of his own soul until it was almost impossible to get out of bed in the mornings. He'd heard nutters in his hometown talk about how they became deadened to a life of crime, that the shutters go down, but he felt every one of them passing as if it were a dear friend he killed.

He looked at the bag again, at the dying green embers floating in the air between them. He stood, picked up the bag, and slung it over his shoulder.

"That's a good boy," she said. "You go collect those desperate, tasty souls."

·········

9.

"Never thought you'd ditch me for the pub." Patty grabbed his wrist as he stepped out into their narrow hallway. "Come back to me, Bobby. I'm falling apart on my own here."

He stopped, glared down at Patty's hand, noticing how veiny and old they were. He slowly raised his head and looked into her panic-ridden eyes. Something screamed within him to take his coat off and pick up his wife, hold her tight, and not let go.

"I need to find her."

"You're giving up on everything else to chase a ghost. I hate seeing you die like this. I know it's hard, but you need to focus on something else." She let go of his wrist. "But no. You just go get mashed at the pub. Forget about real life. Forget about trying to move on. About me."

He opened his mouth to speak, closed it again, then walked past her. Violet's bedroom door lay open a crack. He couldn't help but peek in. A shiny Daft Punk poster reflected the dull light that came in through a window. The room always looked to him like a rainbow threw up all over it. Everything was neon bright. Ticket stubs from the Prodigy, Pendulum, and other thumping music acts he couldn't stand stuck out from the side of a mirror.

If she did come back, everything would be like it was when she'd left. He stood in the doorway, itching to feel the muggy summer air, but unable to move. Soon, he stood in the centre of the room that smelled of hairspray and glue. On her bedside table, he picked up an out of place book.

He'd laughed at Patty's attempts to make a reader of their daughter. Books were *boring*, and *pointless,* until she finally won her over with a collection of John Collier stories. Violet hid the book as if scared to reveal to the world she actually enjoyed it. Short stories were something she could dip into quickly and dip out again without interrupting her schedule. He found himself reading a few of them, and soon, he, too, was hooked.

He brought the book up to his mouth, inhaling the dusty vanilla scent of pages. He cherished the short time they'd spoken about the stories. Her eyes would light up, revealing there was something deeper under all the shallow partying.

The pressing wind slammed the front door shut behind him. It was as if the pelting rain tried to push him back into the house. He leaned into the wind all the way to the International where he'd spent the last two days waiting for John to show up.

A few of the regulars nodded at him as he entered the pub. Though no one spoke to him, he felt something like a camaraderie with them all. They all had eyes that shared secret pain of some sort.

A lager tops was waiting on the bar for him by the time he got there. Chuck took his money and nodded at an empty table in a shadowed corner. Bobby took his pint and sat at the circular table with its etchings of band names and lurid invitations.

He took a sip of his drink, tasting the sweet lemonade that had been added on top. The past two nights, he'd drank one for every four the others in the pub drank, making them last. When he met this John, he didn't want to be stinking drunk.

"I didn't take you for a drink," he said to himself.

The realisation struck him like a physical blow to the stomach. He'd never been much of a drinker, but it was a rite of passage having a scoop with your old man.

He eyed the empty stool opposite him. He'd find her and make up for lost time. Relax himself a little around her. Not give her any reasons to run off.

He could almost feel her presence. She had a tale to tell about everything. Always something to say, and never boring. If you let her, she wouldn't stop, just keep cracking joke after joke, sharing memory after memory. He'd spent many a night wishing she'd just shut up, but now he ached to be in the shower of her unrelenting words.

The door clapped shut. A trail of wind flowed through Bobby's hair. Some of the punters near the door froze, holding their pints by their mouths.

A stalky figure with a backpack looped tight into his shoulders moved towards the end of the bar. The bag seemed to cling on to the man like a kid holding on for dear life.

This was it. This was John. The man with the answers.

The temptation to down his pint in a oner was strong. He downed only half of it instead, praying it would ease his nerves.

Chuck poured a pint as the big man took a stool at the end of the bar and almost slammed the bag to the ground by his feet.

It had grown library silent. John played with the condensation running down his pint, itching to get up and confront the man, cautious to play it right.

He watched as Chuck leaned into the big guy and whispered something in his ear. John turned and looked at him. There had been the same life-deadened look in Violet's eyes the last time he'd seen her. Like nothing could make her care for the world again.

John turned back to the bar. The other punters started sipping their pints again.

Bobby took a sharp blast of air through his nose, then let out a slow, shaky breath. "Peace. You got this."

He set his pint beside John's on the bar top. Light glinted from a buckle on the bag, catching his eye. It felt as if he'd walked through an icy spider's web. Something about the colour of the material made him think of dead skin.

"Ugly bastard, isn't it?" said John.

The voice surprised Bobby. Given his huge frame and the silence that seemed to follow him, he'd expected something gruff, but there was a musical quality to it.

"What?" said Bobby.

"The bag. Follows me everywhere." John turned back to his pint, downing a long gulp. He wiped foam from his mouth on the back of his hand and gazed at Bobby like he was surprised he was still there. "You after something?"

"You could say that."

"Better go somewhere we can talk then."

·· • • • • • • • · ·

10.

Dust bothered the back of John's throat when he pushed the door open to the back room. He pulled the bag by its strap, dragging it along the floor like a dead dog on a leash. Warm air puffed out the seat that looked more like it belonged on a bus than a pub. He gestured for Bobby to take a seat opposite him.

When Chuck had told him the man's name, he had a dry look of concern in his eyes. Watching the fluid and controlled way Bobby moved, he could see why. It was the taut, broken expression in the man's eyes and the ropey figure that said he was coiled for a fight and that he knew how to handle himself. He was nothing like the other desperate souls after the fix of a lifetime.

"You forgot your pint," said John as the door swung closed.

"Don't want it."

John took a long drink of his own pint and set it on the table between them. "What you after then, friend?"

"I'm not your—" Bobby screwed up his face then stared at the ceiling. "I just need to talk to you."

A flash of anger wanted to boil its way out of John's mouth. It felt as if he was at the station getting interrogated by the cops. "Go on then."

With a shaking hand, Bobby reached into a pocket in his expensive looking jeans. He placed a photo on the table and slid it towards him with two fingers like a cop presenting damning evidence. "You spoke to my daughter before she went missing. I wanna know what happened."

The bag revved up against his foot. It made a cold sweat rush its way all over his skin. John stared down at the photo. He remembered exactly what had happened to this one. He remembered what happened to all of them.

"Her name's Violet," said Bobby, returning the photo to his pocket.

"Violet."

She'd been a scratchy little thing when he'd seen her. The haunted look in her eyes told him she'd never stop chasing, no matter how good the high was. This was one who always needed more. He remembered the gooey, childish way those eyes went as she took out the bag's gift. Its blaring lights beamed all over her face, lighting a wonderful smile that had fish-hooked his heart. And then she was gone.

John took a gulp of air, tasting the humid, ashy room. Here was another family broken because of him. How much longer could he sacrifice other people's happiness to make sure his family were okay?

A groan built in volume, rumbling up his throat. He turned in the seat and kicked the bag. The deadweight of it echoed pain up his foot. Across the table, Bobby stared at him, not blinking.

"Can't have you empty, chap," said John, standing. "I'll grab you a pint. Lager tops, is it?"

"You know where she is."

It was a statement, not a question. John's eyes filled with tears. He collapsed back into the seat. "Got me a daughter, too."

He watched Bobby, who sat with his hands clasped together, his breathing barely audible. The way the man held himself screamed a warning in the deep centres of John's brain.

Cold lager scratched the back of John's throat as he took a long drink, not taking his eyes from Bobby. He set the pint down again, wiping his moist palm on his leg, waiting for any kind of response.

"My little Bonnie," said John, "she's back in Liverpool. I'll never see her again. I'm told she's okay, but I don't really know if she's alive. Know the worst part? It's all my fault. I gave up the quiet, happy life we had cause I wanted to give them more. What dad wouldn't, right? That so wrong? To wanna spoil your family? See them smile. She got me bad. Hooked me into this."

"Into what?"

"I'd give anything to play a duet with her. Carve up an old Oasis song, me with my guitar slung across my lap and her strumming her ukulele. I was teaching her. I'll never play with her again. I—"

He swigged the last of his lager, trying to swallow the avalanche of emotion.

"You saw Violet last," said Bobby. "You have to tell me everything you know."

The reek of dust stung John's eyes like someone toked a joint. He pressed his knuckles into his eyeballs until purple and green clouds strobed in his vision.

Bobby slapped the table. "Where is she?"

"I don't think she's coming back."

John waited. He couldn't remember the last time he'd ever felt a fear like this. When he looked down at the bag, tendrils of white mist reached out like ghost hands.

"Tell me what you know," said Bobby, his mouth barely moving as he spoke through gritted teeth.

"You don't want to know, mate. I can't—"

Pain exploded in John's face. Bobby had thrown himself forward, cracking him on the nose with a solid hook.

John tumbled to the floor. His knee landed on the bag. A whoosh of pungent, hot air billowed out of it and into his lungs, mixing with the blood taste at the back of his throat.

Bobby sent his boot crashing into John's side. John placed his palm on the dusty floor, trying to stand, but Bobby kept on kicking with practised, deadly speed.

He threw himself at Bobby's leg, tackling him by the knee, dragging him down to the floor. John grabbed a fistful of Bobby's t-shirt, raising his fist to deliver a blow, but couldn't bring himself to do it. Bobby's eyes grew pained, like he wanted John to fight.

John let him go and they both got to their feet, staring at each other.

"I wish I could bring her back," said John. "Trust me, I do. I know what it's like to try and carry on."

Knotted strings of muscle stood out on Bobby's neck. His face contorted into something visceral, something murderous. He growled at the ceiling. John leapt back a step, expecting a rush, but Bobby threw himself back on a seat and tugged at his grey-speckled beard.

"I really wish I hadn't started this," said John, "you know? It's the bag. I—"

The door flew open, smacking against the wall. Chuck stepped inside, his eyes panicked. "Out. Now."

"Sorry, Chuck. We're done. Swear."

"I've a mind to bar the fuck out of you, John. Gonna be the end of me. Promise you're not gonna tear this room to bits?"

John stared at Bobby, whose eyes said he was far from done.

"As long as you come clean," said Bobby. "I'll stop. Well, in here anyways."

John stepped forward and placed a hand on Chuck's boney shoulder. Chuck's breathing slowed, his shoulders relaxed. "Honest, Chuck. I'm sorry. We're done. Can you grab us a couple of pints? I'll pay you double."

"There's no need for that, John. You's alright, though, aye?"

"We're gonna have ourselves a long talk."

···•••••···

11.

'Patty ;-)' flashed on Bobby's phone again. He turned it face down on the table. It was the first time he'd blatantly ignored his wife's messages. He could see her pacing their living room, squeezing her own phone so tight her knuckles bled white.

His mind was a fog, not helped by the sharply cold lager tops John had bought him. They'd gulped at their drinks, not saying a word in the back room. Every other minute, Chuck peered at them through the small glass pane in the door.

He stared down at his hands. The skin between his knuckles was red and close to splitting. It had been decades since he struck someone in anger. "Why didn't you fight me? Had the chance to knock my teeth through my nose."

"Wouldn't help none," said John. "Can't do it anymore."

Bobby stared at a broken man. John stooped like his bag was permanently on his back. He'd cracked John clean across the face, not holding back, then walloped him in the ribs with all he had. John had popped right back up like he'd been jesting with an angry cat. He'd hate to see the damage the guy could cause if he let fly.

"Why don't you—" Bobby started.

The bag at John's feet pulsed with white and green light as if a thunderstorm rolled around inside. The spoiled battery taste of ozone lay thick on his tongue.

"Best if you don't look at it," said John.

"Tell me how you know Violet's never coming back and why…" he trailed off, staring at the bag John had blamed after they'd gotten into it.

"I've ruined so many people with that bastarding thing. I'd say I can't remember, but that would be a bald-faced lie."

"H-How?"

"Gives them whatever they want. Sometimes she sends me on jobs to dust certain people, sometimes desperate people find me. Sense me, somehow. I don't know."

"You… dust them?"

John glared down at the bag. His jaw clenched as white-hot hatred flared across his face. "Bag gives them a gift. Something that eats them in real life. And then…"

Bobby closed his eyes. Violet's hardened expression from the last time he saw her stormed through his mind. She'd been so hellbent, so desperate to be away from him. "What did Violet get?"

John sucked in a sharp breath. His voice trembled when he spoke. "I… I tried to tell her to leave. They never listen."

"What did she get?"

"A-A party boat. Like an Ibiza booze cruise, you know? Light oozed from its windows like some kinda spaceship. I wish I could take it back. I wish I could take it all back. Boss said she'd kill my family if I didn't keep going." John's hand shook as he raised his pint to his mouth. He tried to take a drink, but the emotion tensed up his chin so much he set it back down again. "Violet's gone, Bobby. Turned to ash like the rest of them. I'm so fucking sorry. That's what the bag does. Gives them their heart's desire and sucks the life from them."

"How do I know you're not telling—"

He was about to ask if John was having him on, covering up for stealing his daughter away. He held his palm towards the bag. Icy mist prickled his hand as if he held it out to an impossibly cold fire. Something scurried around inside it like a rat tried to push its way free.

A sniffling sound made him tear his gaze away. John was crying. Silvery tears slid down his face. Bobby stared into the bubbly depths of his pint, trying to let it all sink in.

"How long is she going to make me do this?" said John. "I've turned into one of those baddies my mummy warned me about. Caused so much anguish around here. Like yours…" John trailed off, angrily batting the tears away from his cheeks with the back of his thumbs.

"Why not just go to the police? Tell them—"

"That I killed those people? Can't prove nothing. They'll think I'm a whacko. Lock me in Stratheden with all the other loonies. No way out for me. No way."

"So, you're just gonna keep going? Keep taking people?"

"If I could spend my life behind bars, knowing my family would be safe, then I'd happily cut that deal. Boss needs her precious collector boy. I signed my life over, thinking I'd be joining them, but no. Trapped me. The little witch."

"I guess I know how it feels to know you'd do anything for your family. For a second there, I was ready to—"

"Kill me?"

Bobby gripped one of his wrists and twisted until skin burned. "I'm begging you. Can you bring her back? If that bag is magic, can it work the other way?"

John shifted in the seat and puffed out a deep, calming breath. His brows furrowed as he stared down at the bag. "If there's anyone who could, it's that little demon thing. Maybe. Maybe there is a way."

Bobby leaned forward, almost falling off the edge of the seat. "How?"

"All she needs is someone to collect the dust. Scoop it into the bag. One more kid or priest and my brain might sail away forever. I love my Bonnie so much, but can I really keep spreading misery to protect her? And I don't even know if she's protected, that's the worst part. I... I'm done." John rolled his shoulders and looked Bobby in the eye. "I'm done. Maybe if you—"

"Don't."

John leaned down and grabbed the bag by a frayed strap. Its material crackled like dry twigs.

Bobby leaned back in his seat, placing his hand over his mouth. "You're daft if you think I'm reaching into that thing."

John stood, knots of muscle standing out on his bicep as he held the bag by its strap out to Bobby. "Take the bag."

"What?"

"It's yours now."

"How would that—"

"Listen to me. Cut a deal with the demon bitch and maybe you can see your Violet again."

"S–She can do that?"

"You said you'd do anything. The boss, she's unnatural. A little nightmare thing. Might be a long shot, but it's worth it, right? Maybe this way she won't touch my family. If she has a new collector."

Bobby stared at the bag, at the flap that looked as if it would fly open and cast him in blaring light. His mouth went cold and watery. His skin felt like a thousand ants marched across every part of him.

"Take it," said John. "It's the only way I can think of. Maybe in some small way it'll make up for all the pain I've wreaked."

Mist puffed out gaps in the bag like breath in midwinter night. A part of him wanted to leap from this back room and be as far from that bag as possible. What else was there? If Violet was gone, turned into dust, didn't he owe it to her to try at least, even if it sounded like a ridiculous long shot?

"I… I said I'd do anything," said Bobby. "Wife doesn't believe how hard I meant that."

John lowered the bag. It scratched the side of his jeans. "Maybe it's not a good—"

"Give me it."

"You're sure?"

"No, but give me it before I change my mind."

John held it out to him. Bobby's hand shook like an old, bed-ridden man as he reached to take it. John let go. The bag landed in his lap, heavy as a bowling ball. Bobby let out a sharp yelp and shoved it off. It landed on the floor, looking like a pile of trampled, dirty washing.

Relief flooded John's eyes. He stood taller and easier. He closed his eyes and sunk his big frame back into the seat opposite. A billowing smell of must filled the room. John leaned back, staring at the damp-marked ceiling, resting intertwined hands on his large stomach.

"My Bonnie had some talent on her," said John. "Was going to rip up concert halls just like me, but she'd take it all the way. Should've seen her blue eyes light up on stage. She belonged there. My little angel. We'd started playing duets. Me on my crusty old guitar, and Bonnie on her ukulele. She was only six, but she was already making her own sound, if you get me. Unique. She was really getting there with it. Close my eyes at night and it's like I can still hear her pluck those strings in her gentle way."

Bobby stared at John's thumbs that spun around each other. It was like he sat in a favourite chair after Christmas dinner, content as can be.

Violet had never found her passion. Another failing of his to add to the list. He should've pressed her more when she was younger, challenged her into finding it. A memory hit him. He watched a hall full of kids in their crisp white uniforms going through their katas, calm concentration in each set of eyes. He could almost feel the slightly hardened material of the black belt around his waist, smell the high smell of sweat mixed with wooden floors.

"I'm ready," said John.

"For what?"

"There's something in that bag for me."

"Wait. You don't have to—"

"I dream about each person that's gone into that bag. They're all with me. This way, I can finally rest, knowing we at least tried. That maybe I helped at the end."

"But... But..."

"Don't let the boss fool you. She's a vicious little thing. Cold. Maybe if I dust myself, it'll break her hold over my family. It has to." The seat creaked under John as he sat forward. "Do it."

Bobby picked up the bag with a hand that didn't seem to be his. His biceps protested at the weight of it. It pendulumed like something zipped around inside. He set it on the table. The bag seemed to sigh in on itself, like it trembled with anticipation.

He looked over the top of it at John who only nodded back at him. He undid the frigid, golden clasp, ignoring the hissed fumes that gushed around his hand when he pushed the flap open.

"It's funny," said John, staring into the depths of the awful colour that spumed up his face. "This is the bit I always warn people off. Try to tell them to leave me alone. Never thought I'd be on the receiving end."

"You don't have to. There has to be—"

"No." John's eyes held the gleam of tears. "This feels right."

John reached over and stuck his hand in the bag. A feeling of unreality washed over Bobby. Half of John's arm seemed to be consumed as he fished around inside. It should've poked out the bottom of the table.

Bobby resisted the urge to cluck his tongue, get rid of the deadened, heavy taste in his mouth. He eyed the door to make sure Chuck wasn't watching.

John gasped in a shocked, pleased way. "Oh, look at it."

Bobby heard a hollow, wooden sound as John took out the object. It was a white ukulele with spiralling flowery detail around its fret board. John plucked at the strings with a practised hand, filling the small room with its tinkling sound.

John closed his eyes, sending fresh tears down his face. Bobby had to gulp down his own wave of emotion. The instrument filled the room with sweet melody as John played.

"My Bonnie lies over the ocean," sang John in a surprising, sweet voice. "My Bonnie lies over the sea."

Powdery grey gnats shook loose from John's shoulders as he played on, his broad arms making the ukulele seem miniscule. The clammy air made Bobby sweat at the temples. His eyes stung like he stood too close to a fire.

"John?"

"My Bonnie lies over the ocean. Oh, bring back my Bonnie to me."

A wind moved through Bobby's hair. John smiled an easy smile and ran his thumb along a string. A sound like someone blowing through their hand seemed to echo in Bobby's mind. A wind of dust swirled around John like he had his own weather system. The dust became thick as it multiplied in the air, spinning around John until he could no longer see him.

The wind died.

A gleaming ukulele sat atop a mound of grey ash.

Bobby stared at it. The small room felt like it had had the air sucked out of it.

"Shit." He stared at the small window, praying Chuck or anybody else wasn't watching.

He stood and tugged at the hair at the sides of his head. Something inside him told him to bolt. Get out as soon as possible. He took a step towards the door.

The bag made a chuffing, growling sound that he felt through the soles of his boots. It lay on its side, flap open towards the mound like a snail trying to devour it.

The words John had spoken came back to him.

All she needs is someone to collect the dust. Scoop it into the bag.

He looked around for a shovel and brush, anything to scoop up John's remains. Deep down, he knew he had to get away from the bag, but worse would be the questions he'd face if someone stumbled into this room right now.

He couldn't find anything.

The fine dust seemed to stick to his fingers as he piled heaps of it into the waiting bag.

When he scooped as much dust as he could manage, he ran out of the room, leaving the bag behind.

······

12.

Bobby fought the frothing water as it pulled him under its silver-green surface. His arms ached as the unrelenting water played with him, tugging him into its murky depths like a monster wrapping its tentacles around his ankles.

The taste of vital forest filled his lungs as he broke the surface, gasping air. Figures lined both sides of the river, glaring at him with glowing, green eyes.

"Violet?" he spluttered. "Help!"

He stared at the impossible images of his daughter as the river pulled him onward. Each version of Violet slowly turned its head, following his progress. They all mouthed something in unison, but all he could hear was the crashing violence of water.

No matter how hard he fought to reach one of the banks, the current stayed him in the river's centre. "Violet? I can't reach. Help!"

Violet's huffy final words boomed inside his skull.

See you later.

"No, I'll—" muddy water shoved its fist down his gullet. He spluttered it out. "We can make it out of this."

See you later.

"Don't go!"

See you later.

The endless figures of his daughter burst into ash.

"No!"

He gasped awake, sitting up, clutching at his chest. The muddy water taste still circled the back of his throat. As he sucked in breath, his lungs returning to a calmer state, the taste of water was replaced by the leather of the couch and the ginger-scented candles Patty loved so much.

A mirthless chuckle broke from him.

John. The International. The bag.

It all came crashing back. The lager he'd drank rose to the top half of his stomach. He clapped a hand over his mouth to keep it from sailing out.

When the feeling past, he rolled his aching shoulders. A heat like the start of pins and needles wormed its way up his arms. He tracked its warm path up to his shoulders. The bag hugged its long, alien limbs around him. It tightened its grip, making a sound like wrung, creaking leather.

He slapped at the straps, forcing his way free, and kicked the bag away. He sat on the corner of the couch, drawing his knees against his chest, staring down at the bag on the living room floor.

"I left you there," he said, his voice strained.

After he'd shoved John's remains into the bag, he ditched it under the table where they'd talked, then ran home like a coward. He couldn't remember getting home or crashing on his couch.

He'd never been one to believe in fairy tales or magic. His dad had beaten the kid out of him at a very early age. If it wasn't for finding Shotokan and its teachings of a zenful, peaceful way of being, he knew he'd have followed in his father's footsteps, doing stints at Broadshade.

Cut a deal with the demon bitch and maybe you can see your Violet again, is what John told him before singing his final song.

"And how do I do that, exactly?" he said. "Can't be real. Patty's right. I've just about lost all my marbles."

He stared out of the large window at the blanket of miserable clouds. For once, rain didn't sting the glass. The bag looked as shrivelled as a dead, dried-up spider. He stepped over it and went over to a small alcove in the corner of the room.

Beside one of Patty's massive candles was a silver picture frame. It was a goofy photo he'd captured at the perfect time. On the beach at Blackpool with the pier behind them, Patty had just tripped over her own feet and Violet reached down to help her up. They were both hollering with laughter, huge smiles showing their back teeth. For the first time, it struck him just how alike mother and daughter were. He ran his thumb over the photo, remembering the salty beach smells and the ready laughter.

The frame cracked under his grip as the bag caught his attention – the bag where Violet's remains had been scooped into. John had said he'd given her a cruise ship with vibrant colours coming out of its windows. They'd let her go to Ibiza with her friends, which he'd fought against. She'd done nothing but rave about the booze cruise when she returned, bronzed and a shade of happy Bobby had never seen before. It didn't take long for that happiness to sour.

Sounds of rummaging and sorting snapped him out of his thoughts.

"Babe?" he said, stepping into the empty hall.

The sound came from Violet's bedroom. Patty didn't step into their daughter's room anymore. She wanted to clean up, bag Violet's life and keep it in the attic in black bags. He'd refused.

A jolt of red anger swarmed up his spine as he shoved the door open. "Patty, you can't—"

Violet lay on her single bed, arms folded behind her head, staring up at the ceiling. Her heels lay in a tumble by his feet

– the same eye-watering yellow one's she'd worn the night she went missing.

She hauled herself up onto her elbows. Her sandy hair tumbled over one side of her face. "What?"

He strode over, threw his arms around her, gripping her in a hug that made her shoulder crack. "Never leave again. Never again." He heaved in a lumpy breath. "Never."

She lay limp in his arms while he fought back tears. Her cold hand patted him on the back. "Jesus, Dad. Get off. Since when were you a hugger?"

He broke the hug, gently holding her by both shoulders, looking into her questioning, amused eyes. "I-I'll change, alright? It was all my fault. I drove you away. I'm here now, though. Sorry for being such a crappy dad. Just... Don't run off, okay? Promise me."

"You're scaring me now."

"I can't go that long without seeing you again. It was hell on your mum and me. Just promise not to—" he let her go, swallowing the need to admonish her, to force her to promise. "Missed you, that's all."

"What? Dad, I was only out one night."

"One night?"

"Aye, one night."

"But you—" he held his clenched fist against his mouth, feeling the rough texture of nearly broken skin.

Had magic really brought her back? Had the demon that John talked about heard everything they'd said? Impossible. A cold feeling licked at the back of his neck. Violet had just decided to come home after all. The adventure was over.

Only she hadn't changed a single bit since the last time he set eyes on her. And wore the same skimpy clothes as before she left.

She stared at his beard like it offended her. He prepared himself for a scathing comment. "Dad?" she said, peering at him with a raised, false eyebrow. "What's going on?"

He stood by her bed, resisting the urge to pat her head or knuckle her chin. To touch her to make sure she was still there.

"My wee angel cake," he said. "You're really here."

"Puke."

"I love you."

"Jesus, Dad. What's up? You alright in the head?"

"I do, though. I know I'm shite at telling you things like that."

She rolled her eyes. "I love you, too. You big weirdo-face."

Patty was in their small rectangle of a garden, attacking a patch of weeds with murderous intent. When she spotted their daughter, she blinked heavily, then fell on her arse. The trowel tumbled from her hand, sticking into the wet dirt like a sword stabbing the earth.

They helped her up and had a family hug in their grey kitchen. Soon, Violet's tongue was in full flow, regaling them with tale after tale, joke after joke. Bobby had a vague memory of Violet sharing the same joke about the difference between a frog and a music teacher from the summer before she'd vanished.

The rest of the day went by in a roaring dream. They opened a bottle of wine and tucked into munchies that he placed on the kitchen counter. Violet's sweet voice echoed in the space, filling the house with substance once more. As he listened, unable to take his eyes from her, he thought she could be a singer.

The thought made a shudder whip its way through his chest.

"Alright there, Pop?" said Violet, wine glass held close to her lips.

"Ehm, aye. Just missed you I guess."

"Missed me like a ghost just walloped you in the pus, aye? Cheer up, you auld baboon."

"Be back the now."

Bobby walked down the hall to the living room with a bounce in his step. She was back. He'd done it. He—

A strap curled its way round his foot when he walked by the couch. His other foot thumped the floor, stopping him from crashing to the ground. The bag sat under the couch like a waiting monster. The skin where the strap touched his shin burned.

Light twinkled off the bag's golden clasps like fire. He hefted it over to the window. Again, the feeling like something was lively inside the bag made it pendulum in his grip. He prayed the souls John had taken weren't trying to burst free.

Beside the window was a small chest where they kept random odds and ends. He opened it up and chucked the bag in. Before he closed the lid, a flicker of green light lit the dusty space. He slammed it closed.

The sweet sounds of Violet and Patty ribbing each other, merrily calling each other names trickled its way to him. No sound had ever been sweeter. He closed his eyes, listening to it, wanting the moment to last.

The letterbox squeaked then clapped shut. He peered out the window. No one walked down the path onto the street.

He stepped out into the hall. A solitary letter with swooping handwriting greeted him.

Roger Hanson.

"Roger," he said as he bent to pick it up.

Roger had been a bit scruffy around the edges, but keen to learn Shotokan when he'd first started. Like so many other kids, his mother had sent them his way because their kid was getting bullied and needed to learn how to stick up for themselves, fight back. Roger seemed to be one of the only ones that took in the lesson that karate was for self-defence, not a weapon to be honed and used to get to the top of the pecking order. He was a bright kid.

A pang of sadness hit him hard in the chest. Maybe after he'd gotten over the shock of Violet being back, he'd start giving karate lessons again.

The paper crackled as he opened the envelope. Inside was a square of paper with an address.

Below the address:

(-: Welcome, new boy :-)

He crumpled it up in his fist.

·········

13.

Three days later, Bobby ran his hand down smooth, freshly bared skin. A clump of his salt and pepper beard lay dying in the sink. Now he'd shaved, he could see the easy smile that had been there since Violet came home.

He looked at his reddened face in a small, oval mirror that he'd fixed to the wall at Patty's request. There was a line of shaving foam where his chin met his neck that he'd missed.

Since their daughter had returned, he'd been proud of his restraint. His instincts told him to sit her down, go over the dangers of running off alone, the evil forces out there ready to pounce. When he set the cool blade under his chin, a shudder ripped its way through him.

"Shit."

He seethed in a breath. A line of blood fell down his neck. He picked up a towel and held it to the small wound.

Cold curled its fingers around his intestines. Despite his restraint not to be all fatherly and preachy, something was up with Violet. Slowly, the spark in her eyes dimmed. Her need to interject herself into every conversation vanished.

When the small slice on his chin stopped bleeding, he paced the hallway outside Violet's room, clutching the book of John Collier stories. He held the book close to his nose. There was a lingering trace of her perfume on it. He breathed it in, then knocked on the door.

"I noticed you left this on the couch," he said, holding the book up. "You been reading it again? Gotta tell you, that one about the black parrot really got me. Was well cool."

Violet lay on the bed. She pinched the bridge of her nose, let out an annoyed groan before dragging herself up on her elbows. Her half-lidded eyes made it look like she'd been toking weed all day. She stared at him like he spoke some alien language.

"Never mind," he said. "I'll just, ehm…"

"Oh, my, God, you're such a Lemsip."

He scrunched up his face and closed the door in retreat. He flicked to the story *Bird of Prey* he'd mentioned to Violet. Her handwriting was scribbled all over that one.

They hadn't left the house in the three days since Violet walked through the door. With each day that passed, Violet seemed to sink more and more into her mattress. It ate at him. She'd been a handful since she was a toddler, always into everything. It felt like they'd had fiery arguments since she learned how to talk. This melancholy was new and foreign.

Patty appeared in the hall, running her thumb over the hole he'd plastered over. "Did she just—"

"Call me a Lemsip? Aye."

"That's a new one."

"Do you think she's—"

"She's fine, Bobby." Patty walked up to him, tilted her head, then wrapped her arms around his neck. She had to stand on tiptoes to do it. "Now that's a face I've missed. My hunk who used to fling me over his shoulder when we—"

"Gross!" Violet called through the door. "Take it somewhere else. You're old and it's disgusting."

"Can't help that your dad's got a skelpable arse."

They giggled their way to the couch like a couple of teenage virgins. He kissed her long and hard. She held his face in both hands, digging her fingers into his cheek, pulling him close.

Something glimmered in the corner of his eye. The bag leaned against the bench seat by the window.

He flinched. Patty uncurled herself from under him.

"What's up, long, tall, and handsome? Hello, trying to chat you up here. Used to you ducking me for the pub."

Numbness crawled along his scrotum, tingling his belly. He tore his gaze from the bag and looked down at his wife, planting a kiss on the crown of her head. "Got everything I need right here, doll. No need for the pub now princess dour is home."

"Nice," said Violet standing in the doorway.

Patty held a cushion over herself as if she'd been caught naked. "Sneaky pants."

"I'm off out. Back in a wee bit."

"Be care—" Bobby started when Patty dug an elbow into his side.

When the door opened, he heard the wash of rain that teemed it down outside. The door slammed shut.

"Now then," whispered Patty in his ear. "Where were we?"

They made love for the first time in months. Afterwards, drowned in a loving silence, he stared up at the ceiling in the bedroom, his heart still racing. They'd rushed and fumbled at each other's clothes, laughing all the while.

He hadn't noticed just how much Violet's disappearance had taken from him. It consumed every facet of their lives. Looking back now, he could see how close they'd come to stepping over a dark edge and into divorce territory.

They lay side by side, talking for hours about everything and anything until Patty nudged him on the shoulder.

"Would you quit looking at the time so much," she said. "Violet's fine. Only been gone a wee while. You're giving me the shivers."

Later, Violet burst into the house looking like a drowned rat. He ran up to her and folded her into a big hug. She smelled of summer and apples and wet cigarettes.

He waited for her to fight him off, but she chuckled instead.

"See," said Violet. "Total Lemsip."

That night, he sipped at a beer, watching mother and daughter throw strands of cooked spaghetti at each other. The kitchen was filled with a raucous laughter he felt in his bones. The smell of tomato and garlic lit his stomach. He took his phone out and snapped a picture right as a strand of stringy pasta landed on Patty's shoulder.

He looked at the photo and choked. Frothy beer dripped down his chin. In the reflection of the fridge, two green orbs shone. He turned to look for the source. In the window behind him, a girl stared at him with burning eyes beneath a large hat.

It was impossible. The window was at least ten feet from the ground. When he cleaned them from outside, he had to use a ladder. She floated like an apparition on thin air. She nodded her head in the direction of the front door, calling on him to join her.

"You alright, my guy?" said Patty when he stood.

"Just gonna grab a bite of fresh air."

He gently closed the front door behind him and stepped down the steep stairs. She stood in the centre of their tiny, chipped front garden. The rain needled his shoulders as stones crunched under his boots. The scent of warm, wet stone met him as he stared into the girl's green eyes.

When she spoke, a current of maddened electricity buzzed inside his skull. "Quite the happy family in there."

Rain stung his eye. He blinked it away. "I don't want you here."

"Don't want me? Oh, my little, ickle heart breaks. It would be a shame if I were to take your slutty daughter back—"

"Leave her out of this!"

When she smiled, faint green light glowed behind her teeth like her tongue was a bioluminescent slug. "I'm gonna like working with you. Yes, sir. More fiery than the other one. Such a pity what happened to him. That's the way the cookie crumbles. And that poor Bonnie."

"D-Did it work? Is John's family okay?"

"How the hell am I supposed to know? Outside of my jurisdiction, one might say."

"What? But he said—"

"He said, he said. Drop it, monkey. I hate losing a staff member, but as long as I've got someone to sling that bag and collect my earnings, it's all good in the hood, dude. And you can keep your precious slut-bag daughter. Have you any idea how many guys she banged when—"

"Stop it." Bobby covered his ears, but it didn't drown her out. The voice came from inside him somehow.

"You said you'd do anything for her. Anything to get her back, right?"

"A-Aye. I did."

"Well, then. Welcome to the team. You start right now."

When she held out her hand, the rain went through her, dropping to the stones beneath. He was tempted to slap that small hand away, see if she had any substance at all.

"I… I can't," he said. "Don't make me."

"Oh, you'd be surprised at what you can do when you really need to. That's what a father does, is it not? Protects the chickens."

She twirled her hand with a magician's flourish. A crisp envelope appeared. The name Roger Hanson written in the same curly script as before.

"I won't," he said, although he hated the weak defeated note in his voice.

She dropped her hand. The fires in her eyes doubled. "Crap-a-slap. Do you have any idea how hard it is to go down there and grab a soul back up? You owe me, mister. You owe me everything. Play ball, be my collector boy, and you'll keep everything you ever wished for." She held out the envelope again. "Don't test me, boy."

"And if I don't?"

"Ding, ding, ding. I take everything from you and make you watch while I dish out two of the most horrific deaths you'll ever witness. And I don't muck around." She nodded down at the envelope in her outstretched hand. "Take it. Be a good lad."

He took the envelope. A weight tugged his stomach closer to the ground.

"What are you?" he said.

"Sugar and spice, folding rust, roll the dice, turn to dust. Now, go bring me my dues."

"But—"

He was left holding the card. She'd blinked out of existence.

The sounds of merry singing and bursts of laughter drifted out to him. He went inside and slung the bag's straps around each shoulder.

"I'm gonna pop down the street for a wee bit," he called and stepped back into the rain.

· · · • • • · • • • · ·

14.

The bag felt like the clawed hand of a demon tried to pull him down through the ground and into hell, and the only thing stopping it was his backbone. The rain had ceased its torrent, but he longed for a drenching downpour to cool his clammy skin. He marched on down a quiet street.

Images of Patty and Violet dying slow, imaginary deaths kept him moving towards the address the demon-girl had written for him. He slid his thumbs under the bag's straps, feeling relief flood his muscles.

Roger's house stood before him, large and silent. The house was on a street considered to be the good part of Balekerin, away from the bustle of the town centre and its flow of drugs.

He wondered if the kid still had the copy of *Zen for Beginners* that he'd lent him just before he stopped giving lessons. Roger's brown eyes had gone wide, like no one had ever cared enough to give him a book before. He thought Roger was a good kid. No reason why he couldn't find himself and have a good life.

"Except I'm here to steal it up," he said to himself, rolling his shoulders.

The nose-twitching odour of fresh-cut grass hit him when he walked the cobbled path to a blue front door. Through the living room window, he saw Roger's mum laying on the couch. She was horizontal, her neck at a sharp angle, as she watched the telly over her stomach and the glass bottle of Buckfast that rested there. She sipped through a long straw as she zoned out, completely oblivious to him.

She was on her own, if he remembered the story correctly. The husband made a killing offshore. In the divorce, she'd won this house in this nice neighbourhood, raising Roger in drunken silence. Those drunken stories had been the reason he'd taken such an interest in the boy when he showed up at the sports hall for his classes.

He snuck around the back of the house, praying they didn't have a dog. The garden was secluded and overgrown. Grass tickled his shins as he stared up at a room with flashing lights.

Through an open window, he heard the popping of video game gunfire.

He clenched and unclenched his fists, breathing in deep of the muggy, summer air. How could John have done this for so long? It felt like his nervous system was going to fall out his arse.

"A man does what a man needs to do for his family," he said.

Unkempt ivy wove its way through a wooden frame attached to a section of wall. Gunfire continued to erupt between groans and swears. It sounded like the game wasn't bringing him any joy.

He eyed the road through the narrow walkway at the side of the house, wishing that a police car would blare its siren and come take him away. See how the little girl would deal with that one.

The bag became almost weightless as he hauled himself up. The frame shifted and protested under him but held firm. He climbed up it like a ladder, wondering why people with money bought stupid things. Things that made it easier for him to sneak up and steal their kid.

"Don't think," he said, clinging on. "Don't think."

The trestle took him to the room opposite Roger's. The window was open, and he slid inside what must've been his mother's room. Cans of Tennents Super covered the floor. The stench of strong lager seeped from the carpet as he tiptoed over the cans, out to the hall.

He listened for any signs of life from downstairs. He couldn't hear anything except canned laughter and prayed the mum had drunk herself into a stupor.

The white wood was cold on his ear as he pressed against Roger's bedroom door. The boy continued to thump buttons on a controller, cursing and getting angrier.

"For my family," he whispered. "It's all for Violet and Patty."

The door gave an ear-splitting creak when he pushed it open. Roger didn't notice. He sat hunched in a small desk chair, his face inches from a massive telly. He punched the small buttons on the controller as if pushing them harder would make the game work better.

A spike of anger welled up within him. How could a mother drench her guts in Buckfast while she left her son vulnerable?

He thought about turning around. Sprinting away. Burying the bag.

Roger threw the controller on the ground and yelled up at the ceiling, clawing at his frizzy, black hair. The chair swivelled under him, and he faced Bobby.

"Mr. McClanahan," said Roger, standing. "What you up to? Here to see my mum?"

"Just wanted to pop up and say hey, is all." The skin on his shoulders felt like it was close to ripping off when he peeled the bag loose. "In fact, I've got something for you, if that's cool?"

"Starting up the karate again?"

The eagerness in Roger's voice melted something within him. He stood with his mouth hanging open, holding the bag in one hand.

"Being kinda weird, Mr. McClanahan."

"Sorry." He shook himself out of it. "Guess I am. Feel a bit guilty about cancelling the lessons, to be honest." Through the bag's strap, he could feel the bag buzzing to life. His hand shook as he undid the clasp. He turned his head away from the awful light that illuminated Roger's face. "It's why I got you something. Go on. Reach in and take it."

Roger gasped like a kid getting just what he dreamed of for Christmas. "No way! Whoa."

The boy shot his arm inside the bag, heedless of the piercing green light. He took out a huge video game controller with neon lights buzzing around its edges.

A sound like swarming bees grated inside Bobby's skull. The air thickened, growing hot. The boy held the black controller close to his face, his brown eyes large and hungry. He sat down on the seat and danced his fingers along its buttons. The screen stayed on a static pause screen, but it seemed like Roger played a different game inside his head. He ducked, then shoved himself to the side. The little boy laugh he blurted out belonged outside in summer night, not locked up in here.

"Roger," said Bobby, his hand hovering close to the kid's back. "I–I'm so sorry."

The boy was locked inside the game in his mind. The controller crackled, steam rising from it as he tap, tap, tapped away. Motes of dust fluttered from his shoulders, spinning around him.

Pressure built until an ear-popping whoosh filled the room. A mound of dust sat on the chair where Roger had been. The controller shot bolts of tiny lightning from the end that stuck out from the ash.

Bobby fell to his knees. A kid. He'd just dusted a kid. A kid he knew. A kid he had hopes for.

"Hey, maggot-boy!" Roger's mum yelled from the bottom of the stairs. "Man with the dinner will be here in two seconds."

A tightness gripped Bobby's chest. His heart raced so hard he felt it in his neck. He held the bag open towards the chair and tipped it over. The dust crawled into the bag along with the controller.

He stood, kicking at the dust marks on the floor. The bag felt light as he put it around his shoulders.

Creaking floorboards marked Roger's mum's ascent up the stairs.

She shouted again. "Goddamn, you wee prick. Spend all day and night lost in those games of yours. Switch it off now. Get downstairs before I have to come drag you away."

A tear slid down his cheek as he made his way out the window.

·········

15.

Drifts of dirty summer rain rose from his clothes as they ate dinner in stoney silence. He lied out his arse, mumbling something about needing to clear his head for a bit. How the last few days had been a bit much. The taste of chalk and ash stayed in his mouth no matter how much bolognese he put away.

After a few bites, he noticed the silence wasn't just his. Patty and Violet attacked their meals at opposite ends of the table, clattering their cutlery like each sound was a note in an argument.

He tapped Patty's foot under the table and gave her his best *what gives?* look, but she shook her head and twisted spaghetti round her fork like the pasta offended her.

They huffed off in separate directions as he tidied and started the dishes. The joy on Roger's face when he played his game haunted him. The way he'd looked so longingly at it – like it was the missing piece in his life. The Buckfast his mum drank would be wearing off. How worried would she be right now? How long until Patty heard something?

Ceramic split apart in his grip. He'd pressed down so hard on a small plate he broke it clean down the middle.

After pacing the living room, he rapt gently on Violet's door. It creaked and swayed open. After a few silent seconds, he peered into the dark room. He knocked again, then pushed the door open with two fingers and stepped inside.

"You alright there, angel cake?" he said.

She was cloaked in darkness. Covers tautened as she turned her back on him. He watched as the covers moved in time with her sobs.

"Hey, what's up?" he said, placing a hand on her side that she jerked away from.

"I'm fine."

"Don't sound fine."

"Beat it."

He straightened, watching as Violet curled in on herself like she used to do when she was a little girl. Back then, he'd run his fingers through her hair and sing her a daft song. Whatever nonsense came into his head. Stupid stuff about squirrels and ponies and farts. Anything to snap her out of a funk.

The floorboards moaned under him as he made his way to the open door. He paused and spoke over his shoulder. "I get you're still coming to grips with what happened, but you have to realise how demented we were when you were gone. A year is an awfully long time to be going out your head."

"Wasn't a year," came the muffled reply.

"It was. Trust me. I felt every slow, aching hour of it. But you're back now. We'll get through this life thing together, right? Me, you, and your mum. I wasn't exactly the best husband when you were… away. It was hard on all of us. I—" He swallowed a rising lump in his throat. "I know I need to treat you better. Might not stop calling you things like angel cake, but I can do my best to treat you like a grown up. Give you space."

"You can start right now."

"Right-o."

His wedding ring clinked off the metal door handle. He stood in front of the door so the light from the hall wouldn't spill over Violet.

"Dad?"

He spun round. "Aye?"

She hauled herself up, lay back against the headboard, clutching her pillow like a long-lost stuffed animal. "It… It feels like part of me is missing, you know?"

"No but go on."

"Had a dream once. Was at school. Primary. Back when it was all Lego and story corners. I'm walking into the school, my backpack straps so tight I can barely breathe."

The hairs around the back of his ears felt as if someone blew frigid air at him. "Then what?"

"They can't see me. I walk in, talking to the teacher, but she looks right through me. Kids skitter around, not letting me play. No one watches me dance or sing or whatever. I… I don't exist."

She stared up at him with a look of such fear he had to stop himself from going to her.

"That's how it feels now." She held her hands before her face like they belonged to someone else. "Like, I'm not even here."

"It'll pass."

"How do you know?"

"Can't begin to imagine all the feelings jumbled up inside you. Bound to muck you up in some ways. That's to be expected. From where I'm standing, you're handling it rather marvellously."

"It's just… Never mind."

"What?"

"Nah, it's too weird. Forget it."

"I've always thought you were weird."

"Dad!"

"Big raging weirdo. Nothing can shock me now. Shoot."

"I keep dreaming about her."

The smile slipped off his face. "Who?"

"This wee lassie playing her ukulele. She can sing. Like, sing sing. Dreamt about her since I got back." She looked him square in the eye. "You know more than you're letting on. Why else would you look like I just whacked you in the nuts?"

He set his hand on the door handle and stepped into the doorway. "Don't you worry about a thing, angel cake. I'll always be here, doing whatever it takes to keep this family together."

He closed the door.

·· • • • • • • ··

16.

Weeks passed by in a collection of souls. John was right, each one was harder than the last.

He saw them at night when he snuck back into his house. It was as if they all hovered above his bed, tormenting him. In his sleep addled state, he thought he saw glimpses of them like agonised wisps.

Worst was Becky Wilson. A girl the same age as Violet. They'd chummed about at one time but drifted apart. The image of her clutching on to a little black horse, weeping with joy before she blew apart seared itself onto his soul.

The demon girl had summoned him for that one. It felt like a warning shot. He'd dusted four at her request, including wee Roger.

Old Berty Manilow was bedridden in a nursing home. The gasp he'd sucked in as Bobby presented the green toy gun seemed like it nearly offed him. Bobby had to place the gun on his chest, his hands were so weak. He'd sung marching songs while breaking apart into dust.

Guilt and shame needled at him when he'd dusted PC Berg. The officer who'd 'led the hunt' for Violet nearly conked him out in a back alley when he approached her. Drool trickled down her chin as she eyed the cookie jar the bag gifted her.

He could almost see Patty biting her tongue through her cheek when he said he was stepping out once again. They'd barely touched each other since the time they'd made mad, desperate love just after Violet got back. She didn't understand he was doing it all for them. It was the price he had to pay. The burden he carried.

He found himself back at the International, sinking pint after pint, trying to make sense of what to do next. How John had lasted so long, he didn't know. The souls seemed to haunt him like physical things. His inner peace was shattered. He didn't belong to himself anymore.

Chuck eyed him suspiciously as he sat on John's barstool. Bobby raised a silent toast for him with each fresh pint. He'd been the one to dust Violet, but he'd had no choice. They were both just father's trying to do their best. Trying to protect their families.

He would do no killing today. Despite the demon girl's threats and instructions, he left the bag at home. There had to be a way of undoing it all. He'd searched on the internet, browsed the library, but couldn't find anything that even hinted at what he should do.

"Tequila, please, Chuck. Chop chop," said the demon, sitting next to him.

A molten nightmare sensation melted over Bobby's shoulders. The demon, the girl, the thing with the green eyes hovered beside him. She leaned twig-like elbows on the bar-top, sitting on a non-existent barstool.

He stared with his jaw hanging open as Chuck simply nodded and poured all three of them a shot of golden tequila. The girl and Chuck saluted their drinks and downed them. The demon hardly reacted while Chuck blustered and thumped his chest.

"You always refuse a drink? How rude," said the girl, eyes bright under the brim of her black hat.

"Chuck? What you up to? You can't serve her, she's only—"

"Oh, don't bother with him," she said. "They only ever see what I want them to see."

"What are you?"

"Your boss, you insignificant prick. Now, drink your medicine."

Bobby held the shot between thumb and forefinger and downed it. It burned fire down his gullet. A shudder ripped its way through him.

He stared at the punters in their silent corners, hunched over their beers. They looked on with disinterest, not seeing the little girl that had been served alcohol.

"Another please, oh bar keep," she said, slapping the bar. "And keep the change. You need it for that child support money, eh?"

She turned to Bobby and tipped him a wink. Crow's feet scrunched at the corners of her eyes like dried plasticine. Chuck poured another, although there was no money on the bar. They downed it. Bobby coughed away the harsh fumes of tequila that tried to claw its way up his nose.

"Bag should be with you at all times," she said. "That's the rule, cause it's cool. Terms of your employment, you might say."

"Employment." A sour giggle escaped him. "If that's all it is, then I quit."

She licked her lips with a slim, black tongue. "Nah. It's one of those forever type thingies. Good job on that Becky, by the way. I could feel her from miles away. She and Violet used to be besties. Good stuff, good stuff."

"I... I'm not sure how long I can do this. Watch them dust away to nothingness. I can still feel them."

"Aye, souls are right buggers that way. You'll harden yourself to it. Once you get a couple hundred on your belt."

"W-What?"

"Big gains planned. Big gains. Gotta climb my way up. Pay back for hauling Violet away. Wasn't easy, you know. Lucky you've got a boss looking out for you like I do."

"You're mental."

"Watch it."

He stared into the bubbly depths of his pint. What else was there to do? Find a way to fight. But how? Keep looking. Do what she asks. Find a way.

The girl rubbed her eye like a tired toddler. She kept at it. It made a sound like wellies squelching mud. "Why, oh why, do I get the feeling you're gonna make my life difficult? It's easy, big one. Dust 'em up, scoop 'em up, and I won't make you watch as I boil your family alive in a cauldron of my choosing. You might as well stop searching at the libraries and all that. You think I'd let word of me survive after all this time? Give me a break."

His shoulders sank, bringing his chin close to the bar and its lemony cleaning product smell. "I can't."

"You've seen the state of this place? Balekerin, I mean. Countless other shit holes around these parts. That's why the old team flourish here. And what's a few extra deaths in a dour place like this? Think it matters in the long run?"

"You can't just kill people when you feel like it."

"Says who? Death is a fact of life, my man. All day, every day. One. Two. Twenty. Forty. No one bats an eye. It'll go on with or without you." She itched at the side of her face. Her sharp nails seemed to pass through her skin. "Take a moment to think, Bobby. Think hard, I implore you. You're such a good wee fish, I'd hate to chuck you back in."

"I'll do anything—"

"Great!"

"—to get out."

Her tongue poked out the side of her face. Her growing scowl made her eyes flare green. "How about this? John didn't get many requests from me. You know why?"

"Why?"

"He carried that bag with him all the time. Attracted all sorts of numpties. Keep the bag happy, dust a few people who'd likely end up dead in a shooting gallery anyways, and I let up on the requests. John learned real quick that makes life easier. Or we can go on like we are, where I tell you exactly who needs dusted. And I pick 'em good and heartachey."

"You're pure evil."

She stared down at her feet floating by the bar, seeming to contemplate something. "Some people are just lost causes."

When she leaned closer like an old man with a secret, he caught the smell of decaying oranges and mould.

"Tell me," she said, "how's Violet, really? Was it worth it? All those innocent souls dead, just to keep her. What's she doing that's so important? Making her way through Tinder in record speed? Ticking off all the drugs on her bingo card so she can say she's done them all?"

"She's not like that. She never got the chance. I never gave her the chance."

"Had to trick my way past the big guy to get her back. Wasn't easy. And now, this…"

An icy stone touched the pit of his stomach. "What do you mean?"

"I can see how the cards have fallen." She pushed herself from the bar as if standing from a real barstool. "I wonder, I wonder. What's she getting herself into now? Better hope you've not left anything lying around."

·· • • • •· • • •· ··

17.

He bolted out the door of the pub. The rain fell like a white curtain before him. The slick concrete made him slip, almost going over on his ankle, but he ran on.

The taste of rainwater and muggy summer filled his lungs as he closed the front door behind him. When he was done leaning on the door, he straightened, leaving a wet handprint on the wood.

He stomped into the house, calling on his family. His mind felt like it was on the edge of some vast chasm, and it wanted to jump off. He couldn't live like this – frazzled and sleepless.

He ignored the sound of his wife's voice in his mind as he trekked through the house, getting mud and rain on the carpet. He stopped by a picture in the hall of Patty and Violet kicking a ball about at a park.

"Discipline," he said to the reflection he saw in the glass of the photo. "Calm down, you idiot. They're fine. It was just to get me back to work. You can stomach it. Eat it up. A man does what he needs to protect his family."

He took his phone out to look at the time. Midnight. Just as well he hadn't woken Patty up or she'd claw his eyes out.

All he could hear was the unsteady sound of his breathing and the drumming rain outside.

He could almost hear stomping little feet as a memory of Violet running up and down the hall hit him in the chest. First, he was nervous she'd topple over, and then he chased her to make sure she wasn't getting into anything or climbing what shouldn't be climbed.

The streetlight from outside the kitchen window cast the room a soft orange. From the window, he could see the moon blazing behind a cloud.

He'd spend the day with Violet tomorrow. Let her see how he'd changed. Maybe even grab that official first drink with her. Make a start to building memories, building back to happy. He'd do what he needed to do to protect her, but he'd leave his secret occupation out of their lives.

As he walked to the fridge to grab a beer, his foot shot forward. A harsh, scraping noise broke the silence as he put his arms out to catch himself from landing on his arse. He stared down at it. It felt as if his soul was being pulled out the top of his skull by an invisible string.

The bag lay with its mouth open. A mound of ash was next to it.

"No," he said, clamping his hand over his mouth. The hand was covered grey.

A party boat with dimmed neon lights sat atop the dust.

ACKNOWLEDGMENTS

A few of these stories were published in magazines and anthologies that I never thought I could reach. Through doing this, I've slowly made friends in the horror community, which has meant a lot. So, I guess I'd like to acknowledge those editors who gave me a chance. The communities over at *Eerie River* and *Crystal Lake* have particularly been helpful, making me feel a little less lonely.

A big thanks to Jaime Powell for helping me whip these stories into shape. Any mistakes found are mine's.

And to my wife, Zoe, who continues to put up with me writing these weird tales. I love you.

The biggest thanks go to you, dear reader. Thank you for spending some time travelling my dark imaginings.

Until next time.

About the Author

Paul O'Neill is a writer of short horror stories from Fife, Scotland. His day job involves battling the demon of corporate speak.

His stories have appeared in Crystal Lake's *Shallow Waters*, Eerie River's *It Calls from the Doors* anthology, Scare Street's *Night Terrors*, the NoSleep podcast, the Horror Tree and many more. His debut collection, the Nightmare Tree, won two prizes at the firebird awards for *best horror* and *best short story collection*.

Besides reading and writing, he can be found pretending to be a dinosaur to make his sons squeal-laugh.

You can find him at pauloneillwriter.com, on Twitter @PaulOn1984 or Instagram paul.on1984.

Printed in Great Britain
by Amazon